Story Overview

The last thing Lindsay expects when she visits Milly's home in New Hampshire is to be thrust back in time to thirteenth century Scotland days before the Battle of Stirling Bridge. Worse yet, captured by the English. Using her wits and ability to wrap men around her little finger, she survives long enough to be rescued by a band of Scotsmen. One of them, a rigid Highland chieftain determined to protect his country, rarely lets her out of his sight. A man, as it turns out, who is immune to her allure...or so it seems.

From the moment Clan MacLomain decides to save Scotland's history, Laird Conall Hamilton knows he needs to be a part of it. What he does not foresee is a beautiful twenty-first century actress crossing his path. More so, that they end up caught in an obligatory kiss that sparks an infamous battle. A kiss, as Fate would have it, that takes them on an adventure through time to both the Action at Earnside Skirmish and the Action at Happrew.

Joining first Sir William Wallace then King Robert the Bruce, Conall, and Lindsay end up on a journey that will leave neither unscathed. Though determined to keep each other at arm's length, desire simmers, reeling them ever closer. Inner demons are faced as they navigate a powerful connection neither saw coming. A bond so intense and passionate that it might very well help them defeat the enemy and save a nation.

~Taken by a Highland Laird~

Series Overview

The term *a new beginning* brings to mind many things. Hope and opportunity. A fresh start. For the MacLomains and the rest of Scotland, the year twelve ninety-six meant anything but. Instead, it marked the beginning of a new and oppressed era fraught with two long wars with England. This particular series revolves around the First War of Scottish Independence that took place from twelve ninety-six to thirteen twenty-eight.

Heroes are often lost to time and folklore, especially when magic is involved. *The MacLomain Series: A New Beginning* shares those mystical tales. Stories about Scottish lairds that came to the aid of Sir William Wallace and King Robert the Bruce. Brave warriors and their lasses who single handedly changed the face of history…or so the story goes.

Taken by a Highland Laird

The MacLomain Series
A New Beginning
Book Two
By
Sky Purington

Edited by *Cathy McElhaney*
Cover Art by *Tara West*

Published in the United States of America.

Name Pronunciations

By popular demand, I'll now be including a glossary of pronunciations for Scottish and Viking words that are a little trickier to enunciate. The following words are ones that you'll run across in this particular book.

Iosbail (ees-*uh*-bel)
Aðísla (*ah*-ue-ee-slah)
Naðr Véurr (nahr vuu-*ah*)
Rona (rohn-*ah*)
Geamhradh (gee-ahr-ick)
Faroese (fâr′ō-ēz′,-ēs′)

If you come across words you'd like to see included when reading my books, please shoot me an email because every story's pronunciation glossary is a work in progress. I love to hear from readers and consider your feedback valuable. Thank you so much for reading!

Email me anytime at Sky@SkyPurington.com or message me on Facebook.

Introduction

Having already been whisked back in time by a magical Claddagh ring, Lindsay has been navigating medieval Scotland by relying on her skills as an actress. More so, by utilizing a powerful magical gift she has long kept secret. One that helped her not only survive an English encampment on the brink of battle but also to manipulate its very commanders.

Soon after, she was rescued by a band of Highland wizards determined to save Scotland's history. Now she's on the opposite side of the River Forth facing the Englishmen who so recently held her captive. Knowing full well she can help in ways no one else can, she has offered to put her life on the line to aid the Scots. And so the story goes…

Prologue

11 September 1297
Stirling, Scotland
Hours Before the Battle of Stirling Bridge

WILLIAM WALLACE SAT back, crossed his arms over his chest and gave her a look she would never forget. An opportunistic expression mixed with surprise and confusion. "So you will be my spy?"

"I will," Lindsay confirmed. "While Adlin and his friends seem nice enough, it's safe to say I know them about as well as I know you."

"And the more friends, the better, aye?" Wallace gave her a look. "Some would say a *good* friend would give me insight into the upcoming battle."

"A *good* friend would do the opposite." Lindsay issued a knowing grin. "But I'll be sure to tell you everything that happens between now and the next time we meet."

"Which should be hours from now," he said.

More likely years but he didn't need to know that.

"As far as I can tell, Adlin has been very forthright with you," she remarked. "So I'm curious why you would ask this of me to begin with."

A puzzled expression flickered across his face then vanished before he shrugged. She had seen that look countless times before. The face of a man being unknowingly compelled. It was a gift of hers to get men to do things they otherwise would not. Right now, that was making sure she and William formed an alliance. Spying seemed as plausible a reason as any.

"There are always things to be heard," William murmured. "Even from those such as Adlin." His eyes leveled with hers. "Especially about future battles and where they might be, aye?"

She nodded but offered no further comment as they resumed eating breakfast. Because she was so important to today's battle, William had requested that she remain in his tent the night before. Though unorthodox, she agreed. As it was, she had spent the night in far more threatening tents lately.

"I should go check on Milly," she finally announced as she dabbed a cloth daintily on either side of her mouth and stood. "Before things get, well, you know…too busy."

"'Tis a brave thing yer doing luring the Sassenach, lass." William escorted her to the entrance. "Stay safe, Lindsay."

"I'm sure I'll be fine with one of Adlin's cousin's protecting me." She just hoped it wouldn't be the one she figured it would be. Since she was mysteriously whisked back in time from the twenty-first century, taken by the English then rescued by the Scots, Bryce, Graham and Conall had been vigilant protectors.

"Aye, especially the one." William grinned. "Ye know he's been eying this tent all eve wondering about us. I might not be able to see him, but I can feel him."

Oh, she knew.

And Laird Hamilton would soon find out exactly what she thought about that.

Unfortunately, by the time she had her say it was already too late.

Chapter One

"YOU COULD SLOW down some," she muttered under her breath as none other than Laird Conall Hamilton yanked her through the woods toward Stirling Bridge less than an hour later.

"Not if they are to believe you are my prisoner," he stated blandly, his hold on her wrist an unbreakable vice grip. Like a chain already trying to lock her down.

Naturally, ever the hero, he had volunteered to bait the English alongside her. At least six foot five with broad shoulders and endless muscles she was no match for him physically. But mentally? Time would tell. Lindsay sighed as she stumbled along and put up a believable struggle. The truth was, Conall was as smart as he was strong and that, amongst other things, was getting on her nerves.

Sure, being flung back in time to days before one of the most famous battles in Scottish history was daunting, but she had handled it. She had worked her magic on Hugh Cressingham then on John de Warenne, the Earl of Surrey. She had been what they needed her to be. But then that's what she did for a living.

She acted, and she did so very well.

Again and again, over and over, no matter where she was.

"The bloody Sassenach are watching you, lass," Conall muttered. "They want you back."

"That's what we're counting on," she reminded, nearly tripping on a root.

Fog drifted in thick waves through the damp, pine-scented forest, obscuring far more than she would like. It hid things from her. Kept something from her. Up until this point, she had been strong but something about that, not being able to see beyond the fog, sent shivers through her. A chill and dread that, of all things, had her clutching the ring in her pocket for comfort.

15

Guidance.

Protection.

But why would she feel that way?

Even as she shook her head against the idea, she slid the Claddagh ring on. Unfortunately, it didn't affect her fear in the least. If anything, it made her feel more vulnerable. Or was it *really* the ring? She frowned as her eyes went to Conall.

"So what is your plan once we get close?" she said. "Because I thought I should be the one to put on the show since I *am* a professional actress and you're ah…well, rather transparent."

"I suspect you *will* put on a show," he acknowledged, clearly not all that impressed as he pulled her along. "I'll be curious to see how well you perform."

Like Adlin and Bryce, he said 'you' instead of 'ye' when speaking with her. Evidently, it was how medieval MacLomains made it easier for twenty-first century women to understand them.

"So why are you so upset?" Lindsay arched her brows, about over his attitude given their current circumstances. "Might it be because I spent the night in William's tent?"

Conall scowled. "Why would I care if you spent the night in his tent?"

Lindsay rolled her eyes. "Because you have been smitten with me since the night all of you saved me from the English."

"Is that what you think?" His voice remained bland. "Or could you have misconstrued my vigilance in protecting a lass who tempts her own demise at every turn as affection?"

She dodged another root, growing more irritated by the moment. "So ending up in the enemy's camp against my will was tempting my own demise?" She inhaled deeply at his gall. "Are you serious?"

"Ending up in Cressingham's arms was tempting something," he returned. "And God only knows what you were up to in the Earl's tent."

She narrowed her eyes at the back of his head. They might have met a few days ago, but this was the most he had ever spoken to her. Where she had hoped they might be able to speak sooner, now she was of the mind that he had spared her.

"Why don't you say what's really on your mind, Conall," she said. "Because I highly doubt it has anything to do with me being in anyone's arms but William's—"

16

That's all she managed to get out before he whipped her around and backed her up against a tree. Half a breath later his lips were on hers. Stunned, she started to push him away but soon realized what he was up to. He was trying to make her former captors act rashly out of jealousy.

Enough so that they would storm the bridge.

So she acted for all she was worth and struggled. It wasn't the first time she played this sort of part. She could do it. Kiss a stranger and make it believable. Just picture someone else in her mind. Someone worth kissing.

The only problem was as her lips softened beneath his, she could only picture one man.

Conall.

Frustrated, but at the same time drawn, she was fairly certain she overacted the whole thing as she struggled against him while at the same time enjoyed it far more than anticipated. He tasted like some sort of mint and that tongue of his. When it teased along the thread of her lips, she found herself teasing right back.

She couldn't remember the last time she had actually enjoyed kissing a man. More so, that it was a man who had given her nothing but attitude since they met.

Well, mostly.

Several nights ago when she had been under the influence of herbs, she recalled flashes of him being tender as he carried her across the River Forth. Then she remembered his warm arms around her as they traveled south and his soothing presence as she slept.

So there *was* a softer side to him.

It was that side she sensed in his kiss along with an unexpected jolt she had never felt before. A rush of heat and desire that caught her totally unaware. The vivid sensations were so strong that she completely forgot to struggle and became lost in the feel of him. Her entire world dwindled down to the talent of his lips and tongue and the warmth of his strong body so close to hers.

In truth, nothing got through until a harsh chill met her skin and he stilled.

Totally out of it, she struggled to catch her breath and gain her bearings. Were the English attacking? Was someone right behind her holding her at sword point? A few blinks later, she realized that wasn't the case at all. In fact, she was no longer leaning against a tree but by the looks of it in a dimly lit jail cell. A torch hissed and spit from a nearby wall bracket, adding a smoky scent to the musty dampness.

"Bloody hell," Conall murmured as he stepped away and frowned.

"Where are we?" She met his frown and looked around. "Please tell me we didn't end up in an English castle somewhere."

"Nay." Conall grabbed the torch, opened the rusty cell door and headed down a stone pathway, leaving her in utter darkness.

"How chivalrous," she muttered under her breath as she started feeling her way along. Unlike most, she found comfort in darkness, preferred it actually, not that anyone knew. After all, she made a point of putting herself in the limelight often and standing beneath the brightest lights possible.

"Conall," she called out, sure to sound distressed. "Where *are* you? Where *are* we? How could you just leave me—"

"I'm here, lass," he replied. His torchlight reappeared moments before he did. "Though I dinnae know the year with any certainty, I would say we've returned to my era. Thirteen twelve."

So she had traveled through time again. "What makes you say that?"

"Because 'tis my castle," he said as he replaced the torch. "After I had this section sealed off."

"Sealed off?" That didn't sound good.

"Aye." He gestured that she follow him then headed back down the hallway. It seemed he had lit more torches in a larger but just as dismal area with no windows.

"I can only assume we're in your castle dungeons then," she remarked as she watched him. He felt along a stone wall, murmuring chants.

"Aye," he muttered. "Like Castle MacLomain 'tis one of verra few in Scotland that have dungeons."

Lindsay sighed as he tried to get beyond the wall with magic. Though it should be the last thing on her mind considering their circumstances, she kept replaying their kiss. Who knew Conall had it in him? She never would have guessed considering his stiff behavior.

She licked her lips and eyed him, knowing full well it was the last thing she should be doing. The last thing she ever did with any man for that matter which probably should alarm her even more. Yet it didn't as she fully appreciated how handsome he was. Better looking, in fact, than most actors she came across in Hollywood which was saying something.

With his height and build, he could be cast in a great number of parts. Her eyes trailed up his long, well-formed legs. They weren't body-builder muscular but lanky in a good way and led up to an ass that most male actors would gladly use as their butt-double in screenshots.

He might be overly tall, but all his proportions were dead on. Enough so that he could pull off a wide variety of roles from action to even romantic drama. Her gaze went to his face. Oh, yes, he would do well in a romance. Cowboy, Sci-fi, Fantasy, it didn't matter. Those classic yet rugged features would fit the bill across all spectrums. The jaw, cheekbones, sensual lips, thick dark brown hair with a hint of auburn then last but certainly not least those eyes.

As if he knew she was checking him out, those eyes turned her way accompanied by a scowl. Even miserable, those icy orbs of his were stunning. Minty light sage with just the right amount of sexy crinkle at the corners, they were thickly lashed and made for the camera. Eyes like his would jump off the screen with the right lighting.

"Och," he muttered and shook his head. "You dinnae need to put on a show anymore to get what you want. I'll protect you, lass."

Lindsay frowned, not following. "And what show am I putting on?"

"The one you put on with every man." He continued studying the wall before he moved to another.

She perked her brows. "Excuse me?"

"You are whatever we need you to be," he explained as he crouched, touched a particular stone and murmured another chant. "You adjust accordingly to get what you want."

True. To a degree. But the way he said it made her feel dirty.

"So what are you implying?" She inflected an edge of sarcasm and gave it right back. "That I am adjusting to you?" Then a dainty snort. "As if such a thing were possible."

Still crouching, Conall rested his elbows on his knees, eyed her and shook his head.

Did they not just share the same kiss? Was he truly so unaffected by it?

"Please, Laird Hamilton, share your insight into my character." Lindsay arched one brow in mild curiosity, refusing to let him get her riled. "I *insist*."

While she sensed his irritation had more to do with where they were, it quickly found an outlet in what had troubled him prior.

"Which character should I share insight about?" he said dryly as he stood. "Because there are so many."

Stung but determined to roll with it, she offered him a tepid smile. "I have to wonder what bothers you more. That I, a woman, was able to take care of myself and get out of some damning situations." She pouted, sure to look sad for him. "Or that you, a man, were completely unneeded. That all you did was help your grandfather carry me across a river. An old man, by the way, that carried me further than you and with more compassion than you likely have in your little finger."

"Compassion is it?" He offered a stiff smile. "I dinnae think you worry all that much about such a thing."

Lindsay narrowed her eyes and shook her head. She might want to tell him where to go, anyone would, but he was likely waiting for that. Hoping for it. Because he was clearly attracted to her and did not want to be. And she wanted to know why.

Time to test some theories.

"Who broke your heart?" she said softly, adjusting her posture to one less confrontational as she touched the wall and shifted closer to him. "Because I suspect someone did."

Conall leaned his shoulder against the wall, crossed his arms over his chest and eyed her with unexpected amusement. "Aye, someone did."

"I thought as much." She kept her tone gentle, her curiosity piqued as she shifted even closer. "How long ago? Are you all right?"

"Good days and bad." He shrugged a shoulder, a hopeful gleam in his eyes. "But rumor has it, she wants me back."

"That's good, right?" She tried not to frown when a nugget of disappointment made her shoulders tighten. For God's sake, this was a *good* thing.

"Aye." He nodded. "'Tis verra good had she not already agreed to marry another."

"Oh, I'm so sorry."

Just like that, her muscles loosened. Damn it.

"Och, 'tis nothing to be sorry over," he commented as he resumed studying the wall. "I'll marry as well, and she will become my mistress."

"I see," she murmured, biting back a frown. That sort of thing was common enough in just about any century, but for some reason, she had not thought Conall was the type. But then, what did she really know about him? Nothing evidently.

"'Twas easier than I expected," he muttered as he felt along the wall more insistently and grew more frustrated with their prison.

"What's that?"

"Simply saying what needed to be said to pacify and interest you," he said. "To direct your mind in another direction altogether."

What the hell was he talking about?

Yet as their eyes met, his expression a bit too smug, she suddenly got it. "There is no great love loss or another woman, is there?"

"Nay, but there *is* the satisfaction of seeing you experience what you do to others," he said. "'Tis like that for most, I imagine. Being led in one direction by you only to realize 'tis all false. That you simply had them where you wanted them."

Her heart thundered into her throat at his gall and insensitivity, but she kept her cool. Deep down, it was easy because she knew he was right. Yet no man saw it let alone called her on it. They were too enchanted, too easily swayed.

All but Conall even *after* that kiss.

Something that most certainly had not affected him like it did her.

Or so it seemed.

She narrowed her eyes.

While some might argue it out with him and call him all the names he deserved, she did things differently. Arguing never got you anywhere. If he intended to think her incapable of feeling, because that's what it sounded like, she would do the opposite to him.

"Obviously we're stuck," she murmured, her voice raspy and seductive as she rested her shoulders against the wall, thrust out her chest just enough and gave him a look from beneath her lashes than no man could refuse. "Maybe if you kiss me again we can magically whisk our way out of here."

Conall gave her a look that spoke volumes. "You dinnae get put off that easily, do you, lass?"

"No," she said softly as she rested her hand on his strong forearm. "Not if I see a possible way out."

Lindsay didn't miss the way his muscles tensed beneath her fingers or how his jaw clenched ever-so-slightly. She might not be able to get to him with words, but touch was a different story. So she sidled along the wall even more until she was nearly between him and the stone. Lord, he was large, but she liked it. Far more than she expected.

"We can't get out of here, can we?" she whispered as she rested her hand on his chest. "At least not in the way you're hoping."

Conall's eyes dropped to hers before they fell to her hand, more so her ring. "Mayhap not."

"So you think it was the gem that shifted us through time?" she murmured as she moved her hand higher, more aware by the moment of the heat and strength beneath her fingertips. Here she was trying to seduce him simply for payback but was turning herself on instead.

"I think 'twas likely the gem," he conceded, his voice not quite right as his eyes remained locked on her hand. "That's the only thing that makes sense."

"But why at that moment?" she purred, now squarely between him and the wall. "What made it so special?"

Conall's eyes rose to hers and held. "'Tis hard to know." His brows lifted. "If I were to guess I would say standing on the brink of war, aye? Mayhap a need to protect you from imminent death?"

"Assuming the English meant to kill me." Just look at how he navigated around talk of that kiss. "Which never would have happened with you protecting me."

She kept her voice husky and her eyes with his. Though typically this would be the moment in a movie she pretended heat simmered between them, she realized she wasn't doing that in the least. Yet heat was still there, rolling over her skin like a fiery wave.

This would also be the moment the man fell under her spell.

22

"I wasnae protecting you," he said, dry amusement in his voice yet again. He was clearly not under any spell as he stepped away. "I was helping the cause."

How did he *do* that? Why was he not completely taken with her at this point? And that wasn't a cocky thought in the least. Not really. But more of a confused one because she had yet to meet a man she could not enchant if she set her mind to it.

Though tempted to give it another shot, she was just too curious. About many things actually. Mainly him but she would get back to that. "So we're in your dungeons, and we can't seem to get out." She shook her head. "I don't understand."

"Nor would I expect you to," he murmured as he frowned at the wall and kept muttering chants that were doing no good.

Hell, did he ever quit being an ass?

"All right, I've had just about enough of this." She crossed her arms over her chest and frowned. "I refuse to be treated so rudely anymore. Especially when I just put *my* life on the line to help *your* country and *your* family."

"Aye, you *did* do that," he agreed, crossing his arms as well as he squared off with her. "And 'twas the only thing you've done where I havenae been able to figure out your motives."

"My motives?" She rounded her eyes. "I thought that was pretty clear. Get the English to rush Stirling Bridge, so history unraveled like it was supposed to, not how it was going to had I not put my life on the line."

She did not raise her voice.

She wouldn't give him the satisfaction.

"And while we're on the subject of you questioning my motives with such distrust," she continued. "What was your take-away from me doing my best to make sure your cousin, Laird MacLeod was not tortured to death by the English? Because I get a funny feeling you weren't all that impressed by that either. That my motives weren't what they seemed to be." She planted her hands on her hips and shook her head. "Because God forbid it be basic human compassion."

"I am grateful for what you did for Bryce," he said softly, yet that same edge leveled his voice. "As I know he is too."

"Oh, right," she whispered, eying him. "He's a sore subject, huh, because I might be his to claim if the gem in my ring shines the color of his eyes?" She yanked the ring off and shoved it in her pocket. "Well, don't worry about that because this ring will dictate my love life over my dead body."

Like Milly's had, it seemed the gem at the center of Lindsay's Claddagh ring would eventually match the eyes of her one true love. To hell with that. She chose who she loved. No man, not ever, and it would stay that way.

"Why did you risk your life at Stirling Bridge?" Conall said, back on topic. "I truly want to know."

"And *I* want to know why you want to know," she countered.

"I already told you," he replied. "Because 'tis the only time I cannae quite ken your actions."

"I love that you think you understand the other times," she muttered, trying to come up with some excuse for her actions at the bridge. "If you truly want to know, I did it for Milly."

His brows snapped together. "Milly?"

"Yes." She nodded once. "I knew she would be staying in Scotland and the only way for that to go smoothly was if I helped history get back on track."

"You are lying." Arms still crossed over his chest, he cocked his head and narrowed his eyes. "Why will you not tell me the truth?"

How could he possibly know that? What was with this guy and his ability to see right through her?

"I am," she said.

He shook his head. "You are not."

They eyed each other as she continued to search for an excuse. Yet as the moment stretched and she considered the conversation she'd had with Grant, Lindsay realized he had never told her *not* to tell Conall. Even so, something held her back. Unexpected compassion for him despite what a douche he was being to her.

"What is it?" he said, his voice a deep rumble of unease as he clasped her upper arms. "What are you keeping from me, lass?"

Lindsay again held his eyes for a long moment before she finally came clean. "Your grandfather and I were able to talk on occasion when we were in the English encampment." She swallowed. "Grant told me things. About how all of you are on a mission to save Scotland's history. How your country would be wiped off the map if you didn't. It would cease to exist in the future."

"But that is not why you did what you did," Conall said, his grip firm but not painful. "Is it, lass?"

His ability to read her was getting a little uncanny.

"No," she finally relented softly. "I did it for you and Grant."

"I dinnae ken." She was surprised by a flicker of something other than distrust and dislike in his eyes as they searched hers. "Why would you do it for my grandfather? For me?"

"Because," she managed, her heart suddenly in her throat. "You deserve to have your father back...and the only way that might ever have a chance of happening is if that battle took place like it was supposed to."

Chapter Two

CONALL MIGHT HAVE imagined Lindsay saying a great number of far-fetched things, but certainly nothing about his father. What purpose did that serve? What had his grandfather said? Because his father, Darach, had gone missing a few years ago and hadn't been seen or heard from since.

Instead of questioning Lindsay further because she likely lied yet again, he did his best to ignore her and resumed searching for a way out. Of all the places they could have ended up, why here?

"This was where Grant was held prisoner when he was young, wasn't it?" she said softly.

He clenched his jaw and murmured yet another useless chant to free them, but like the rest, it did no good. They were going nowhere, and as Lindsay implied, it had everything to do with that bloody ring. He crouched and watched her out of the corner of his eye as she kept touching the stone.

From the moment his grandfather had handed her over to him in the midst of the River Forth, he was just as she said…smitten. Just not in the sense she meant it. Or so he hoped. Yet Conall knew as he inhaled deeply and tried to keep his eyes off of her, it wasn't all that different from her version of it. Whatever else happened that night, the second he felt the weight of her in his arms and her cheek rested against his chest, he was gone in a way that irritated him to this day.

While none could deny Lindsay was a remarkably beautiful woman with her pale blond hair and silver eyes, it was more than that. Instant. Unavoidable. He had carried her in his arms on horseback all the way to the abandoned English castle, fearing for her life the whole time. Though only under the influence of herbs, she had seemed a million miles away from him and that bothered him greatly.

A lass he had just met.

Since that moment, he had kept a close eye on her. None were so courageous or foolish. Because the more he watched the way she interacted with people, men in general, the more he realized what she was all about.

She used men to get what she wanted.

That meant doing whatever was necessary to stay safe.

Or so he thought at first until he began to sense far more. While, yes, Lindsay feared for her own safety, it was subliminal. Which somewhat explained why she risked her safety at every given opportunity with her foolhardy behavior. Did she seem to have a gift when it came to men? Aye. Had she been lucky so far? Aye. But it was only a matter of time before that good fortune ended.

"Well?" she prompted, interrupting his thoughts.

"Well, what?" Conall kept his eyes trained on looking for a way out that would never be there. Not via his magic anyway.

"Dear Lord, you make this difficult," she murmured as she placed her hand against the very wall he had created and sighed. "*Was* this where Grant was imprisoned? *Did* you create this wall so he would never have to look at this place again?"

It seemed her, and his grandfather had talked plenty.

"I did," he confirmed as he stood. "And we will not get past it."

"What about your family? Maybe they could help." She frowned as she gave that more thought. "Do you think they're still at the battle? That what we did worked and the English started coming over the bridge?"

He could only hope.

Right now, however, he had bigger concerns because he couldn't sense his kin within his mind. While his cousins were likely still at Stirling Bridge, at the very least, he should be able to connect with his mother. Or even his aunts and uncles. Someone. But there was nothing out there but silence.

"Conall?" Lindsay prompted. "Are you even listening to me or am I wasting my breath?"

He sighed, leaned back against the wall and contemplated their next move. Unfortunately, he had no idea what that should be. They were completely trapped without magic which meant there would be no manifesting food or drink or anything else.

"You should sit," he said at last. "And rest."

"Sit and rest?" she said, surprised. "What good will that do me?" She frowned and shook her head. "No, I'd rather be useful. How can I help?" Though it was clear she did not want to, she pulled the ring out and eyed it. "Or should I say how can *this* help?"

Conall narrowed his eyes at the ring, not sure what the bloody thing was up to. All he knew was that repeating what he suspected got them here was *not* a good idea.

"Oh, just come out with it already," she said, her tone exasperated as she leaned against the wall beside him. "We both know it was probably the kiss combined with this ring that got us here, to begin with." She gave him a pointed look, challenging him to say otherwise. "So maybe that's the way to get out too."

"Och," he muttered, avoiding her luminous eyes. They were half the reason he imagined most men got in trouble around her. "So your solution is to kiss our way out of here, aye?"

As if he would stop at a kiss if he did it again.

He was somewhat surprised he made it out of her arms the first time. If she had kissed Hugh Cressingham or the Earl of Surrey like that, there could be no doubt they would storm Stirling Bridge to get her back. He reined in his aggravation at the thought. At how many men she had likely kissed since traveling back in time to get her way. Though he knew bloody well he should be thankful she was willing to do anything to stay alive, it irked him to no end.

He scowled and shook his head. The last thing he should focus on right now was Lindsay kissing other men...or kissing him. Yet all he could think about was the taste of her soft full lips and the feel of her lush body as she melted against him. Aroused despite their dire circumstances, he sat against the wall and rested his elbows on bent knees to hide an untimely erection. One, much to his dismay, he had been battling on and off since he met her.

"I've kissed men for lesser reasons," she muttered as she roamed the rectangular room, eying it dubiously. "This place is awful." Her eyes went to his. "I'm truly sorry Grant was imprisoned here for so long. I can't begin to imagine how terrible that must have been."

If he wasn't mistaken, she genuinely meant it.

Kidnapped from MacLomain Castle when he was only eleven winters old, his grandfather had indeed spent several long years down here. The first two winters he never saw the light of day. After that, he used his wits and became everything his captor Keir Hamilton needed him to be. Eventually, he became first-in-command of the warlock's army. Of course, it had all been an act until he was able to come together with his MacLomain kin and defeat Keir. By then the people here had come to love him, and against all the odds, he became Chieftain of Hamilton Castle, even taking the name Hamilton.

When Conall did not respond to her statement, she continued. "You must love your grandfather very much to have gone to such lengths."

He knew what she was thinking. Why hadn't anyone blocked this off before him? Grant included?

"But then I know you love Grant despite how cold you seem to him," she said softly, not afraid, it seemed, to say what was on her mind. Even if it was none of her concern.

"I know you went back to keep an eye on him after that first battle," she continued. "First, you made sure I was safe, then you left."

Conall again remained silent. She was referring to the battle he and his cousins had fought days before the main battle at Stirling Bridge. A secret battle that history would never know about. Grant had subjected himself to the frigid river and was far too old to have done such. Grandmum would have had a fit. So Conall kept an eye on him.

Lindsay sat across the chamber from him, tucking her skirts around her legs primly as though she were not a sumptuous vixen. As though she had not kissed him in such a fashion that he knew she wanted more. That had he persisted, he could have willingly spread her legs and...

"Bloody hell," he whispered and braced his head in his hands. While he was not entirely opposed to being meant for a woman from the future, Lindsay was not the right choice for him. Milly would have been a much better fit because as far as he could tell, she did not purposefully and constantly put herself in harm's way.

"I didn't mean to pry about Grant or make you uncomfortable," Lindsay said softly. "I'm sorry."

Uncomfortable about Grant? That was the last thing she was doing. Uncomfortable in general? Aye. He shifted, hoping she could not see what was becoming damn hard to hide. Her sitting where she had did not help matters any. Mayhap, however, if he went along with her assumption, it would get his mind off her body.

"I dinnae overly like speaking about my grandfather," he said, sure to keep his tone as stiff as his stubborn cock. "He is well now. That's all grandmum will want to hear."

"Grandmum?" she said. "She's from my era too, right? Just like your mother?"

"Aye," he said. "Grandmum was born in nineteen eighty nine."

"Wow, it's so strange how that works," she whispered. "I was born a year later in nineteen ninety."

Other than a brief blip when his parents came together, time had resumed passing as it always did for medieval MacLomains and modern-day Brouns. Time went by much faster here so a man could live twenty years and it would only be a few years in the future. The premise was that time was trying to catch up with itself.

"Aye, 'tis strange," he agreed. "Ma was born in nineteen eighty eight, so a year *before* my grandmother...at least in twenty-first century terms."

"I'll be damned," Lindsay murmured as she continued to eye him with a look he knew all too well by now. She thought she had found a way to get closer to him. Therefore, a means to eventually get him to do anything she wanted.

Almost as if she followed his thoughts, she cocked her head. "You don't like that do you, Conall?" Her lashes dropped a scant fraction as she seemed to see right through him. "You don't want me to get too close." The corner of her lip curled up slowly, and her knowing eyes sparkled with newfound power. "Why do I get the feeling it's already too late?"

He frowned and knew he should not entertain her but did. "Too late for what?"

"Too late for you to stop wanting me," she whispered, her large sultry eyes shimmering in the torchlight. "Because you do, don't you, Conall?"

Aye. He did. With everything in him.

Like always, it was nearly impossible to pull his eyes from hers, but he did. As it was every time, he had to fight to keep from looking at her again. Gazing at the lass muddled his mind, and right now it needed to stay level. More than that, he had to remember she was not the lass for him.

He would never survive her.

She inhaled deeply and murmured to herself. Words he could hear with his superior hearing. Words that caught him off-guard. Against his better judgment, he looked her way again. "What do you mean you dinnae understand why I'm different than the rest?" He frowned. "Explain, lass."

"Oh, I think you know." She stood, her movements fluid and seductive as she sauntered his way. "I think you *very* well know."

Though the dress given to her at camp was too big, it didn't hide her full breasts or her perfect hourglass figure. She was built for a man's hands and hell if she didn't know it as she sat beside him, close enough that their shoulders touched. Her slender hand slid onto his thigh dangerously close to his eager cock. If he didn't know better, he would say she knew *exactly* what state she had him in.

"You are wearing the ring again," he managed, irritated by his thickening voice, and the stark lust she provoked.

"I am," she concurred as her hand slid a fraction closer to his manhood. "Do you know why?"

"Aye." Conall put his hand over hers and shook his head. "But we will find another way out of here."

Any way but how they likely got here in the first place.

"You enjoyed that kiss, Laird Hamilton," she murmured, her voice whisper soft, and seductive. "Don't tell me you didn't."

As she intended, his eyes drifted to her lips. When they did, the tip of her dainty pink tongue slipped out and ran along her plush lower lip. He didn't realize he had clenched his hand around hers until she jerked ever-so-slightly. When she did, he pulled away only for her to try to stop him which, as it turned out, conveniently put her hand right alongside his rigid cock.

He clenched his jaw and remained very still as her eyes dropped and her breath caught.

If he had any willpower left, he would push her hand away. He would remind her that unlike most men, he did not want her. Yet she was already blatantly admiring proof that said otherwise. A maneuver he knew she did on purpose to reel him ever closer. Regrettably, it was working because he had not moved an inch.

He tried to focus on the hiss of the torches, even the chill of the stone at his back, but all he could see was her hand. How small and delicate it appeared beside the heavy ridge of his cock straining against his breeches.

"Well, well," she said softly, her voice raspy, sensual and knowing. "It seems you're stiff in more ways than one, Laird Hamilton."

Had she been any other lass, he would have pulled her onto him, freed himself and plunged into her sweet heat, but this was Lindsay. An actress from the future that was *not* the lass for him. In truth, he had done well to keep women away. On occasion, he took a whore, but that was it.

He sought no connection.

Nothing that could be taken from him.

Nothing he could lose.

"You've put the ring on, and now you try to seduce me," he managed, his voice hoarse though he was trying for bland. "You must be verra convinced a kiss will free us from here."

"I think it's worth a shot." Her pinky finger shifted just enough to make his cock leap. "Unless you have a better idea."

Unfortunately, he did not. But he had finally summoned enough strength to remove her hand from its precarious perch so he could inspect the ring more closely. Held by two hands coming from opposite directions, its heart encased gem was supposed to seal her fate.

Milly's had, at last, glowed the color of Adlin's eyes, but only after they vanquished the evil that had infected it. Dark magic it seemed. Warlocks. Bastardly things that somehow caught wind of Grant and Adlin's original creation of the rings and tainted the process. While their foul influence could be overcome, it would not be easy. Grant speculated Adlin had dealt with the weakest of the warlocks, so that meant Conall and his cousins would face far worse.

More alarming? Lindsay and her fellow Brouns would as well.

Yet it was that, her Broun ancestry, that was so powerful in combination with its MacLomain counterpart. Her one true love. So no matter what happened, Lindsay was destined to be with him, Bryce or Graham. If all went as it should, the gem would change color, matching the eyes of the man meant for her. In Adlin's case, it had not worked that way. Milly's ring claimed several men, but only until the evil was conquered.

"I think we need to set aside our personal differences and keep our eyes on the bigger picture," Lindsay said, interrupting his thoughts once more. "If I was brought back in time by this ring that means I'm supposed to help in future battles so that Scotland's history doesn't become obsolete, right?"

"Aye." Her hand remained in his as he eyed a gem that made him feel more conflicted than he vowed he would ever let it. "'Tis daunting, is it not? 'Tis so verra much for a twenty-first century lass who knows nothing of this era. Nothing of the enemy or evil that abides here." His eyes met hers. "Yet still, you rush to save a country that is not yours. You seem so eager to put your life on the line for people that arenae yours."

While his words sounded challenging and he kept his eyes hard, he was at heart, truly curious about her reasoning. Her motives. How she could possibly be so brave considering where she came from and worse yet, what she did to make money. It made no sense.

"It *is* daunting," she conceded as her fingers curled against his. Her fingertips brushed his palm and lingered as her eyes softened to shimmering pewter. "But what choice do I have? There is nowhere to go but forward and believe it or not, I'm not the coward you think I am, Conall." Her eyes dropped to their hands as she swallowed. "Because though you question my heroism, I know deep down you think I'm merely a survivalist at best."

A *survivalist*? In her case, he could only hope that was true. If so, he bloody well wished she would start going about it without putting her life on the line so much.

"I have not exhausted all our options to get out of here yet." He stood and again muttered pointless chants at the wall.

Anything to get away from her.

"You and I both know you have," she said, her soft, breathy voice behind him far faster than he anticipated. "And we both know this ring is our only hope."

A ring that saw fit to put them here, to begin with.

To what purpose?

"Why were you the first to do it?" she said softly.

He frowned at her over his shoulder. "Do what?"

"This." She gestured at their surroundings though her eyes never left his. "Why were you the first to block off something that had caused Grant so much pain? His family so much pain?"

Their eyes held as he battled emotions. "It doesnae matter."

He turned away and started to chant only for her to step around him, put her hand on his chest and meet his eyes again. "It *does* matter, Conall." She shook her head. "Why was it you?"

When he didn't respond, she continued.

"Grant didn't want to, did he?" she whispered. Her eyes never left his. "He told me he visited here often after he became laird. That it was his way of reminding himself where he got his strength…his perseverance."

"Nay, he didnae want the area sealed off." He meant to keep his silence, but something about the look in her eyes made him speak. She was open. Different. Not acting. "I wanted it sealed." He shook his head. "But never grandfather."

Lindsay said nothing but listened, her eyes steadfast on his.

So he kept talking.

"There was no need for this dungeon," he said, more emotion in his voice than intended. He curled his lips in disgust as he looked around. "It took Grant from Clan MacLomain for far too long. It nearly killed him. Yet he still visited it before I sealed it off and I dinnae think it did him any good." He clenched his jaw and shook his head. "I believe what it represented weakened him so much his own son was taken from beneath his verra nose. To this day he doesnae seem to care about whether or not his son lives."

Lindsay did not respond right away. She didn't touch him, bat her lashes or do anything that hinted at an ulterior motive. When she did speak, her voice was without the octave of flirtation that seemed to be in everything she said. Instead, she was curt and to the point.

"You might not respect or even like me, and it's fair to say I know nothing about your past, but I *do* know one thing." Her eyes never wavered. "I have *never* met a stronger man than Grant."

He was surprised by the vehemence in her voice and the sudden fire in her eyes. Though it might have been more beneficial to agree with everything he said and perhaps lure him into another kiss, she quickly came to his grandfather's defense. "While I appreciate that you were worried about his state of mind, I applaud a man courageous enough to face his demons and not hide from what kept him oppressed for so long."

She pulled away and looked around, her tone still unique, still *her*.

And still sharp.

"Furthermore, the man I met, the Grant Hamilton who never abandoned Bryce or me when we were taken by the English..." She shook her head and jutted out her chin. "That is a man who would do anything to protect not just his kin but those he doesn't even know. He would always protect the innocent." Her eyes shot to Conall, and she rallied more nerve than he saw coming. "I know most people better than they know themselves and I can say without a shred of doubt that Grant would *never* allow himself to become weakened nor would he willingly allow *anyone* to take his son."

Like her voice and eyes, Lindsay's posture was different. Ferocious but kept in check. Her shoulders were back, but she wasn't braced for attack. Rather, she almost seemed to be looking down her nose at him with disappointment.

Though tempted to lash back, he was close to yanking her into his arms and giving her that kiss she was looking for. He might not agree with her assessment, but her valiant defense of his kin impressed him greatly. And, it seemed, aroused him even further.

He narrowed his eyes.

Could it be that was her intention? To get what she wanted by manipulating him this way?

Her head whipped back as if she knew what he was thinking.

"You're hopeless," she said softly, amazement in her eyes. "You can't see past your pre-conceived notions of me, can you?" She shook her head. "Nothing gets through but what you expect of me."

Perhaps that was true, but it was safe. It kept him from pulling her close and heading down a path he refused to take. If he was meant to be with one of Milly's friends, so be it, but it would *not* be Lindsay.

"We have more important things to focus on than your insecurities," he muttered, back to searching for a way out that did not exist.

"Dear Lord above," she exclaimed and threw her hands in the air in exasperation before shaking her head again as she paced.

"How do your kin tolerate you? Because you have to be the most pig-headed ignorant fool I've ever met! Not to mention insulting beyond reason."

Conall nearly grinned. *Now* they were getting somewhere. Or should he say, she was done playing games and by the looks of her red cheeks, done trying to woo him into a kiss. Unfortunately, his only remaining theory on how to get out of here was to use that ring. Yet how to do so without physical contact? Without pulling her into his arms and never letting go?

"I need to see your ring," he stated, without looking at her.

"I'll bet you do," she replied, her voice unsteady as she kept pacing.

"As you said, 'tis likely our only way out of here," he relented, confident enough in her distaste for him now to look her way and hold out his hand. "Mayhap if I hold it I can find a way to utilize its magic."

"Sounds good to me," she muttered as she tried to pull it off. "Anything not to risk seeing your eye color reflected in its gem because heaven knows, that wouldn't do either of us any favors."

He could not agree more.

Conall frowned as she kept yanking at it. "'Tis not usually an issue getting the ring off, is it?"

"Obviously not, as you very well know."

The minute she sucked her finger into her mouth to lubricate it, blood roared straight to his cock yet again. So much for self-control. All he could see were those full, sensuous lips wrapped around where he wanted them most and those sultry eyes of hers staring up at him.

"Bloody hell," he muttered and tried to look elsewhere, but his stubborn gaze was glued. Worse than that, his feet were moving of their own accord. Lindsay's eyes widened, and she had just enough time to pull her finger free before the last of his willpower snapped, and he yanked her against him.

"You'll get your way then," he growled before he did what he swore he never would again.

He closed his lips over hers.

Chapter Three

HERE SHE WAS yet again kissing a man she should *not* be kissing.

Yet unlike before she wasn't putting up a fake struggle. This time she returned the kiss with everything she had if it meant freeing them from this dungeon. Or so she kept telling herself as she stood on her tip-toes to get even closer. As she wrapped her arms around his shoulders and lost herself in the moment.

He might be a grouchy, stalwart man, but Conall knew how to kiss. Lord did he ever as their tongues wrapped and he pulled her more tightly against him. Overly aware of his thick erection and the blazing need between her thighs, she groaned.

"The Battle of Stirling Bridge was won," came an amused voice. "So ye can stop kissing now if ye like."

Conall pulled back so abruptly at the sound of Grant's voice, Lindsay nearly toppled over.

"Och, lad," Grant muttered, closing the distance quickly and steadying her with a hand to her elbow.

"Thank you, Grant," she murmured, gathering herself in front of what turned out to be several people. As far as she could tell they had not traveled anywhere at all.

"Of course, lass." Grant smiled and was about to say more when Conall cut him off.

"What year is it?" Conall shook his head. "And how did you get through my wall?"

"Dear God, Son." An older picturesque woman with hair a mere shade darker than her own extended her hand to Lindsay. "Forgive my son's rudeness for not introducing everyone. I'm Jackie, Conall's mother." She gestured at a lovely woman closer to Grant's age. "This is his grandmother, Sheila." Then her eyes went to a solemn but stunning woman with long, flaming red hair. "And that is Conall's cousin, Rona."

Lindsay nodded graciously in greeting. She did her best to seem unaffected by both the kiss *and* the fact his family had met her for the first time while doing such. "I'm Lindsay. Nice to meet you all."

Conall kept scowling at Grant. "Well, Grandfather, how did you get past my magic?"

"'Twas just good timing, I'd say." Grant held out the crook of his elbow to Lindsay. "Come, lass, so that we might, unlike my grandson, offer you a proper welcome to Hamilton Castle."

"Thank you." She dished out a genuine smile as she accepted his arm, ignored Conall altogether, and left a dungeon now lacking the stone wall that had held them prisoner. They climbed an old, worn set of stairs that led to a vast courtyard. Though there was plenty of activity, she sensed tension. The portcullises were closed as well as the gate.

"What year is it, Grant?" she said softly. "Did your success at Stirling Bridge help things at all?"

"Aye, 'twill in good time," he assured. "And the year is thirteen twelve. The current year for Conall and his kin."

Though she was afraid to ask, she had to know. "And what of Milly and Adlin? Are they safe?"

"They are," he confirmed. "I left them verra happy indeed at MacLomain Castle. I'm sure you'll see them again soon enough."

"Good." She nodded, relieved. "I'm so glad to hear it."

"Aye, all went as it should," Grant assured as he redirected her attention to a castle that made her stop short and her breath catch. "Welcome to Hamilton Castle. I'm sorry you had to see it for the first time from the dungeon.'"

"Me too but only because of what you suffered there," she said softly, taking in the beauty of what was now Conall's castle. It sat on a cliff overlooking the sea, its very structure stunning yet defiant. That was the only way to describe it as it was weathered yet stalwart. In some ways, it reminded her of Conall. Though he might not look weathered on the outside, she suspected he was on the inside.

"We're in northwestern Scotland," Grant said. "MacLomain Castle is further south and MacLeod Castle is on the eastern side of Scotland overlooking the North Sea."

For a brief flicker, Lindsay felt a nugget of disappointment that Grant was showing her this for the first time and not Conall. Yet as she watched Laird Hamilton stride up the castle stairs with one too many doe-eyed women trailing after him, she shoved thoughts of him firmly aside.

"Dinnae hold it against him," Grant said softly. "He has suffered much and doesnae know how to handle the likes of you, lass."

While she wanted to tell Grant how unimpressed with Conall's behavior she was, she bit her tongue. Grant deserved better. Yet she wouldn't sugar coat things either. Her new friend would see through it anyway.

"No worries." She patted Grant's arm and winked. "I know how to handle Conall."

"So you do," Grant murmured, eying her. "Better than most I'd say."

"All right, husband," Sheila said fondly as she and Jackie fell into step alongside them. "I think it's time Lindsay took a break from dashing Hamilton men and spent some time with twenty-first century women."

Lindsay looked around for Rona only to see her striding after Conall. Rona was Graham MacLomain's sister, but she knew very little beyond that.

"Aye, then." Grant smiled, pulled Sheila close and gave her a kiss that almost put the one Conall had just given Lindsay to shame. Go, old people. When she glanced at Jackie, she only shrugged and smiled, so it seemed this was the norm.

After the kiss ended, Sheila offered her elbow to Lindsay. "Walk with me?"

"Of course." Lindsay slipped her arm into Sheila's and started up the stairs with her and Jackie.

"I'm sure Grant's told you enough about Conall, but I would like to further add to what he may have said if it's all the same," Sheila said, her voice both soft and firm as she kept her eyes on the stairs.

"If she's of a mind to hear it," Jackie said, her tone not quite as gentle.

"Are you then?" Sheila cast Lindsay a sidelong glance that told her she would hear it either way. "Are you of a mind to hear why Conall's such a jackass?"

"Sheila," Jackie chastised, but there was amusement in her voice and approval in her eyes.

Though Lindsay fully intended to say she would rather not hear another word about Conall, she said the opposite. When she did, it was in a way she didn't expect. "Yes, I'd very much like to know why Conall's such a jackass. Beyond the pain he must still be feeling after losing his father. And let's not forget his cousin, Fraser."

Why on Earth was she defending him? Because she was.

While Jackie looked at her with surprise, a wistful smile of approval came to Sheila's lips as she said, "So you *do* care about him."

"Enough to explain away some of his poor behavior," she said, ignoring the endless stares she got from men, most of whom stopped short on the stairs and watched her pass. Though curious about the particulars of his father, Darach's disappearance, she would not ask it of Jackie any more than she would have of Grant. Fraser, however, was another matter. "I heard Conall and Fraser declared themselves blood brothers when they were young, so I can't imagine what it was like for Conall to lose him. How that must've felt."

"My husband shared much with you." That same wistful smile hovered on Sheila's lips. "Now I understand why."

Lindsay was about to respond, but Jackie spoke first. "Yes, my son and Fraser were very close. Losing him..." She sighed and shook her head before she continued. "Losing Fraser then his father set Conall on a path we all pray he'll break free from."

She remained respectfully silent as Jackie continued.

"While I do not think my husband is dead, you should know Conall believes the opposite." Jackie's voice trembled slightly, but her posture remained strong as they neared the top of the stairs. "Conall adored Darach and took what happened so deeply to heart that it changed him." She shook her head. "Before that, Fraser, who was not only his cousin but his best friend, was killed before his very eyes. That alone took away a good portion of the son I knew and did nearly the same to Rona." Her eyes met Lindsay's. "The three of them were very close."

So that was why Rona stayed on Conall's heels.

As to Darach being dead, Grant was convinced he was not, and had told Lindsay as much. He also said, as she tried to share with Conall earlier, that if the Battle of Stirling Bridge went as it should and history began to correct itself, his gut told him Darach would be found. That he would return.

"I'm so sorry," Lindsay said softly to the women and meant it. She wasn't acting in the least. "I'm sorry for both of your losses…and Conall's."

"Thank you." Jackie received a mug from a passing servant and handed it to Lindsay as a random Scotsman leapt to open the door for them, his eyes locked on Lindsay with avid appreciation.

Sheila chuckled and muttered, "I wonder how long it will take my grandson to put an end to this."

Likely around the time hell froze over, Lindsay thought.

They might have chemistry, but she had no desire to be tied to a man and Conall had not changed that perspective in the least. If anything, he reminded her why being single was the way to go. Did she have sex? Of course. Though it had been some time. A long time actually. Sex just wasn't a priority.

Or so she had always thought.

She bit back a frown and kept a pleasant smile on her face as her thoughts returned to the kisses she and Conall had shared. The way her body reacted. The pure intensity and desire she felt. It was different. Poignant in a whole new way. The lust she usually felt with a man was part of the persona she embraced. *Nobody* could fake an orgasm like her. Yet her lust for Conall was *very* real, so she could only imagine what else might prove authentic.

"Welcome," Sheila said as she ushered Lindsay into a great hall she never could have anticipated. With endless, ornately designed stained glass windows, sky high ceilings and a grand staircase leading up the center, it was the most majestic space she had ever seen. Sort of a cross between a medieval hall and gothic church, the effect was absolutely stunning.

The rest of the castle, as it turned out, was just as mesmerizing. Who knew she liked gothic? And who knew such a castle even existed in medieval Scotland? But then, as Jackie explained later that evening, the castle's interior had been strongly influenced by a warlock named Keir Hamilton who had been the archenemy when Sheila and Grant first met.

"Things didn't end well for Keir," Sheila commented as she helped cinch up Lindsay's dress. "But at least his offspring haven't been so bad." A small grin curled her lips. "I believe you've met his granddaughter, the Viking Aðísla?"

"More so, granddaughter to former Viking King, Naðr Véurr Sigdir," Jackie added.

Aðísla, it seemed, was the reason for all of this. She was the prophet who foresaw an alternate history for Scotland that involved it ceasing to exist. *She* was the reason Milly and Lindsay were already here and that their friends were sure to be next.

"I have met Aðísla," Lindsay confirmed, as she recalled traveling along the River Forth with Andrew de Moray and Aðísla mere days ago. "She's definitely unique."

Sheila and Jackie chuckled but said nothing more. Yet Lindsay remained curious about the Viking woman. Why was she here and not in Scandinavia with the MacLomain's Viking ancestors? She had been able to glean very little about it from Grant and never had the chance to question Adlin.

"Well, if this doesn't get my son riled up, I don't know what will," Jackie murmured as she stepped back and they looked her over. "You're an exceptionally beautiful woman, Lindsay." A soft smile came to Jackie's lips. "And one I very much like by the way."

"Thank you." She smiled. "I like you as well." Her eyes went to Sheila. "Both of you."

While she meant her response to a degree, she tucked away any legitimate emotions. It wasn't that she felt nothing because she did. They were nice. Everyone here was. People who meant well. It was just hard to truly connect because long ago she had taught herself to disconnect from anything too real.

Which, as it turned out, made becoming an actress the perfect profession for her.

She ran her hands down her dress, impressed with the smooth material considering the era. It was a light silvery shade of gray that highlighted both her eye and hair color. And the fit? Very flattering. But then she was blessed with a figure that made most clothes look good. It wasn't a cocky thought but the truth and yet again, only complimented her profession. A career that kept her safe and difficult memories at bay.

"Do you wish to wear your hair up?" Sheila asked. When her eyes met Lindsay's, she had the strongest feeling the woman might have sensed all those thoughts. "I know it's still damp from your bath earlier, but we can dry it with a chant."

Right, because they were witches.

Something she knew about all too well.

"I'd prefer to leave it down," she replied as her eyes drifted to the window and she remembered a time she would have done anything to have hair let alone wear it down. She fingered a lock. Now it was a reminder. A shield. A mantle of protection she had earned the right to wear.

"Are you okay, Lindsay?" Jackie said softly.

Startled out of contemplation but quick to mask it with a smooth, cordial expression, she smiled at Conall's mother. "Of course. Just tired I suppose."

"I'm sure." Jackie's eyes never left hers. "After dinner, you should get some rest."

Something about the look in Jackie's eyes gave her pause. As if the woman could see right through her and knew who she was at her core. Who she was beyond the acting.

"Rest sounds good," Lindsay agreed though she wasn't really all that tired. If anything, she felt restless and out of sorts. Edgy almost.

"I would say you're ready to join everyone in the great hall." Sheila smiled warmly as she looked her over one last time before they headed downstairs. "It's a shame we can't properly celebrate yours and Conall's safe return, but as I'm sure you know, saving Scotland's history is top secret. Even from its own people."

"So I've heard," she murmured as they descended. As always, men turned their heads to admire her. She sometimes wondered if they saw beyond her beauty to what lay beneath. By no means was she referring to her personality either but something she suspected Grant and Adlin had already detected and likely even Sheila and Jackie.

Magic.

Lindsay's brand of magic.

Despite the thick crowd, her eyes found Conall almost immediately. He stood in front of the great hall's monstrous fireplace with his legs braced, and his arms crossed over his chest. Though a few scraps of Hamilton plaid tied off tiny braids in his dark hair, he didn't wear a tartan but trousers, boots and a black tunic. As usual, he was as stern as ever and surrounded by a harem of adoring women he didn't overly acknowledge. Though he spoke to Rona and never glanced her way, Lindsay knew with certainty he was aware she was there.

Lindsay, Sheila, and Jackie had only crossed half the great hall, meeting many along the way, when a well-muscled wall of a man cut Lindsay off. A wide smile split his face as their eyes met.

"So good to see you again, Laird MacLeod," she managed to get out before he scooped her up.

"'Tis good to see you too." He kept grinning. "I was worried about you, lass." The crowd parted in curiosity as he made his way toward Conall. "'Tis unwise for you to be left alone anywhere, lassie, so I'll see you where you need to go safely, aye?"

Lindsay only smiled in return. Bryce MacLeod was hoping she might be his one true love. And honestly? She wouldn't be so opposed to the idea. Even taller than Conall by a few inches, Bryce was a damn good looking man in a ferocious sort of way with his tattoos and unpredictable nature. But then, that nature was half dragon which intrigued her to no end.

While she might have enjoyed his attention more a few days ago, the truth was, Bryce was interested in her for no other reason than to get out of a marriage pact. As soon as Milly's ring shone the color of Adlin's eyes and he knew she was no longer available, Bryce's attention turned Lindsay's way. Now here they were with Bryce putting on a show to win her over. One, she could tell by the tightness in Conall's jaw, that displeased the Hamilton laird greatly.

Let it. At least Bryce had greeted her *somewhat* properly.

"So what brings you this way, Laird MacLeod?" Lindsay asked as he lowered her alongside Conall and Rona. She met Bryce's eyes, sure to hide behind her lashes just the right amount.

Dressed in a black and yellow tartan that signified his clan's colors, he looked very impressive. Unlike when she met him before, he didn't seem overly subdued but a bit mischievous and even boisterous. She would guess he'd had some whisky. Not enough to make him drunk, but enough to make him the life of the party if he so chose. Based on the adoring looks he was getting from women, it would be most welcome.

"You brought me this way, of course, lassie," Bryce said in answer to her question as he stayed close enough to let any man interested know she wasn't available. "The moment I realized you were here, I came and will protect you as valiantly as you protected me. You have my word."

"As will I, lass," came another all-too-familiar voice before Graham MacLomain appeared through the crowd with a charming smile. With his swarthy good looks and flirtatious nature, it was no surprise he had a trail of female followers.

"So good to see you again Graham." She stood on her tip-toes and kissed his cheek. "I was under the impression when we last spoke that you were going to be protecting MacLomain Castle during Adlin's possible absence."

"So I was." He shrugged. "But it seems our aunts and uncles have that covered." His warm eyes met hers. "We are all to travel together once more to other battles."

"'Tis good news indeed," Conall murmured yet she heard a little something in his voice that said he might not be as pleased as he seemed. "Do you know when we travel?" He looked between his cousins. "What word is there from Laird MacLomain?"

"Adlin and Milly will be joining us soon," Graham informed, his liquid black eyes never leaving Lindsay. "Then we will know more."

"Aye, then." Conall gestured at the tables of food, purposefully not looking at her. "Eat and drink, my kin, then get a good night's rest."

"Aye," Graham and Bryce agreed as they ushered Lindsay in that direction without a backward glance. Nonetheless, she felt Conall's eyes on her. He might not want her, but deep down, he didn't want his cousins to have her either.

Lindsay remained pleasantly cordial as they sat her between them at the head table. Moments later she had a plate heaped with food and a mug of ale in front of her. Neither of which she particularly wanted.

"You need to eat, lass." Bryce gestured at her plate. "You will need your energy."

"Aye," Graham agreed and pushed her mug a bit closer. "A wee bit o' alcohol couldnae hurt either."

She had not known either of them long, but she knew enough that their hearts could only be in the right place. So she buried a sigh, nibbled on a piece of bannock and took a small sip of ale, flinching at the taste.

Graham looked at her in question. "Ye dinnae like ale then, lass?"

"Not really." She shrugged. "If anything, I prefer whisky."

"Och, well you should have said so." Bryce switched their drinks and smiled. Like his cousins, and bizarrely enough in this day and age, his teeth were straight and white. Grant had issued a wink when he explained it was both a wizard and dragon thing and to count her blessings.

"Thank you, sweetheart," Lindsay said to Bryce and sipped the whisky. "This is *much* better."

Graham cast her a sidelong, amused look. "Ma always said our whisky was awful compared to modern-day whisky."

"Then we have a difference of opinion," Lindsay said, knowing more than any one woman should about whisky. Yet she would not make Graham's mother, Nicole, look bad. Instead, she used the opportunity to flirt if for no other reason than to see if Conall reacted. Because she knew very well wizards could hear better than most. "Let's just say I have a *unique* taste for things made in Scotland."

Both Bryce and Graham perked their brows at that, but Conall seemed to have no reaction.

Not outwardly that is.

If she had learned nothing else about him, it was that he was very good at repressing things.

Bryce rested a protective arm on the back of her chair while Graham leaned just a smidge closer. Like Bryce, however, Graham had his own agenda. What that was, she had yet to figure out. What she *did* know, despite his flirtatious behavior, was that Graham wasn't entirely on board with this whole MacLomain-Broun connection. Yet he continued to play the part despite the whore who had snuck out of his tent at the last battle.

Lindsay continued to flirt as she ate and drank very little. Once finished, Bryce convinced her to dance with him then soon after, Graham. While both were very attractive and entertaining, her eyes continued to wander to Conall. She might not like him very much, but something about him drew her.

He never left his perch in front of the fire beside Rona as they spent the evening either talking to one another or to others. Conall's expression remained stoic but kind enough she supposed as he chatted with various women.

As she watched him, Lindsay realized they really weren't all that different. Like her, he was going through the motions when it came to everything around him. Doing what was expected. Nevertheless, she knew he saw the world from a distance though he was right here. She disliked that she had something in common with him. That she understood him. Yet she did.

As if he heard her thoughts, his eyes met hers across the room, and a brief scowl flickered across his face. Moments later, however, his attention was drawn elsewhere when a commotion sounded at the door. By the time Lindsay glanced in that direction and back, Conall was gone. She scanned the crowd, convinced he must be heading that way, but saw no sign of him.

"'Tis the bloody Sassenach!" a woman wailed before the whole place broke into chaos.

Bryce and Graham drew their swords and positioned themselves in front of her.

"Go with Grandfather," whispered through her mind seconds before Grant pulled her after him up the stairs with Sheila and Jackie in tow.

A slight shiver rippled through her at what she knew had to be Conall's voice within her mind. She was well aware these wizards could speak telepathically with their family but was under the impression it usually only happened beyond that with their one true love. She frowned and shook her head in response to that thought.

No way, no how.

They were about halfway up the stairs when loud booms echoed outside, and the castle shook. Women and children screamed and ran every which way as men in armor started pouring in the front door.

The English were here.

She finally located Conall near the entrance fighting with vigor alongside his cousins. Ever the berserker, Bryce roared and slashed. Graham chuckled, a wild look in his eyes as he ran his blade through a man's stomach. Conall, though, was unlike the rest. He didn't fight with heart but entirely with his mind as far as she could tell. His expression remained stoic as he sliced a dagger across one man's neck before parrying with another.

Lindsay clenched her teeth against the worry she suddenly felt for him. It was clear he was an excellent fighter and could handle himself. Yet her eyes remained glued to him as Grant tried to pull her up the stairs.

"He will be fine, lass," Grant muttered. "But only if you follow and allow me to work my magic."

"Of course," she whispered, ready to do just that but something caught her eye. More so, *someone*. A little girl near the door, her eyes wide with terror as she watched a man who must be her father, get run through with a sword.

Something inside Lindsay stilled as she watched the girl shy away in fear, her round eyes frozen in horror as her father's blood poured at her feet. Seconds later, a woman who had to be her mother tried to scoop her up, but another sword ended her life just as quickly.

"Oh, God, no," Lindsay whispered. "Not again."

From somewhere far away, she heard Grant roar in denial and Sheila and Jackie call to her to come back, but it was too late. She was flying down the stairs and heading for the little girl.

The great hall had turned into a war zone as men and women battled. She couldn't tell if the Scots were pushing the English back or the other way around. All she could see was that little girl she raced toward. The shock as the child stood absolutely still caught in a place Lindsay knew all too well.

An indescribable limbo.

Pure shock.

Lindsay dodged and ducked and raced, slipping on blood the whole time, until she scooped the child up and managed to make it a few more steps before she fell to her knees. Meanwhile, the girl never made a sound, her wide, frightened eyes still locked on her parents.

"No," Lindsay whispered as she cupped her cheeks. "Look at me, not them."

When the girl didn't listen, she began trembling and made her voice firmer. "Right now," she ground out. "*Look* at me."

The girl's eyes snapped to hers, terrified.

"That's right," she whispered. "Just keep looking at me, *not* them. Stay *strong*."

She was about to say more when a sharp pain lanced her lower back. At first, she thought she had pulled a muscle in her struggle to get to the girl, but realized when she tried to talk it was far worse than that. Her throat felt thick, and pain spread like blazing wildfire through her torso.

Yet she never took her hands off the little girl's cheeks.

She never stopped trying to soothe her.

Or at least she thought so until she found herself flat on her back, the child gone and Bryce and Graham kneeling over her. They spoke, but she could not hear them. For that matter, she couldn't hear anything. She could only assume they had won the battle but Lord they looked concerned. Why? She tried to ask but couldn't seem to form the words. Her throat was nearly clogged at that point, and something warm trailed out of the corner of her mouth.

A heartbeat later, Conall fell to his knees and pulled her head onto his lap.

"I'm fine, really," she tried to whisper, but nothing came out. Moreover, she was fairly certain her lips never moved.

Conall spoke, but like the others, she never heard his words.

Everything was silent.

Dwindling away.

That's when she began to panic.

"*Lindsay, can you hear me, lass?*" whispered through her mind. "*Because I'm right here. I've got you.*"

Conall.

She knew it was him as his concerned smoky green eyes stayed with hers.

"I'm scared," she tried to tell him, but again, nothing came out. Yet as their eyes held, and he showed far more emotion than she thought him capable of, she knew he heard her.

"*I know you're scared,*" whispered through her mind. "*But ye dinnae have to be.*" He shook his head and clenched his jaw, his brogue growing thicker with emotion. "*I willnae let ye go, lass.*"

"*But you'll have to,*" she whispered, hoping he got the message because she suddenly understood what was happening. "*Because I'm dying, aren't I?*"

"*Nay.*" He shook his head vehemently and pulled her further into his arms. "*Ye arenae.*"

"*Protect the little girl,*" she whispered as his hand squeezed hers and he kept shaking his head. "*Remind her that she's strong.*"

Conall responded.

She knew he did.

Yet everything grew further and further away.

Even the sound of his voice.

Was the pressure dropping? Had the floor fallen out from beneath her?

The last thing she felt and saw before darkness took over was his eyes.

More so, how sad he was to let her go.

Chapter Four

Strathearn, Scotland
Off the Banks of River Earn
September 1304

CONALL HAD VOWED he would not tolerate Lindsay being tucked away in William Wallace's tent again, yet there they were. Better yet, there *she* was. The only difference this time was that Aðísla was in there with them.

Like before, they had been pulled through time against their will. Thanks to Milly's insight, Grant and Adlin believed that Adlin's foster sister, Iosbail was doing this from the afterlife. Transporting them where they needed to go at the appropriate time. This, of course, was just speculation. Because, oddly enough, they were at a battle that occurred nearly six months after the one they would end up in at Happrew.

"She *will* bring Lindsay back, Cousin," Bryce assured softly. "If anyone can…"

What neither voiced was the will of Fate. Aðísla had cared for Andrew de Moray, yet could not bring him back. Even with her advanced skills at healing and magic, some souls were destined to move on. The thought of Lindsay being one of them seemed impossible. They might not get along, but to lose her now, so soon, bothered him beyond reason.

It upset him so much that it took both Graham and Bryce to hold Conall back when Aðísla ordered that he stay out. William was allowed in, but not him. It didn't matter in the least that it was

Wallace's tent, Conall should stay with Lindsay. He had held her in his arms as she faded away and by all that was holy, he should be there holding her to the end.

She's not yours, he reminded himself. Anything to keep from storming in there. To keep from feeling so strongly that it was his right. That she should be in his arms if she slipped away altogether. If she didn't survive. He ignored the tightening of his chest at the idea and redirected his thoughts. Best to think differently so that he didn't end up cutting down his cousins to get to her.

Even if she survived, he did not want her.

She was better off with one of his kin.

He scowled at Bryce and Graham remembering all too well how they hung all over her like fools in his great hall. More than that, how they were *not* there to protect her when a Sassenach ran his blade through her. Just like that. One second she had been holding a child, the next, bleeding out on his castle floor, the life draining from her glorious silver eyes.

A sight he better bloody well never have to witness again.

"She will be all right," Rona said softly from beside him. "I would know otherwise, Cousin."

When Rona said such a thing, it was typically worth heeding. Rare was the day she was wrong, or so said her cursed gift of seeing life come and go before it actually happened.

Conall refused to look at her. Refused to be hopeful until he was sure.

When Aðísla finally stuck her head out and gestured that Conall enter, his heart about stopped. Was her expression grim because Lindsay was dead?

He stepped inside the tent and immediately went to the cot. She looked pale. Was she breathing? Though tempted to use magic he knew better. They had traveled back to a crucial time in history which meant there could be a warlock or two about. If he used his magic, it might draw unwanted attention.

Aðísla's magic apparently followed another set of rules.

"She's alive, Conall," Aðísla said softly. "More than that, she is nearly healed."

"So your magic—" he began, but she cut him off.

"No, it was not only my magic," she responded. "But the ring's as well I believe."

His eyes shot to the Claddagh then its stone. He wasn't entirely sure he wanted the answer to his next question. "Did it glow? Take on a different color? Is that why it healed her?" Conall frowned at Aðísla. "I didnae know the rings were capable of healing. Is this new?"

"Look at the gem in the ring for yourself." Aðísla gestured at the bauble. "It *is* a different color, and if Rona is correct, it makes no sense."

Not that he would ever admit to it, but now that the sheer panic over Lindsay's potential death was past, he was beginning to see things clearer. She lay peacefully on William's cot beneath a blanket. Color had returned to her cheeks, and her chest rose and fell slowly as she slept. He crouched beside her, his eyes lingering on her lovely face before he looked at her ring again.

"'Tis grayish." He shook his head and frowned at Aðísla. "So 'tis doing what Milly's ring did then? Being undecided?"

"Yes, in a way." Aðísla appeared troubled. "But not like you're thinking." She shook her head. "Not to match a man's eyes I do not think. Not yet."

When he kept frowning in confusion, she continued.

"According to Rona, the ring glowed in your great hall," Aðísla explained, her eyes on Lindsay's face as she pondered something. "It shone the color of that little girl's eyes. The one she tried to protect...comfort." She crouched beside him and gestured at the gem in the ring. "It remains that very color now." She arched a brow at Conall. "A shade remarkably similar to Lindsay's."

Conall studied the gem and tried to remember the child's eyes, but everything had happened so fast. The Sassenach had somehow slipped by his castle's defenses, and he still had no clue how. Outside of MacLeod Castle, Hamilton Castle was the most impregnable fortress in all of Scotland thanks to its location on a seaside cliff. So it made no sense.

Not yet anyway.

He ground his teeth and brushed aside his emotions. They would serve no purpose right now. Not until he had more answers.

"What does this mean then?" His eyes went to Aðísla's, and he shook his head. "That a warlock might somehow be controlling the ring yet again?"

"I dinnae think so," William murmured softly, the first words he had said since Conall entered. "I think Lindsay controls her ring so far and nobody else."

Naturally, Wallace would give his opinion. As it was, he almost ended up with Milly because her gem shone the color of his eyes.

It seemed William had no recollection of seeing them at any battle but the one in Stirling. Because according to Grant, they would all be traveling to two skirmishes. Earnside and Happrew. They were in Strathearn now to fight at the Earnside skirmish so that meant they would eventually travel back in time six more months to Happrew. Based on the fact that William did not recall seeing them there, one of two things happened. Either they would not survive this battle or Adlin and Grant had somehow altered William's memory. That, he surmised, was the more probable of the two scenarios.

Or so he hoped.

Either way, it was always best to remain vague with well-known historical figures while traveling through time.

As it stood, the last time William had seen Lindsay was in his tent before the Battle of Stirling Bridge in twelve ninety seven now it was thirteen hundred and four. A day or so later for Lindsay and Conall but much longer for William. Yet Wallace seemed just as fixated on her. And just as fond.

"I think you are right, William," Aðísla agreed. "In fact, I know you are. At this point, Lindsay does still control her ring yet something tugs at her power. Something determined to get past the walls she has put up. The defiance that is second nature to her."

Walls? Defiance? While Lindsay could get a little heated, as he saw recently in his dungeon, she did not strike him as overly defiant. Why would she be when she could so easily enchant every man around her?

"Can she be moved?" Conall eyed her. "'Twould be better if she was housed with Rona, would it not?"

"'Twould be best if she stayed here," Wallace started, but Conall interrupted him.

"Ye've a sizeable enough band of men." He quirked a brow at William. "Men who will likely be in and out of yer tent, aye?"

"Nay." William frowned at him. "They shall meet me elsewhere."

"So ye say," Conall began before Aðísla cut him off.

"She will wake soon enough. Within hours I imagine." She looked between them. "When she does, *she* will decide where she would like to continue resting. Do you understand?"

It was clear his Viking ancestor would make sure that happened whether or not they agreed.

They both nodded, scowling at each other as Conall debated his next move. Though loathe to leave her alone with Wallace, staying would not be wise either. If she were to awake with him watching over her, it would work against his plan to see her safely in the arms of one of his cousins.

"Until she awakes, I will stay with her," Aðísla continued, not asking William's permission. It seemed she did not need to based on William's grateful look. But then Aðísla had taken good care of his friend, Moray, at one time and Conall knew Wallace would never forget it.

William nodded. "Then I will see to my men." His eyes met Conall's. "Join me, Laird Hamilton."

Not a request but an order if he were not mistaken.

Nonetheless, Conall nodded and followed. He might not have liked Lindsay spending the night in William's tent in Stirling, but the fact remained that William Wallace was to be respected. Revered. The sacrifices he had made for Scotland, the ones he *would* make, were heroic.

As they exited the tent, he noticed his cousins weren't too far off. Ever vigilant. Though he could not help but wonder why Rona was here as well. Was it because she had been in the great hall when they were transported back in time? Or was it, mayhap, because they were so close?

As he and William joined his kin, Conall noticed that Wallace didn't eye Rona as most men did when they met her. Then again, now that they were out of the tent and away from Lindsay, he could see William. Really see him. Though he was seven years older, he seemed aged beyond his years. Tired. But then, if history served correct, Wallace had been on the run for some time and was, by far, the most wanted man in Scotland. Now another skirmish lay on the horizon.

One that history was quite undecided ever took place.

More than that, if this was even the location.

Here they were though which told him all he needed to know. Something would happen. Something important enough to warrant him and his kin being here. Though he had claimed the number of Wallace's men sizeable, they were not. He counted two hundred at most and by the looks of them not the strongest fighting men, either.

"'Tis my hope more come," William said, clearly aware of how ragged his bunch looked. "But then, ye four have come, so that is a good start."

"So yer expecting the Sassenach, aye?" Graham said as they walked through the encampment. "Have ye a battle strategy?"

"Aye, rumor has it a garrison will be passing through." William gestured at the trees around them. "We will fight them by using the forest to our advantage."

It was a tactic often used in these times and Conall well understood it. Guerrilla warfare his mother would call it. In his opinion, it was bloody smart, and he nodded his approval. "What of the tents, though? Will they not be obvious?"

"Props only. Soon to come down," William said. "We're housed in caves not far from here."

"Ye've Lindsay resting in a *prop* then?" Conall stopped short. "Vulnerable to the enemy?"

"Nay." William shook his head as they stopped at a small fire and he handed them a few skins of whisky to share. "I have verra dependable scouts. The Sassenach are still a ways off."

"What about rogue bands?" Bryce growled over his shoulder, already heading back in Lindsay's direction.

"None are about," William called out. "I can assure ye,"

"How would ye know—" Graham started when Rona interrupted him.

"I would say with Adlin's help."

"Aye." Adlin grinned as he and Milly joined them. "All is clear right now."

"When did you arrive?" Conall asked.

"Not long before you."

Before them?

"Did the ring pull ye here too, then?" Graham asked as Milly hugged first Graham then Bryce. Rather than embrace Conall, she eyed him with what he knew were bound to be several uncomfortable questions.

So he said something he hoped she didn't know so she would take her questions elsewhere. "Though she is all right, Lindsay is in William's tent after a difficult ordeal. Mayhap you should be there when she awakens?"

"The ring didnae pull us here, we just knew to come here next," Adlin reported as Milly answered Conall's question without budging an inch. "I know Linds is okay and I intend to go see her soon." She made a gesture back toward the river with her head that meant he would not be escaping so easily. "Meanwhile, I was hoping to speak with you alone, Laird Hamilton."

Her use of his title told him much. She was not feeling all that cordial.

Conall looked at Adlin and made it clear with a stoic expression that he did not think now was an appropriate time for this. Adlin, however, in typical Adlin fashion, merely shrugged and grinned. As usual, he had absolutely no intention of making Conall's life easier.

Fine then. He and Milly didn't go far before she stopped, crossed her arms over her chest, narrowed her eyes, and said the last thing he expected with a glint of humor in her eyes. "Thank you for what you did at the Battle of Stirling Bridge, Conall. Thank you for...protecting Linds like you did."

Before he could respond, she shocked him when she stood on her tip-toes, kissed his cheek then took his hand. "I did not see that coming." She shook her head, a sparkle in her eyes that reminded him far too much of Adlin. "None of us did."

"Aye," he murmured and merely nodded, not sure how else to respond.

"You thought I was upset with you, eh?"

"I didnae know what to expect," he said, preferring to be blunt. "I kissed Lindsay against her will. 'Twould be fair if you were upset with me."

Milly twisted her lips against what he surmised was suppressed amusement before she smoothed her expression and nodded. "I was...more surprised than anything." She perked her brows, clearly trying to remain serious. "I hear after the kiss you ended up in your dungeons..." Her lips twisted again, that same fight in her eyes to remain serious. "Then I hear it took another kiss to free you two."

Damn his bloody grandfather. His eyes swept over the forest. Where was he?

"He's not here. Not yet." Milly tapped her temple and quirked the corner of her mouth. "Grant told Adlin everything telepathically."

Naturally.

"So where is Grandfather?" he said dryly. While tempted to cross his arms over his chest in a defensive posture all too familiar to him, he preferred to keep his hand close to the hilt of his blade. Though Adlin assured them that the Sassenach were not about, he would not risk Milly getting hurt if his cousin was wrong.

"I'm not entirely sure where Grant is," she said softly, her eyes on his. "I'm sorry about what happened at your castle in the great hall, Conall." She shook her head and swallowed hard. "More than you know."

He clenched his jaw, his eyes drifting into the woodland as though he could look forward in time and see what had been left behind. Now that he was no longer distressed over what happened to Lindsay, he should be pestering Adlin to send him home. He should be doing whatever he could to get back to his people. To protect them. Yet he was not, and he loathed the reason why. He detested that he put protecting one life ahead of protecting so many others. His *own people*.

"It hasnae happened yet, Cousin," came Adlin's soft voice from behind him before he joined them. "The battle that just happened at your castle, the lives lost, doesnae happen for eight more winters."

"Why are you telling me this?" But Conall already knew. Because something might very well happen here in thirteen hundred and four that could change the fate of that night.

"You know why." Adlin handed him a skin. "Take a sip or two, Cousin, before we join the others and prepare for what is to come."

They both knew he had barely touched alcohol since Fraser died and though tempted to take a hearty swig now, he would not. It was best to keep a clear mind, especially during such precarious times.

"Nay," Conall replied. "Thank you, Laird MacLomain."

Adlin frowned as Milly chuckled and shook her head, murmuring, "Laird MacLomain again is it?" She cast Adlin an amused look. "I think that's Conall's way of saying let's get serious and damn fast."

Adlin met her amused look with one of his own. "Were we *not* serious then?"

Though he'd had about enough of this conversation, Conall would not head back to the others first. Not until Milly was done speaking. But how was he supposed to know when that was when it seemed she joked just as readily as Adlin now? And it appeared more and more likely they had forgotten he stood there since the two of them kept gazing at each other.

Likely aware he needed saving, Rona appeared, blade in hand as her eyes met his. "Sorry to bother ye, but I could use a hunting partner when yer done speaking with..." Her pointed eyes went to Milly who wasted no time introducing herself.

"I'm so sorry." Milly held out her hand to Rona. "I'm Milly Broun."

"Aye." Rona offered a forced smile as she shook Milly's hand. "I am Rona, daughter of Niall and Nicole MacLomain."

Milly smiled. "Nice to meet you."

Little was said after that, and thankfully the awkward meeting soon ended. He and Rona did not go far before he crouched beside a small stream and splashed cold water on his face. As was her way, Rona said nothing at first and waited him out.

"'Tis all right," he muttered, still crouched as he stared at the water, frustrated.

"Nay." She shook her head, white-knuckling a blade as she eyed the stream for fish. "None of this is, and well ye know it, Cousin."

The battle that had taken Fraser's life had changed them both. And not for the better. They were hollow shells of their old selves, seeking answers to questions they knew may never be answered. It had taken away the light in an already dim situation. In some ways, it had brought them closer. But he often wondered if he should be more alarmed. Where Fraser's sister, Blair, had embraced a warrior's attitude, determined to avenge him, Rona had done something different.

Something...hard to explain.

She had embraced a caustic and sometimes morbid persona.

But then her magic was markedly different than everyone else's. To sense life and death was no small thing. Based on the sudden silence she experienced before her gift ignited, Grant suspected it was born of her mother's semi-deafness. Either way, possessing such magic could by its very nature turn a person more somber when they struggled with grief.

"Grant and Adlin keep more secrets," she spat as she crouched and splashed water on her face as well. "Ye know they do."

"Aye." He frowned and stood. "That is nothing new and willnae help us right now."

"Because we dinnae know what they're hiding." She shook her head and eyed him over her shoulder. "Ye know God sent me along with ye to keep ye safe, Cousin. Ye do know that, aye?"

"Aye," he murmured as he sat on a rock and set to sharpening his blade. "And I am thankful yer here, Cousin. Never doubt that."

Conall scowled at the small voice in his mind that wished she were not. Wished that she was back at MacLomain Castle spending time with her parents healing. Like all of them, Uncle Niall and Aunt Nicole were still struggling with the loss of Fraser and in many ways the loss of their daughter. Rona never went home. She always stayed at Hamilton Castle close to Conall. And close to her memories. Especially those last few moments when they still had Fraser with them.

"Ah, here it comes," she whispered. "Death."

Some might find her words daunting but not Conall who knew she would spear a fish moments later. He sighed and eyed her as she stared at it hanging off her blade. Like every time she had killed something since Fraser's death, there was a bored, dull look in her eyes. As if she felt her prey was where it would ultimately end up anyway. Death spared no creature, human and animal alike.

"Ye love her already then, aye?" Rona whispered, staring at the fish. "Ye'd risk such?"

Conall knew she was talking about Lindsay.

"Och, nay," he muttered. "She but needs protecting because she is foolish and doesnae ken the true dangers here."

"Here or there," she said softly, her eyes never leaving the dead fish. "Our time or this time or the time that ye kissed her." She shook her head and snorted. "Och, wait, 'twas two different eras ye've kissed her in, was it not?"

"They will want more to eat than that," he said as he stood, not in the mood to explain himself after what he had just witnessed at his castle. The possible future on the horizon. "Come, Rona, let us hunt."

"Dinnae patronize me, Cousin," she muttered as she stood, ripped the fish off the dagger and tossed it his way. "If ye think my mind's not quite right, just say so."

He had stopped saying so a long time ago.

Conall caught the fish and tossed it onto a rock. They would pick it up on the way back if a scavenger did not get it. Right now, Rona needed a bigger kill. Something to help release her anger. More than that, her negative magic. A magic that some already suspected resembled that of a warlock's.

So he ran alongside her until she did what no other human could and caught the scent of her prey minutes ahead of time. Usually, they would slow and enjoy the hunt but not this time. He let her take the lead as she raced forward, whipped her dagger and downed a buck before its instincts ever sensed them coming. It was not a fair fight by any means, but this had been Rona's way since the day Fraser was sliced open in front of them. One way or another, every single moment since then had been payback.

Unfortunately, that meant dealing a blow that left her prey suffering.

Conall closed the distance quickly and ended the animal's torment. Though tempted as always to chastise her for her cruel behavior, he knew it would fall on deaf ears. They'd had this conversation many times before, but it did no good. Rona had and would continue to take out her grief on innocent creatures. Animals were for food and clothing, not an outlet for suffering to match her own. Yet he understood her grief, therefore, continued to defend her to the rest of their kin.

He hoisted the buck over his shoulder and headed back. Like always, Rona was caught up in an adrenaline rush combined with remorse. And, as she did every time, she whispered the same hoarse words as she strode after him.

"I am sorry."

It was always hard to know if she meant it. Right now he had other things to worry about as should Rona. Most specifically, what lay behind and ahead. What had happened at Hamilton Castle and how what they did *now* might affect that.

They were just around the bend from the encampment when a loud wail resounded through the forest.

It was Lindsay…screaming as though she was just driven through with a sword once again.

Chapter Five

"**L**INDS, CAN YOU hear me?" came Milly's faraway voice. "Can you *see* me?"

"Milly?" Lindsay whispered after her scream died off. For a second, she swore she gazed through the woods at Rona before the Scotswoman whipped a blade at her. It had seemed *so* real.

She clutched her chest just above her heart at what felt like lingering pain and gasped as she sat up. "What happened?" She blinked rapidly, trying to acclimate. The forest had been replaced with a dimly lit tent, and a person sat nearby in the shadows. "Is that you, Milly?"

"Hey, sweetie." Milly's face became clearer, her eyes concerned. "How are you feeling?"

"Where…what…" she started to say before Milly squeezed her hand, shook her head, and explained everything.

They had traveled back in time. The battle at Hamilton Castle had yet to happen. There was no way to know if the little girl had lived or died.

"And Conall?" she nearly whispered but didn't mostly because there was no need. He had done what was expected of him and carried her here. Then he left her to Aðísla. That made sense. She knew better than to have expected him to be by her side when she woke. That might mean he cared.

"Conall is off hunting with Rona," Milly said, eying Lindsay. "In case you were curious."

"I was not," Lindsay assured and smoothed her hair back as she sat up, pretending to worry about her appearance when it was the last thing on her mind. "How are you? Adlin?" She met Milly's eyes and plastered on her warmest smile though she suspected it wobbled. "Are you totally in love or what?"

"Totally," Milly assured, smiling. "He's..."

When she didn't finish her sentence, Lindsay did so for her. "Everything you had no idea you wanted, now couldn't imagine living without. Right?"

Milly's smile grew soft and her eyes dewy as she nodded. No words were needed.

"I'm happy for you." Lindsay squeezed her hand. "More than you know, sweetheart."

"Thank you." Milly cocked her head, her eyes still locked with Lindsay's. "So how about that kiss?"

She knew exactly what kiss Milly referred to.

Lindsay merely shrugged, not about to make a big deal out of it.

"Oh, *really*?" Milly's eyes widened with humor. "So no sharing yet, huh?" She winked, baiting Lindsay. "Because rumor has it that kiss was *so* much more for Conall."

She highly doubted that. He might have enjoyed kissing her, but she already knew him well enough to know he would *never* admit it.

Again, she only offered a dainty shrug.

"You're not gonna tell me a thing are you?" Milly appeared totally enthralled as she leaned forward, her sky blue eyes merry. "By the way, you overacted during the kiss I saw." She shook her head, grinning. "I can't speak for the second one."

"I *did* overact," Lindsay agreed then fibbed. "Can you really blame me? As you can imagine, the English had me somewhat nervous."

Milly snorted and chuckled. "Yeah, yeah, sure they did." One brow rose slowly. "Because it certainly couldn't have been that you were so wowed by Conall's kiss that you forgot how to *act* altogether."

Lindsay narrowed her eyes as she swung her legs over the side of the cot. "*Definitely* not. As you saw, my acting skills are flawless no matter the circumstances."

"Typically I would agree." Milly's amusement didn't fade in the least. "So imagine my surprise when I saw otherwise."

She knew Milly was just trying to glean more information, so she kept quiet and focused on acclimating to sitting up then hopefully standing.

"I'm not so sure you should stand quite yet," Milly said as Aðísla entered.

Not one to back down from a challenge, Lindsay brushed off the comment. Yet when she placed her hand on the edge of the cot to stand, she noticed her ring and hesitated.

"Dear Lord, it's gray now." She frowned and looked at Milly, not sure she wanted to hear the answer. "Does it match anyone's eye color?"

"It does not," Aðísla said. "Anyone's, that is, except your own."

"My own?" she replied, surprised. "What does that mean?"

"We don't know yet." Milly shook her head. "But we'll figure it out, Linds."

"Like you figured out whose eyes your ring matched at first?"

"At first," Milly reminded. "But not ultimately."

Lindsay sighed and nodded. There was no point getting stressed over this. She knew the gems in these rings could be fickle. Besides, even if the gem *did* glow, she had no intention of being with any man, period.

"Let me look at you, Lindsay," Aðísla said as she crouched in front of her. "Both your mind and body went through something very traumatic."

Right, she had been on the verge of death, hadn't she? Yet now there was no wound. Though she should be both grateful and alarmed, she felt oddly unaffected. As though it made perfect sense. A fact, she realized as Milly eyed her with concern and perhaps confusion, that must have many wondering what happened.

The Viking looked her over then placed a thumb to the center of her forehead, explaining that she was accessing her third eye. Within seconds she narrowed her eyes, pulled her thumb away and whispered, "You're completely closed off to me now."

That told Lindsay at some point she had not been. Instead of lashing out at Aðísla for invading her privacy, she kept a serene expression on her face. There was no need to let them see her real emotions. Best that she kept those to herself.

"It is okay," Aðísla confirmed as her eyes met Milly's. "She is fully healed and should have no issue standing."

Lindsay could have told her that as she kept a pleasant smile on her face and stood. Though the world swayed ever-so-slightly, everything straightened out fast enough. "I'm fine." She glanced at them both in reassurance when they tried to help her. "Truly, I am."

Though she still wore the same dress, her shoes had been replaced with boots. Aðísla put a fur around her shoulders as Milly held the tent flap open and said, "Let's go see what the guys are up to. I suspect they're hatching plans with William."

Curious, Lindsay glanced at Milly. "It must have been odd for him seeing you again after seven years."

William had been very attracted to Milly and would have gladly been with her had she not been meant for Adlin.

"It was certainly strange," Milly said softly but didn't elaborate as they exited.

She was not surprised to see the same four men that had been at the Battle of Stirling Bridge. Conall and his three cousins. The only ones missing from their last adventure were Grant, Blair, and Jim. As far as she knew, Blair and Jim were still in the future. Though surprised to see Rona here as well she made no mention of it as she joined everyone.

Graham and Bryce were immediately on either side of her. Graham urged her to sit in front of a small fire while Bryce handed her a stick with meat on it. Adlin offered her a skin of whisky with a wide smile. "'Tis verra good to see you up and about, lass."

All agreed.

"It's good to be up." She smiled warmly at them. "Thank you."

His expression as stoic as ever, Conall's eyes flickered over her before settling on the fire again. Yet she saw the tension in his body. The tightness in his broad shoulders. More than that, she remembered how concerned he had been when he knelt over her on the floor of his castle. The stark fear she never would have expected.

"As soon as you've had a bite to eat, Lindsay," William said as he joined them. "We will move to the caves."

Her eyes met his, and she nodded. "Of course. Good to see you again, William."

Though it had only been a few days, it felt like eons since she had agreed to be his spy.

"Aye, lass," William said. "'Tis bloody good to see ye as well. How are ye feeling?"

She didn't have to look at Conall to know he grew even tenser if that were possible. Likely because William seemed so glad to see her.

"I'm feeling much better," she responded. "Thank you for asking."

He nodded and considered her before he turned his attention to Adlin. "Might I speak with ye alone?"

After Adlin nodded and they left, everyone chatted about preparations for the upcoming skirmish. She absently followed it as she nibbled on meat and took a few small sips of whisky. What she wouldn't do for a freshly tossed salad and perhaps some fish.

"Here, lass." Barely glancing at her, Conall handed her another stick with some sort of meat on it.

Lindsay frowned and took the stick, studying its contents. "What is this?"

"Fish." He frowned at her. "Did you not want some then?"

"I did," she said softly, meeting his frown. "Not that I said as much."

Conall grunted something indiscernible before he unsheathed his blade and started sharpening it without casting her another look. Meanwhile, Lindsay handed her meat to Bryce and sampled the fish. It was very good, and she said as much.

"Rona caught it not me," Conall stated and left it at that.

Lord, he was an uncivil beast, wasn't he?

"Well, thank you then, Rona," she said as she enjoyed it.

Rona, it seemed, was as bland as Conall because she didn't bother with a response. The look she gave Lindsay, however, was a giveaway. She was not a fan, and God only knew why. Not one to let another drag her down, Lindsay refocused on Milly, Graham, and Bryce and made the best of the time remaining before everyone was on the move.

Tents were left behind as they made their way deeper into the woods away from the river. The weather was chilly, so she was grateful for the hooded fur Bryce wrapped around her shoulders instead of the one she had been wearing. Though both he and Graham flirted readily, she kept them at bay. After all, she had plenty of practice.

What she had little practice with were men who ignored her especially after kissing her.

Regardless, Conall kept his distance and never looked her way. Or so he wanted her to believe. She supposed that was for the best. She did not want him. And she certainly did not want to promote the desire she knew he felt for her. Keeping their distance was best for them both.

Milly never strayed far from her side, and eventually, Adlin rejoined them. When he did, his brows were knit with concern.

"What is it?" Milly asked.

"There are more Sassenach moving into the area than Wallace anticipated," he said. "'Twill make this battle a wee bit more difficult."

"How can I help?" Milly and Lindsay asked at the same time.

"Och, you're good lasses," Adlin murmured as he steered Milly closer to him. "But there isnae much either of you can do until we know more." His eyes went to Milly. "Mayhap you've a mind to use your witchcraft to keep an eye out for warlocks?"

She nodded. "Of course."

Milly had the ability to astral project out of her body. If the last time she did as much was any kind of example, then it seemed she could also home in on pure evil.

"I can help too," Lindsay said softly. "I am very good at…convincing men to do what I want them to."

She wasn't that surprised when Graham and Bryce adamantly shook their heads no, and Conall doubled back. She didn't have a chance to get another word out before he steered her away from the others.

"Excuse me—" she started to say before he cut her off.

"You will *not* be going near any more Sassenach," he bit out, his hand wrapped firmly around her upper arm as he directed them even further away from prying ears. "Do you ken, lass?"

Here they were yet again tromping off into the woods together with his assertive nature nothing less than overbearing.

"I *ken* that you're being overly dramatic," she bit right back. "If you hadn't noticed, I'm along on this journey, which means it's for a reason." She stopped short and frowned at him. "We all knew what that reason was at the last battle. And we all know I played a very important role." She cocked her head. "Do you think if I have the chance to do that again, I intend to turn into a coward? What do you take me for?"

She could tell by the way his brows snapped together, and his expression grew fierce that she was not going to like his answer.

"I take you for a twenty-first century lass who thinks she will remain unscathed because she is overly confident in her wits, wiles and most certainly her physical allure," he ground out, his hand not budging an inch. "I think you got bloody lucky before and to test that luck again is foolhardy."

Overly confident in *what*? Had he just insulted her not once but three times? She couldn't act calm if she tried and she definitely could not stop a heated response.

"My wits and wiles are what saved Scotland just a few short days ago," she reminded him through clenched teeth. "And we both know all my looks did for me was put me up against a tree thanks to you and your lust."

"I was not lusting," he started before she cut him off.

"Oh, that's right, you were trying to save me from the English." Her eyes rounded. "By satisfying your lust and don't you deny it!"

"Och, 'twas no hardship on you though, aye?" he came right back at her. "You enjoyed the kiss well enough." His actions were contradictory to his words as his grip loosened and became gentler. His thickening brogue, though, was heated and out of character. "But then I imagine ye have enjoyed every kiss ye've given a man since ye traveled back in time."

Lindsay slapped him without thinking twice.

It was the first time she had ever hit a man, and though he might have deserved it, she didn't believe in hitting another. Not like this.

Stunned, he released her arm and simply stared, baffled and perhaps even a little disappointed in himself. It was hard to know with a man like Conall.

Both infuriated and saddened by his words not to mention her own overzealous response, she continued after the others. Milly, naturally, had stopped and looked like she was ready to throttle Conall. So did Adlin, Bryce, and Graham for that matter. Lindsay shook her head as she passed them and kept walking. It was time to focus on other things.

Anything but Laird Hamilton.

Of all people, Aðísla fell in beside her but said nothing. Not at first anyway. Instead, she seemed to be letting Lindsay gather herself. When she at last spoke, they had just entered the cave systems they would be taking shelter in.

"While I do not condone what Conall said to you," she murmured, her tone softer than Lindsay had ever heard it. "I hope you will take into consideration that those words were only meant to push you away not offend you."

"I know." And she did, but that did not make them acceptable. "I know exactly where Conall is coming from Aðísla which is all the more reason it's best we keep our distance at this point." Her eyes met the Viking's in the semi-darkness. "Distance we *both* want."

Though it was clear she wished to say more, Aðísla only nodded in agreement before Lindsay continued on alone. Well, as alone as she could get since Graham walked in front of her and Bryce behind as the way got narrower. They didn't go far before it opened up again into what appeared to be a honeycomb of sizeable caves. Tents were set up to protect against the cold draft billowing through. Not many though. It appeared most would sleep on meager plaids and blankets tossed onto the rock.

"You, me, and Aðísla will share a tent," Milly said as she joined her, eying the area. "Rona can as well, but we'll see."

Translation. Rona would be with Conall. It was obvious she rarely left his side.

"I'm not worried about a tent." Lindsay shook her head. "I don't care where I sleep."

Milly gave her an odd look before she said, "I know you don't."

Well, what did she mean by that look?

"What are your thoughts on bathing?" Milly's eyes met hers. "And maybe having a heart to heart."

"Not if it's about—"

"It's not about Conall," Milly interrupted. "Come on, sweetie. Adlin showed me a spot earlier where you can clean up a little."

Cleaning up didn't sound half bad, so she agreed and followed, not surprised to see Aðísla fall in behind them. Likely Adlin's request for protection if she were to guess.

"I have another dress for you to change into in this satchel," Milly said as she retrieved a torch and they went down a narrow hallway into another chamber. That was her tasteful way of saying it was time for Lindsay to get out of her blood spattered dress.

Like she had been doing all along, she swallowed and ignored the memories. The images of the little girl watching first her father then her mother being murdered. The blood that slickened the great hall floor. The same blood dried and caked on her dress now. She knew Adlin or his cousins would have gotten rid of it with magic if they dared. But there was no way to know if warlocks were about and they couldn't risk Wallace being discovered.

Aðísla didn't join them at the water's edge and remained out of sight yet Lindsay knew she wasn't far off.

"Oh, I imagine this will feel fabulous," Lindsay declared, determined to put on her usual airs in spite of her discouraged mood. "Even if it *is* frigid."

"Aw, it's not that bad," Milly lied as she stuck her hand in then sat on a rock. "But I think I'll pass."

"You intended to pass from the moment you asked me to come here." Lindsay winked and offered a knowing smile as she stripped down. "If I were a different sort of friend, I would say get your butt in here. Misery loves company."

"Thankfully, you're the best sort of friend and won't." Milly gave her an apologetic look. "If you *really* want me in there you know I'll join you."

"Don't be silly," Lindsay said. "No need to freeze if you don't have to."

While she could just crawl into the other dress and stay blissfully dry, Milly had brought her here for a reason. She knew Lindsay would want to wash off what she had seen in that great hall even if the blood didn't literally stain her skin.

"Oh, *hell*, this is cold," she whispered as she waded in. Yet she didn't flinch. Not once. She was made of tougher stuff than that.

Almost as if Milly sensed what she was thinking, she asked the last thing Lindsay expected after she sank down into the water.

"I've never asked you much about yourself in general because I respect your privacy," she said softly. "But based on what happened between Hamilton Castle and here, I think it might be time. Heck, based on everything that happened before that."

Lindsay remained quiet, knowing full well what was coming as Milly continued.

"I could tell as I filled you in earlier that you remembered what happened at Hamilton Castle. Most specifically what happened to *you* in that great hall." Milly's eyes narrowed. "I mean Aðísla is a great healer but aren't you curious why you're wound free, Linds?"

Lindsay considered Milly for a few moments, debating how much to tell her before she sighed and shook her head. It was too hard to share. Her secrets had been hers for so long. "I remember very little about what happened except that it was violent."

"It certainly was," Milly said, eying her with that same curiosity and confusion she had before.

"What I might or might not recall aside," Lindsay said softly but firmly. "I think we can both agree it was traumatic and something I may not wish to chat about quite yet."

"I see. My apologies, sweetie." Yet it seemed Milly would not be put off so easily. Some might say she was being pushy, but her sharp, knowing eyes insinuated she knew full well Lindsay hid things. "If you would rather not talk about that, then how about why I found you sleeping on the floor in my house back in New Hampshire? Because I have a feeling it has something to do with all of this. That it's an important part of who you are."

Lindsay's heartbeat slowed to a crawl as her eyes locked with Milly's. She could lie or tell the truth. The truth wasn't an option, but Milly would see through a flat out lie.

"It's a way to remind me where I came from," she began, trying not to flinch at how cliché she sounded. "To never forget that I didn't always have money."

"I'm sorry, Linds," Milly replied. "I didn't mean to pry, but I'm trying to understand..."

Milly did not entirely believe her. She could see it in her eyes.

"Understand what?" Lindsay kept her voice playful and her eyes daring. "How a gal goes from rags to riches?"

"No." Milly shook her head. "You're an amazing woman, Linds. I've never questioned your success. Not for a second." She frowned. "But I *do* want to know how you survived that English encampment. Then, Aðísla's assistance aside, how you healed so miraculously after being killed." Her eyes grew moist. "Because you died, Linds. You flat out died." She bit her lower lip and shook her head. "And when I talk about your time with the Brits I'm not thinking along the lines Conall did but about what Grant said."

"And what did Grant say?" Lindsay murmured, taking the dress from Milly as she got out.

"About the same thing Jessie implied about all of us Brouns," she said. "That you were special. Exceptionally special." Milly tapped her fingers as she counted off her abilities. "I can reincarnate myself, astral project then actually move myself via magic." Her eyes grew curious. "What can *you* do, Linds? Because I call utter bullshit if you say nothing."

While tempted to buy herself some time by reminding Milly that she knew nothing about her abilities until she met Adlin, she refrained. Instead, as she stared into her friend's eyes and realized there was nothing but death and heartache behind and likely ahead, she said more than intended.

"Though I'm not entirely sure why I'm wound free now, I do have a particular gift I *can* explain," Lindsay admitted. "I have a certain talent when it comes to men, and even women I suppose. I can...enchant them for lack of a better word."

"*Enchant* them." Milly thought that over, nodding. "That makes sense. It's not just your looks or mannerisms, but your magic."

"You could say that," Lindsay said. "I always kind of looked at myself as a succubus without the suck-the-man's-soul-out-of-his-body part." She shrugged. "But that's all I can compare it to, and it works on any man I want it to...or at least it did."

Milly kept nodding, intrigued. "Tell me about it." She tilted her head in question. "It's clear you knew you had a gift, that it was different. When did you first discover it? What happens specifically when you use it?"

Lindsay ground her teeth against painful flashbacks, specifically the night that first sparked her gift, and remained vague. "I was young. In my teens, I think." She redirected the conversation to what Milly would find more interesting. "I was around twenty-one when I used it on a man for the first time. A bouncer at a posh club I needed to get into. I needed to," she made quotes in the air, "*be seen* by those who mattered. Directors, producers, agents, you name it."

Clearly intrigued, Milly propped her chin on her fist and nodded for Lindsay to continue.

"Well, it was like any other night I suppose. I was all done up, and looked quite amazing I might say." She flashed a smile at Milly to keep the mood light and off the dark underbelly of the conversation. "Yet this time when I tossed my hair and met the bouncer's eyes, something...simmered."

"Simmered?" Milly rolled her eyes and grinned. "Like *attraction*?"

"Well, sure, on his part," Lindsay acknowledged. "But it was more than that, somehow, on *my* part."

"So you developed the hots for the bouncer?"

"No, not quite." Lindsay shook her head. "More like I finally perfected my act and convinced myself that I had the hots for him. The moment that happened, a vibration rolled through me as our eyes locked, and after that..." She shrugged a shoulder. "He was mine."

"What does that mean?" Milly sat forward a little, completely enthralled. "He was *yours*."

"I mean after that, he did anything I asked of him." Lindsay tried not to look guilty. "And I mean anything."

Milly's eyes rounded as Lindsay tied up her dress. "Oh, God, what did you make him do, Linds?"

"Mind you, it was for experimental reasons." Sort of. "And nothing so bad as that."

"So bad as what?" Milly shook her head. "Linds, you're not acting right now. It's just me. There's no script. Tell me what you mean and stop being..." She made a dismissive gesture with her hand. "So flippantly vague as if we weren't talking about you bewitching a bouncer...for real!"

"Right." Lindsay paused for effect. "Well, after a few weeks I had him do some odd things in the back room to prove what I suspected to be true. That he was completely under my spell...that I could order him to do anything."

"Oh, no, what did you ask the poor man to do?" Milly asked, her eyes round again.

"Nothing *too* bad." Lindsay smirked as she tugged on her boots. "Just kiss his toes, howl at the moon, stupid stuff like that."

"And he did every last thing?"

"Yes." She shook her head. "Then the next guy I enchanted did, then the next, until..."

When she trailed off, Milly frowned. "Until what?"

"Until I decided I wanted to make it on my own, so I did," she said with a little more vehemence than intended as she ran her fingers through her wet hair and combed it the best she could.

Milly eyed her, understanding where Lindsay's mind was at.

"Linds, almost-succubus-like-magic aside, you're genuinely talented at acting. You know that, right?"

"I do." And she did. "But it took almost more strength than I had not to take the easy way out, Mil. To not bewitch those directors into casting me as the lead when they chose another." She sighed. "And, believe me, there were enough of those."

Milly stood and looked at her with a level of respect that Lindsay still wasn't used to. It was the same look her friend gave her on their last adventure when Lindsay volunteered to bait the English.

"I'm proud of you, hon." Milly pulled her in for a big hug. "Amazed *and* proud. Don't you forget it."

"Don't be," Lindsay murmured, hugging her back. "Not yet. Not until I've ultimately done what I'm here for."

Milly pulled back and frowned. "What do you mean?"

"You know what I mean." Lindsay kept a positive look on her face. "I'm here for a reason, Mil, and you and I both know it has to do with my gift."

"Chances are good," Milly said, always one to be honest. "You, the gem and a MacLomain...or someone with MacLomain blood. You realize that right?"

"Yes, I do." Lindsay nodded. On that fact, she was not deluding herself. The only difference in her case was she fully intended to harness the gem's power then move on.

"Ah," Milly said softly, eyeing Lindsay with that look she got. "You think you'll be able to save the day then use your not-quite-succubus powers to tell your one true love to go in the opposite direction because you don't want a man in your life."

"Well, when you say it like that, yes." Lindsay shrugged as she wrapped a fur around her shoulders and they headed back in the direction they had come. "Not a bad plan, right?"

"I suppose not," Milly conceded before she stopped, touched Lindsay's arm and looked at her curiously. "Have you used this power of yours on Graham or Bryce? Better yet, Conall?"

"Why better yet Conall?" Lindsay frowned. "As if I would want to."

Though she *had* been since the moment she met him. Anything to get him under her thumb so she could steer him away...which he somewhat seemed to be doing on his own anyway. Damn confusing man.

"No, I haven't needed to," she fibbed.

"Liar." Milly's eyes narrowed. "You thought about it with Bryce until you learned he was engaged and maybe even Graham until you figured out he wasn't entirely woo'able either for reasons we're all still trying to figure out." She made a flippant gesture. "You liked them both so left them alone."

A sly smile curled Milly's lips as she continued. "Now if you *truly* wanted to control and redirect any man I would think Laird Hamilton's at the top of your list. If for no other reason than to drive him in the opposite direction..." She slanted another one of those all too knowing looks at Lindsay. "Because despite what an utter dickhead he's been to you lately, you *do* want him looking anywhere but at you, *right*, Linds?"

Lindsay started to answer, but the words trailed away as a shadow brushed by her. What *was* that?

"Linds, are you all right?" Milly asked, but she barely heard her as she spun.

A tall, older but very handsome man in a Hamilton plaid materialized directly behind her. He looked so much like Conall and Grant she knew who he was in an instant.

Grant's son.

Conall's father.

Darach Hamilton.

Chapter Six

"I WAS WRONG," Conall muttered. "And ye bloody well know it."

"Ye were not." Rona scowled as she eyed him. "Ye knew the lassie was using her feminine ways wrongly and ye called her on it is all."

Conall frowned. No, he had done far worse than that and knew it the moment the words left his mouth. He knew it as he watched Lindsay's eyes. She was not the creature he accused her of being and even for the sake of pushing her away, his words were too harsh. But he had been heated, no, infuriated, when he heard her offer to put her life on the line.

Again.

The bloody lass would be the death of him with her antics and heroic ways. Yet when she slapped him, when he felt the sting of her palm and saw the hurt in her eyes, he knew it had gone too far. It was one thing to push away a lass, another to cause the sort of pain he had.

There had to be a better way to keep her at arm's length.

Yet at every turn, she did something to rile him up again.

Almost as if she heard his thoughts, her voice drifted through his mind. *"Darach Hamilton?"*

Caught off guard by both the feel of her in his mind and her saying his father's name, he dropped what he was doing and strode in her direction. She and Milly had only gone a few caves over. By the time he joined them, Lindsay was sitting on a rock, trembling and Milly sat beside her. Adlin was two steps behind Conall.

"What happened?" Conall frowned as he looked around. Only Aðísla stood nearby. Hand on the hilt of his blade, his eyes returned to Lindsay. "You sounded distressed…you said my da's name."

"I did," she whispered and met his eyes, more shaken than he had ever seen her. Genuinely shaken which told him a lot.

"I need to talk to Grant." Her eyes swung to Adlin. "Do you know where he is?"

"Nay, not at the moment." Adlin sat beside her and took her hand. "What did you see, Lindsay? What happened?"

It took almost all Conall had not to drag her out of there and demand answers. This was *his* father they were talking about not Adlin's.

"It…I…" Her eyes went from Adlin to Milly before they met Conall's and she released a choppy sigh. "Then I need to speak with you. Alone."

Adlin didn't quite frown but came close to it as he looked from her to Conall then back again. "Are you sure, lass?"

"Aye, I would say she's sure," Conall ground out. "Laird MacLomain."

Adlin's eyes stayed with Lindsay's. "Are you then, lass? Do you want to be alone with Laird Hamilton?"

Ah, so Adlin *could* use his proper title. Telling. And likely in a way Conall should take more heed to, but he was too concerned about Lindsay. As to his father, they would see about that. As far as he was concerned, her ring could very well be playing tricks on her…on them.

"Come." Conall held out his hand to her. "Let us go talk."

Lindsay's eyes fell to his hand, and she shook her head as she stood. "Thank you but no. I can walk just fine on my own, Laird Hamilton."

He didn't blame her for her distrust of him, her defiance. A defiance he was finally getting a peek at. One she kept well hidden. The *real* her underneath. He realized as they walked away from the others that it had been the real her since she slapped him. Since he saw the raw pain in her eyes that he had no idea existed.

They only went one cave over in the opposite direction. Conall set his torch in a bracket common to these caves it seemed, leaned against a waist high rock and waited while she crossed her arms over her chest, paced and looked anywhere but at him. It was clear she was upset, even agitated, and trying to make sense of something.

"Lindsay," he said calmly. When she offered no response, he repeated her name and decided to be honest. "Lindsay, please tell me what is happening and why you spoke my father's name within my mind."

She stopped short and met his eyes. "Within your mind?"

"Aye," he responded, doing his best to sound calm, not concerned. What if a warlock was inside her head? Infecting her like the last one tried to do to Milly?"

Though inclined to offer her comfort, he figured she would shy away.

"He's alive, Conall," she whispered as her eyes stayed with his. "Your father is alive."

"What do you speak of?" When he stepped closer she took a small step back then one forward, her eyes narrowed. There was more of that defiance he had no idea she possessed. And again, it wasn't an act in the least.

He urged her to sit on a rock. "Sit, and I will stand."

She eyed him for a moment before she did as he asked and sat, her demeanor still very different than what he was used to. Not sultry and enticing, not trying to lure. Not trying to *enchant*. Conall frowned as that word churned in his mind when all he should be focusing on was her reference to his father.

"He wants you to forget about him," she said, her voice soft and hoarse. "You, Grant, Sheila, Jackie...all of you."

"I dinnae ken," he said more intensely than he meant to. He didn't step closer though and never touched her. "What do you mean, lass?"

"He sent a warning," she said softly. "Never look for him, or it will mean your death."

"How did you see him?" Conall kept frowning. "Where did he go?"

"I think..." She shook her head. "I think though he was alive, he was also a ghost...he was transparent."

"Och," Conall muttered, frustrated. "You have been through a lot. 'Twas likely just your imagination."

"I don't think so," she murmured then described the man she had seen. By all accounts, it sounded just like his father. "He told me you probably wouldn't believe me so he shared something only you two would know to prove it was really him."

"And what was that?"

"When you were ten years old you told him that you would never take a wife." Lindsay cleared her throat, clearly uncomfortable. "Not unless she was the faery in the tree."

His blood chilled. Indeed, nobody but his da knew he had said that about the girl he saw on many occasions in the great oak in front of MacLomain Castle. A tree with a rich, magical history.

"'Tis verra likely a warlock has gotten inside all of our minds," Conall said crisply, trying to navigate around this uncomfortable information. "'Tis more likely that than having actually been my da."

"He didn't seem evil in the least, Laird Hamilton," she said, continuing to address him formally. She was putting distance between them, and he deserved it. Distance, he reminded himself, that he wanted too.

"And how familiar are you with evil that you would know the difference?" he asked.

"Familiar enough," she muttered as she started back toward the others.

Conall grabbed the torch and fell into step beside her. "Did this entity say anything else?"

He tried his best to keep his eyes straight ahead and not on her. Strangely enough, she smelled of the very wildflowers that surrounded the oak during summer. And there was something alluring about her thick damp hair. He longed to feel the cool silky weight of it in his hands.

"No, your father did not say anything else," she replied.

"Why did you feel the need to speak with Grant alone about this?" He clenched his jaw. "Then me when you realized Grandfather was not available."

"Because it felt personal." She shrugged. "Private."

"It sounds to me like a warning that should be heard by all."

"Then, by all means, tell everyone," she said, her tone tight. "I just assumed they might want the same proof you did." Her eyes dusted over him. "Forgive me if I figured you wouldn't want them to know you intended to marry a make-believe *faery*."

"She wasn't make-believe," he nearly said but bit his tongue. Lindsay was the last person he wanted to discuss this with. The hairless girl with big sad eyes would always be his best kept secret. A girl he had only ever seen glimpses of, but would never forget.

Lindsay slowed and cast him an odd look before continuing.

"What?" he said.

"Nothing," she murmured. "I'm just not used to…hearing other people's thoughts I suppose."

Conall ground his jaw and asked something he suspected he already knew the answer to. "Are you hearing everyone's thoughts or just mine?"

"Does it matter?"

"You know it does," he muttered, praying she would answer yes.

"So far, I only hear your thoughts." She frowned. "Hopefully, soon enough, maybe I'll hear others. Maybe even William's."

Well aware she had said that on purpose, Conall refused to be baited. If nothing else, he needed to control his behavior around her.

"I will simply tell them what you saw and nothing more," he stated, shifting the conversation away from both William and his childhood faery. "They can choose what to make of it."

"Do what you like."

That was the last thing she said to him before she strode in Milly's direction. He sighed and frowned, annoyed at the feeling he experienced in her absence. The same feeling he had felt since the moment they met. The very same that had turned him into her unseen but vigilant protector.

"Ye ought to just tell her how ye feel rather than being so angry at her all the time," Graham mentioned as he joined him. "'Tis clear the two of ye desire each other."

"Is that what ye gathered from her slap," Conall said, not hiding his sarcasm.

"Ye cannae turn from love because yer afraid of losing it," Graham said, always a little too quick to offer his opinion. "'Twill make a bitter old man out of ye, aye?"

Conall ignored him and headed Adlin's way. Graham had a mission, and he suspected it would not be the last time he tried pushing Conall toward Lindsay. A tactic, he realized, meant to steer her away from Graham even as he pretended to woo her. What was the bloody man up to?

Adlin was once again discussing the upcoming skirmish with Wallace but stopped talking as he and Graham joined them. Both were concerned about Lindsay, so he explained what happened. As she had surmised, Adlin asked the same thing Conall had. So he remained relatively honest.

"He told her information only I would know, but I dinnae think we should necessarily trust it," he reported. "I believe a warlock could have just as easily manipulated her."

"I agree," Adlin said, not pressing the issue. "Yet 'tis nice to have at least a wee bit o' hope, aye, Conall?"

He offered no response. Hope was not something he trusted or embraced easily. Instead, he focused on what Adlin and William had been discussing before. "So ye plan to attack as soon as the Sassenach arrive on the morrow?"

"Aye," William replied. "'Twill be bad weather which will work to our advantage."

Conall nodded, well aware that the air had shifted and chilled even further. A mixture of freezing rain and snow would arrive by sun-up. While he agreed it would help in a spontaneous battle, it was also more suited to seasoned warriors of which Wallace seemed in short supply. The Sassenach, however, were likely traveling with just such warriors and as was grimly reported, more than expected.

"Just tell me what ye need of me," he said to Wallace, "and my blade is yers."

William nodded, briefly caught them up on what directions they planned to come from and which warriors he wanted where. Magic was not to be used unless absolutely necessary or if Adlin said otherwise.

When William eventually strode off, Conall frowned at Adlin. "Yer planning something sooner, I take it?"

"Aye." Adlin looked from Conall to Graham then to Bryce who had just joined them. "After she's rested for a few hours, Milly will be astral projecting to the Sassenach camp. When she does, I will already be there with Bryce, Graham, and Aðísla." His eyes went to Conall. "I would like ye and Rona to stay here and watch over the lasses. Milly most especially."

While he would rather be amongst his fellow warriors spying on the enemy, he was well aware that Adlin had just entrusted him with a great deal.

"Aye, Cousin, I will keep Milly safe," Conall vowed. "Ye have my word."

"And Lindsay," Bryce ground out, clearly not happy with her being left out or, no doubt, Conall's treatment of her earlier.

"Of course I will keep Lindsay safe." Conall narrowed his eyes at Bryce. "As I have since the moment she traveled back in time and better than any other."

"Better?" Bryce narrowed his eyes as well. "Is that what ye call driving a lass to slapping ye?"

"Enough." Adlin frowned. "We all know what we need to do. Bryce and Graham, meet me at the cave's entrance in three hours." His eyes met Conall's. "I'll expect ye at the lasses' tent at the same time. Discreetly, of course."

"Aye," all three replied before they went their separate ways. Or at least Conall tried to before Adlin stopped him.

"How fare ye, Cousin?" Adlin asked. "It couldnae have been easy hearing yer da's message."

"A message I willnae believe until I have more proof," Conall stated. "Until then, I willnae believe 'twas him. I willnae be so foolish."

"No, I dinnae suppose ye will," Adlin said softly, eying him with that wise look he was always so good at. A gaze all that much more intense now that he had come into his full power.

"Ye've an intense way of dealing with Lindsay that I feel needs to be addressed," Adlin continued.

"Is that so?" Conall crossed his arms over his chest and perked his brows. Adlin might have just honored him by asking him to watch over Milly, but that did not give him the right to father him. Or grandfather him, if he were to guess Adlin's thoughts. Because Adlin would do whatever he thought Grant would want done in his absence.

"Not only do I like Lindsay, but I respect her courage," Adlin said. "I'm grateful for the things she's done for our people. As should ye be." His expression tightened. "Though I well ken the reasons ye do it, 'twould be better if ye treated her with less contempt and more kindness."

"And for what reasons do I do it?" Conall asked, wondering if Adlin saw things from his perspective.

He should have known better.

Adlin looked at him as though that was a foolish question. "Ye do it because ye love the lass and dinnae want to lose her if ye let her close." He shook his head. "But 'tis wearing thin and upsetting Milly." His eyes narrowed, and his tone grew stern. "And I dinnae want anything upsetting Milly, ye ken? She is still new to her magic, and though she's astral projected several times on her own since the battle, she hasnae had as much practice as I would like. Even so, she volunteers to help and we should all be appreciative." He gave Conall a pointed look. "More than that, we shouldnae do anything to upset her, aye?"

Though tempted to tell Adlin he was not pleased he had upset Lindsay then, in turn, Milly, he decided against it. Let his cousin think what he would. Frustrated, he merely nodded. "I willnae upset Milly any further. Again, ye have my word."

Adlin eyed him for a long moment before he nodded.

Later, as his cousins snuck off into the darkness and he entered the lasses' tent, he realized what an uncomfortable position he had put himself in. Rona stayed outside the tent guarding it, but Adlin had been very specific. He wanted Conall *in* the tent with his blade at the ready. So here he was, sitting across from Milly and Lindsay, certain he would prefer to be anywhere else.

Milly, it seemed, was well aware of the tension between him and Lindsay as she grinned and looked at them before she took a swig of whisky and made idle conversation. "It took me awhile, but I'm finally getting used to this stuff." She fanned her breath. "Strong though."

When neither responded, she handed the skin to Lindsay. "Have some. I know how much you like it."

"I do," Lindsay agreed, her sole focus on Milly "Thank you, darling."

She took a hearty swig. Several in fact.

"Whoa, easy there." Milly grinned as she took the skin back. "Have as much as you like later. Right now, I don't want you inebriated when I do what I need to do."

"Trust me, it would take a bit more whisky than that to get me drunk." Lindsay offered Milly a warm smile. The sort that made it nearly impossible to look away from her.

"Right. Hmm." Milly eyed her. "How is it again you're such a bad ass when it comes to whisky? I never once saw you drink it at home." She shook her head, baffled. "I couldn't imagine you ever wanting to."

"A girl's gotta have her secrets," Lindsay said a little too gaily as she tossed Milly a secretive look. "Let's just say I had to play a certain part that I refused to fail at."

"And as you would say, how deliciously vague." Milly chuckled. "I'll get it out of you eventually, you know."

Conall did his best to keep his eyes off Lindsay and on the fire as the women continued chatting quietly. Though most were sleeping and the wind whistling through the caves was fairly loud, it was better if they did not cause a stir.

"It's time," Milly finally said. Her voice dropped a few octaves. "Adlin's ready."

Conall nodded and shifted closer to them.

"I find it's easier to do this laying down," Milly explained as she curled onto her side. "Seeing how I'll end up here anyway unless someone holds me up."

Lindsay nodded and shifted closer as well. "What should we do? Anything?"

"Just don't let anyone get to me," Milly joked. "And be as quiet as possible. I've got to concentrate on Adlin."

"Aye, of course," Conall said softly. "I willnae let anyone near you, lass."

For the first time since they entered, Lindsay glanced at him, her concern for Milly evident.

Conall offered her a look of reassurance and put his fur over Milly before settling down beside her. A strained silence stretched as she appeared to drift off. He kept his eyes either on the fire or Milly as they waited. Was it him or was that same wildflower scent Lindsay emitted earlier only growing stronger? It was sweet and warm and reminded him of...

He frowned as a memory hovered just out of reach.

A memory from childhood.

As he often did, he was visiting MacLomain Castle and was out by the oak. It was a warm summer day, one of few that year, and he was practicing whipping his new dagger into a post. He had not seen his tree faery for several long months yet still he went there and waited, sure she would appear again.

This particular day, the wind turned gustier than usual, the sun was brighter and the scent of flowers stronger. Everything was sharper and crisper. Just like it had been on those rare days when he saw her. What he could see of her that is. So he knew without question that they would soon cross paths again.

What he didn't expect was it to come in the form of soft sobs from high up in the branches.

He peered up but saw nothing hidden in the shadows. No faery in the leaves high above. He kept calling out in hopes she might answer though she never did. Even so, the sobs continued and his heart broke for her. Why was she so sad? What had happened to her since the last time they spoke?

Though he had just turned thirteen winters, he was allowed to drink whisky on occasion and had a skin with him. If he could do nothing else, mayhap he could ease her pain with that. So he sealed the top and tossed it up into the branches. The first few times it fell back down. The third time, however, it did not.

So he sat against the trunk and waited. Though he never saw her that day, her sobs faded. He sat there until the next morning, just in case, but he never heard her again. Defended by and even made of magic, he could not climb the tree to see if the whisky might have landed on a limb. So truly, there was no way to know if she ever got it.

Yet the strong scent of flowers on the wind seemed to confirm it.

The same scent he smelled now.

He glanced at Lindsay, confused, only to find her slumped beside Milly. What the bloody hell? He had been so lost in thought he never saw her go down. Was she sleeping? Breathing? Fear shot through him as he pulled her onto his lap and cupped the back of her head, so it didn't loll. Her chest rose and fell slowly. She appeared to be sound asleep.

Yet he knew something was wrong.

"Lindsay." Though tempted to shake her awake, he sensed that was unwise. "Can you hear me?"

Frustrated, unsure what to do, he rested her cheek against his chest and held her. That's when he noticed the gem in her ring. It flickered a unique shade of dark brown. If he was not mistaken, it matched Graham's eyes.

Seconds later, it turned jet black.

"Och," he muttered and called out for Rona. His cousin frowned as she ducked in, assessed the situation then crouched in front of him and Lindsay. Her frown deepened as he pointed out the gem.

"Ye need to reach out to Adlin," she insisted. "Milly could be in danger."

"But what if that's what the warlock is counting on." Because he knew dark magic was involved. "What if I lead it straight back here by doing so?"

"Bloody hell," Rona muttered and nodded. "Yer right." She closed her eyes and became very still, clearly trying to sense if death was close. If danger was near.

She shook her head and opened her eyes. "I dinnae sense anything, and I dinnae trust that."

"We will only do what was asked of us then," Conall said. "We will stand guard."

He went to pull a fur over Lindsay when she whispered, "geamhradh," and something started happening. He saw flashes of the oak at MacLomain Castle. Shadows in the tree as he looked up.

Then he was somewhere else.

He stood beside Milly in a dark forest.

Something was off about her. She seemed frozen in place.

Adlin and his cousins were nearby, and Graham was slumped against a tree wounded.

At first, it seemed nobody could see him, so his eyes wandered. Had he somehow followed Milly's astral projection?

Then his eyes locked on Lindsay.

She was drifting through the enemy encampment, her eyes shimmering, her expression daring. He knew that look. She was enchanting a man. Soon after, he saw someone trailing after her. Or *something*. Tall, sheathed in black from head to toe in a hooded cloak, a man followed her.

A warlock.

Conall shook his head as he realized what she was doing. Using her allure to distract pure evil. Using herself as bait. His eyes were drawn to her ring. How it shined the color of Graham's eyes then suddenly, turned inky black, no doubt reflecting the warlock's eyes.

That's when she stopped, looked directly at Conall, and whispered, "geamhradh," again before she gazed up at the sky and it began snowing. Seconds later, the warlock's eyes whipped in Milly's direction, and he hissed.

Adlin's eyes blazed blue through the darkness at Conall as he roared, "Get Milly out of there!"

A heartbeat later, Conall's eyes snapped open.

"What is it, Cousin?" Rona said, alarmed. It was clear only a moment had passed for her.

"We must go quickly," he said. "Guard me."

Rona nodded and said nothing. He didn't bother with the tent's flaps but ripped the whole thing down. Adlin might have said to get Milly out of here but there was no way he was leaving without Lindsay and Rona wasn't strong enough to carry her.

So Conall intended to carry them both.

Rona's eyes widened as he handed her all of his weapons, except the dagger sheathed in his boot. Anything that could inadvertently hurt the lasses. Then he relied solely on adrenaline as he slumped Lindsay over his right shoulder and Milly over his left. He barely felt the pressure on his knees as he stood, and moved swiftly.

Though tempted, he knew better than to go deeper into the caves. He didn't know them well enough and could very well end up trapped in a corner. And if warlocks were good at nothing else, it was navigating dark, musty corners of the world.

So he headed outside.

While running was impossible between the weight on his shoulders and the slick ground, he kept up a brisk walk with Rona at his side. He headed toward the windy shores of the river. A place he could, if necessary, manipulate his element of air easier. Right now, that was the best possible weapon against the sort of evil he had just witnessed.

Not surprisingly, Wallace joined him within moments. Rona never said a word but got her point across somehow, because William released a soft whistle. He was calling his men to arms.

The battling would begin.

Conall didn't make it that much further before Adlin, and his cousins appeared. Based on the roars in the distance, they had lost the element of surprise.

"What's going on?" Milly mumbled as Lindsay murmured, "Dear Lord, where am I?"

"Set them down," Adlin ordered. "They're safest here surrounded by us."

Conall crouched and did his best to set them down gently but both sort of thumped back on their arses against a tree trunk.

"My apologies lasses," he muttered as he stood and caught his blades when Rona tossed them his way. He tucked several daggers here and there then handed one to each of the women. Disoriented, both glanced around, frowning when Bryce sat Graham on the ground beside them.

Bryce crouched in front of him and wrapped Graham's hand around the hilt of a dagger. "Do what ye can with this, Cousin. Ye'll not be wielding more until Aðísla sees to ye, aye?"

Clearly in pain, Graham grunted his response and nodded.

Next, Rona crouched in front of him, concerned. They had spent very little time together since Fraser's death. Rona was always at Hamilton Castle and Graham, despite being first in command, was often off doing one thing or another. Yet as she pressed her forehead against his and murmured a prayer to give him strength it was clear they were once close. That they could be close again.

Wind gusted harder, and snow fell steadily as Conall and his cousins awaited the onslaught. They were about halfway between the river and caves, and the Sassenach were coming…as was their warlock.

William and Adlin never exchanged a word, but he could tell by Wallace's face that he knew this might happen. As it turned out, those tents at the river were being put to actual use. Where it looked to the Sassenach that the Scots were resting and vulnerable, many were already braced to attack.

What they did not foresee—even their God forsaken warlock—was Grant Hamilton appearing there.

So multiple fronts came together in the midst of a pre-winter storm.

One battle next to the river and one right here in the forest.

Conall braced his legs, held a sword and a small mace at the ready, then took up position in front of Lindsay and Milly. When he met his cousin's eyes, Graham nodded, determined. The two of them had always worked well alongside each other in battle, using their elements of air and water to manipulate what they could. A storm such as this would assist them greatly if Graham were strong enough. Which it seemed he was by the look in his eyes. The sheer will as he held the dagger and turned his gaze to the forest.

Conall never said a word just watched and waited.

"*Whatever happens, Grandson, keep our Brouns safe,*" Grant whispered into his mind. "*They are everything.*"

He didn't bother responding because he had every intention of doing just that. He knew Adlin and Grant would be battling the warlock so it was up to him and his cousins to take care of the lasses.

Bryce, Rona, and Aðísla became his front line as the forest filled with a wall of roaring Sassenach. Conall waited calmly and focused on every little thing about the men coming at them from their sizes to their potential threat. He weighed the air, how it shifted and moved around each warrior. In doing so, he was able to gauge their strengths and weaknesses.

Though plenty of Scots fought alongside, he knew better than to depend on them. Their battle had been long and hard over the past seven winters, and many were losing heart despite their love for Wallace and Scotland. Though they fought, it was not with the same passion he saw in their eyes before the Battle of Stirling Bridge.

So he was prepared to take on every last Sassenach if need be.

Seconds later, it seemed, by all accounts, he would have to do exactly that.

Especially when Bryce, Rona, and Aðísla evidently became victims of the warlock's magic and slumped to the ground.

All three were passed out cold.

Chapter Seven

"OH, *SHIT*," LINDSAY whispered, her eyes wide as Conall's cousins fell moments before a line of English warriors reached them. "That can't be good."

Milly started to respond, but the words died on her lips as Conall unleashed pure hell. Or so it seemed. He remained eerily silent but deathly effective as he began fighting. Despite the horror unfolding, there was a certain beauty in the methodical way he battled. It was calculated and mesmerizing as he fought with everything available to him.

At first, he used his sword in combination with his mace. He thrashed, slashed, and cut men down while simultaneously swirling the mace in an arc. Mostly, he just used it to nick and drive warriors back. Sometimes he would sink it into a neck or thigh, then yank it free.

War surrounded them. Men cried out. Swords crashed together. Yet all she could see was Conall. It was almost as if she felt him. His inner calm mixed with the rush of battle. His expression never changed, he never uttered a word, yet he raged on the inside.

"Damn," Milly whispered, her eyes wide as more men than they could count fell. "Go, Laird Hamilton."

Graham, meanwhile, was clearly in pain but trying not to show it as he shifted closer to them and gripped the hilt of his dagger. From what she remembered, he had taken a wound to the mid-section. One inflicted on him by the warlock.

Lindsay clenched her teeth against the memory and focused on Conall and how she might help. While she found his battle skills beyond impressive, there was another part of her on edge. Worried.

93

Frightened that he might fall prey to one of the many blades coming his way.

More and more men came at him as he ducked and swirled and thrust. One warrior swiped, and Conall ducked beneath his sword. Another came in low, and he jumped over the blade. All the while he swung that mace in all sorts of directions and kept warriors away from the three of them.

Yet she saw the distance between Conall and the tree growing smaller as bit by bit they drove him back. More came until he was so close she could reach out and touch him. But he never stopped, and she knew he never would.

"We're out of bloody time," Conall muttered as he kept slicing and dicing before he shook his head and roared, "Now, Graham."

Then they began chanting.

Moments later, the weather changed. At least over them. They were using their magic to manipulate the elements. Snow turned to ice seconds after Graham muttered a chant, and they were covered with a thick rawhide type of blanket. One, they soon discovered, built purely for protection.

"Oh, dear God," Lindsay murmured as she and Milly braced the blanket up against an onslaught of what felt like golf ball sized hail. When men began crying out in pain yet everything stilled above them, Lindsay peeked out.

"Oh, no," she cried, her voice hoarse as she realized what Conall was doing.

He had his hands braced against the trunk over their heads and was protecting them from large hail stones and razor sharp sleet. Though it was obvious he used magic to protect them, he was clearly running into trouble. If she were to guess based on Graham who had his head braced back against the tree and his eyes closed, Conall used the majority of magic to protect his cousin. That meant he was using his body to protect the women.

Men continued to fall victim to the harsh weather as Conall bore the brunt of his own storm to keep them safe. While she understood why he was doing it, she never felt such rage. At him for taking on so much pain. At all of this.

Though his knees buckled slightly and pain flashed in his otherwise emotion-free eyes, Conall held his ground. His legs and arms shook slightly but he never budged, and he never called off the inclement weather.

Not until a hand eventually landed on his shoulder.

"It is over, Grandson," came Grant's soft voice. He had already turned ice back to snow. "The Sassenach have been defeated."

"What of the warlock?" Conall ground out.

"Gone for now."

Bruised and bloodied, Conall nodded, staggered sideways and plunked down in the snow. Half a breath later, Adlin pulled Milly into his arms, his relief palpable as he embraced her. When Lindsay tried to go to Conall, he put up a weak hand and shook his head without looking at her. Even now, he meant to keep her away.

Soon enough, having awoken alongside the others, Rona was there for Conall, so Lindsay redirected her attention to Graham who had passed out. She felt for a pulse. It was still there. But of course it was otherwise his family would be responding much differently right now. More than that, she suspected if Graham were in real trouble and facing imminent death, Rona would know it and be at his side.

"Let's get them back to the caves and out of this weather," Grant said to Adlin, his voice pained as he eyed Conall. "Aðísla needs to tend to them both."

"We should go to the tents on the river's edge," Aðísla said. "I can help Graham best closest to his element."

Adlin nodded as he helped Conall up and wrapped his arm around his shoulders. In the meantime, Bryce carefully lifted Graham, and they headed that way. It was obvious one hell of a battle had taken place based on the sheer number of fallen on both sides. Wallace joined them, his expression grim but triumphant. He had lost many, but another battle had been won.

Aðísla saw to Graham first, who would make a speedy recovery if he rested for a day or so then she saw to Conall. Rona stayed outside both tents the entire time, unconvinced based on her dubious expression, that the Viking would tend to them properly.

Though the winds had died down some, snow still fell steadily as they converged in William's larger tent. Everyone seemed well enough but very tired as she sat next to Grant. He offered her a warm smile as he squeezed her hand.

"Good to see you well, lass." He sighed. "'Twas not an easy battle."

"Easy enough for me," she said softly. "But then we both know you're talking about Conall and Graham."

"Aye." Grant nodded. "I am verra proud of both, most especially my grandson."

"As am I," Adlin added, pride in his eyes. "I will forever be indebted to Conall for so valiantly protecting my lass." His grateful eyes went to Milly before his genuine gaze returned to Lindsay. "And of course you as well, lass."

"Thank you," she replied. "You have an amazing family, Adlin." Her eyes went to Grant then back to him remembering how they had saved her before. "All of you are pretty wonderful."

"Aye," William murmured, his tired eyes on the fire. "If ye werenae here I dinnae know what might have happened." He looked at Adlin. "Why, after all the skirmishes I've fought since Stirling, was a warlock present now? 'Twas not an important battle by any means." He frowned, considering Adlin. "Or was it, my friend?"

"'Twas a battle that needed to happen," Adlin allowed. "But like the one my kin and I fought south of Stirling Bridge, I dinnae think history will much remember." He shook his head. "Many of the Sassenach were cast beneath a spell so 'tis likely they never reported coming here." A heavy frown settled on his face. "What happened this eve was more a means for evil to weigh us out." His eyes went to Lindsay. "To see what it might be up against this time."

She frowned but was catching on. "Though six months in the past, the next battle we go to is more important, isn't it?"

"Aye." Grant nodded. "William and Robert the Bruce will both be there. 'Tis a prime opportunity to truly alter Scotland's history."

"But it doesn't, right?" She narrowed her eyes. "Because if it had, we wouldn't be here now."

"You would like to think," he conceded. "'Twould be logical." He shook his head. "But time travel and dark magic are anything but logical. We were sent to this battle first, and the warlock followed. That means he is traveling on our time line, not that which happens naturally."

When she frowned, confused, he continued.

"Because we came here first instead of the Skirmish at Happrew, this is our timeline," he explained. "This happened first then that, and the same goes for the warlock. So he has the experience of this battle, a far lesser threat to history, to learn about your powers and Conall's." His expression grew grim. "Expect him to be far more clever next time around." He sighed. "And if he succeeds, 'tis verra doubtful this battle will ever take place. Everything will change altogether."

She stared at him, a little baffled. "If that's the case, and we're assuming good not evil is directing us, it doesn't make much sense to have come here first…does it?"

"Nay," Grant agreed solemnly. "It doesnae." His eyes skirted over everyone. "I can only hope there was a method to the madness. That whoever sent us here knows something we dinnae."

"Right, because neither you nor Adlin transported us," she murmured as her eyes went to William. "And nobody knows why you have no recollection of us being at the next battle…the one that technically took place in your past."

"That is correct," Adlin said softly. "But I'm sure we will find out soon enough."

Her guess? Adlin or Grant saw to it that William didn't remember.

"What happened, Lindsay?" Grant's voice was soothing as his eyes met hers and he changed the subject. "What happened when you were in that tent with Milly and Conall?" He handed her a skin of whisky. "How did you end up in the enemy camp in much the same way as Milly?"

She was about to respond but stopped when Conall entered. She wasn't all that surprised to see him despite his injuries. Adlin and William started to stand, but he shook his head and plunked down in one of the chairs around the fire. He might look pretty beat up, but his chin was still stubbornly notched and his brow furrowed, so he wasn't all that far off from his usual self.

Lindsay did her best to even her breathing and ignore her thundering heart. Until that moment, she had not been entirely convinced he would survive his own storm. It was brutal and had killed many. And until that moment she had no idea she cared so much. She frowned and took a swig of whisky as she eyed him. The last thing she wanted to do was feel anything for a man.

Especially Conall.

"Well, lass?" Grant asked.

Startled, she glanced at him. He had asked her a question, hadn't he?

"What happened tonight, Linds?" Milly prompted. "How did you end up...wooing the damn warlock?"

Right. That.

She debated how much to share but realized as Adlin and Grant watched her intently that lying would be pointless. They would see right through it. So she explained things the best way she knew how after telling them about her ability to enchant.

"Sometimes, on rare occasions, I see things through the eyes of the victims," she said softly, uncomfortable sharing so much. "I nearly did with the little girl in Hamilton Castle's great hall, and I believe I did when I first traveled here...something Rona was shooting an arrow at. An animal I believe." Her eyes drifted to the fire. "Then when the warlock went after Graham, I briefly saw through Graham's eyes."

"Yet you were there," Grant said. "Like Milly, you were there as an astral projection and distracted the warlock. You drew its attention away from Graham on purpose, aye?"

"I did," she whispered doing her best to appear at ease even as a harsh chill rippled through her. "And almost succeeded."

Nothing but frowns met her words as Grant wrapped an extra fur around her shoulders and urged her to drink before he said, "'Tis no small thing enchanting a warlock as you did, lassie. You've a rare gift." He slanted a look at her. "But then I suppose you already knew that."

When Lindsay merely shrugged, Conall spoke, his voice hoarse and his brogue thick, likely from exhaustion. "Ye put yer life on the line when ye dinnae ken in the least what ye faced." There was no missing his frustration as his tone heated. "Have ye any idea what a warlock can do? What that warlock might have done to ye had Adlin and Grandfather not been here?"

Appalled that he would grow aggravated with her considering all they had been through she tried to rein in her temper as she met his eyes. "I did what I had to do tonight, Laird Hamilton. Just like you did. The only difference?" She tried to perk her brows but they sort of fell flat. "I'm thankful for what you did and have no intention of getting upset with you for putting your life on the line. Why would I when I understand that's just the sort of person you are."

Silence fell as their eyes held.

98

She knew he was moments away from a comeback she would not like, but something held his tongue. Something she felt dust her mind. Emotions that were not hers but could have been. Fear. Pride. Defiance. Courage.

Desire.

Both yanked their eyes away from each other at the same time, and Lindsay looked wherever she could next which turned out to be at Milly. Quick to move on from the awkward conversation she and Conall just had in front of everyone, she said, "As to me being there tonight as what seemed like an astral projection, it wasn't quite like that."

Here she was sharing too much again.

But at least it kept her from speaking with Conall.

"Part of my enchanting gift has always been the ability to shift close to those who need me most. I'm not really an astral projection when I do it but more of a...ghost I suppose. Yet I'm very solid." Her eyes stayed with Milly. "Tonight you needed me most whether you knew it or not. The moment you saw the warlock go after Graham."

"This gift of yours might very well explain how I easily brought you back from the brink of death when you were nearly killed," Aðísla murmured. "And why you so readily healed." Her wise eyes met Lindsay's. "Because the wound was inflicted when you were not entirely yourself but somewhere beyond. My guess is close to looking through the eyes of that little girl."

Lindsay shrugged, not entirely sure.

"While I'm grateful you came to my rescue tonight because you thought I needed you most, Linds," Milly said, putting the conversation back on track. "The actual thoughts I was having at the time were more along the lines of Adlin coming to my rescue."

"I'm sure because that's logical," Lindsay conceded. "But the truth is, somewhere in the back of your mind, you knew I had the ability to draw the warlock away." She shrugged. "And though you knew Adlin could fight it, why put him in harm's way if you didn't need to?"

"Lindsay!" Milly's eyes grew troubled along with her tone. "Are you saying that I put you in harm's way to keep Adlin safe?"

"Not intentionally, but of course." Lindsay offered a reassuring look. "And that's normal. I would be worried if you didn't." She shook her head. "Your subconscious would always protect your true love, and I am always willing to help, darling."

Milly and Adlin both frowned, clearly baffled by her declaration.

"So we've something to work on once this is all said and done." Grant smiled softly at Lindsay. "You learning how to control your magic so that you are not summoned by everyone you care about unintentionally, aye?"

"I don't mind—" she started before Conall cut her off.

"I couldnae agree more, Grandfather." His frown was fierce as his eyes went to hers. This time he seemed to have his brogue under control. "Whilst your intentions are noble enough, lass, right now you are a victim of your own magic. That, in itself, is verra dangerous to all those around you."

"Well, I wouldnae go that far—" Grant began before Lindsay interrupted him.

"So what would you have me do, Laird Hamilton?" she quipped, scowling at Conall. "Because as you can see, there isn't a lot of time for training right now. Not when we're constantly being whipped from one time to another, one location to another, one kiss to—"

She snapped her mouth shut when she realized what she nearly said. He knew how to get her going, didn't he? What she needed to learn above all else was *not* to let him get under her skin.

"I will work with you as we travel," he announced. "I will help you learn to control this enchantment of yours."

Everyone appeared amused as they looked at Conall with surprise. All but Grant that is. He didn't appear shocked in the least that his grandson had offered something so preposterous. Rather, as his fond but fleeting gaze flickered over Conall, she had a feeling he had hoped his grandson might offer something so foolish.

"Actually, I'd much rather Grant help me," she began before Grant shook his head and said, "Och, nay, lass, 'tis not wise."

She frowned at him. "Why not?"

"Because I dinnae know with any certainty that I'll remain on this journey." He gestured at Conall. "Where there cannae be any doubt he will."

"Aye," Adlin agreed, a twinkle in his eyes. "Grant makes a good point. I think Conall teaching *and* protecting you from here on out is a sound idea, Lindsay."

"Aye." Grant nodded. "'Twould give me peace of mind to know he's looking after you, lass."

"I offered to teach her not to—" Conall started, but Adlin interrupted.

"The best teacher is always the best protector." He gestured at Grant. "Is that not true? Did you not do that for me often?"

"Aye," Grant agreed. "And did you not do that for me as well in your last life?"

Milly chuckled.

When Lindsay frowned at her, she shrugged. "Sorry, sweetie, but they make sense." Her eyes went to Conall. "Thank you for offering to teach Lindsay how to use her gift. Can I count on you to keep her safe too?"

"Have I not been doing that from the verra beginning?" Conall said tightly.

"You have," Milly acknowledged. "But as we move forward and journey together, Adlin and I are going to want time alone, and Lindsay needs somewhere to sleep."

"Mildred," Lindsay admonished, whipping out Milly's full name on purpose because it irritated her. "Are you trying to push me into sleeping in Laird Hamilton's tent?" She shook her head. "Because I won't."

"Okay." Milly flinched, apologetic. "Then maybe Rona's?"

"Bloody hell no," Rona muttered. "I prefer the outdoors."

Lindsay glanced at the Viking. "Aðísla's then?"

"I prefer the outdoors too," she stated. "And I prefer to be alone."

Her eyes went to Bryce, and she smiled. "Might I stay with you then?"

He smiled right back and said, 'Aye," before William interrupted him.

"Actually, lass," he said. "I would prefer it if ye stayed with me."

William was about to say more when Conall ground out, "I will teach *and* protect you, Lindsay. You have my word."

Translation? She would be sleeping next to him.

Bryce frowned and was about to say something but Adlin gave him a look that evidently stopped him dead in his tracks because Grant talked instead.

"There you have it." Grant offered a heartwarming smile as he looked at her. "You will agree to be protected by Conall, aye?" His eyes grew a little devious as they went to Conall. "And you agree to protect Lindsay, aye?"

Neither answered but continued to bicker with each other.

"It might just work out to be the other way around," she muttered as she eyed Conall's battle wounds.

"Not if I teach you," he muttered right back. "And by doing so, you dinnae end up starting a battle to begin with."

Her eyes rounded on him. "Are you telling me you think I'm responsible for everything that happened tonight?"

"I think unchecked magic can create many problems," he began before Grant interrupted.

"Enough you two." He shook his head. "You have come to an agreement and will see it through."

"We never agreed to anything," they both said at the same time before frowning at each other.

"You did and you will," Grant announced. "So that's the end of that." He nodded his head in thanks as Adlin handed him a skin of whisky, no doubt anticipating what he was about to ask next.

Something she should have seen coming.

"You say you are drawn to those that need you, Lindsay." Grant's eyes met hers. "Why then, did my son Darach need you?"

"I don't know," she said softly. She felt as sad looking into his eyes as she had looking into Conall's earlier. His pain was just as evident. "And I don't know with any certainty that my magic was involved."

"Of course it was, lass," Grant murmured, his eyes a little distant. "Your gift somehow allowed you to summon him and he was able to get his message to us."

"So you believe he's alive, Grandfather?" Though he grunted a little in pain, Conall sat forward, intrigued. "You dinnae think 'twas evil afoot?"

"Oh, evil was afoot." Grant shook his head. "But based on what I saw tonight, it cannae control Lindsay any more than it could Milly. Not yet anyway." His eyes went to Lindsay before returning to Conall. "She is strong, and you would do well to remember that, Grandson."

"I dinnae doubt she is." Yet it didn't quite sound like a compliment coming out of his mouth. "A strong lass in need of protecting, aye?"

Lindsay wanted to throttle him. She really did. But even she recognized Conall's behavior for what it was. He was genuinely scared for her and had shown it with every swing of his blade earlier, with every moment he put his life on the line.

Yet still, he pushed her away.

And she did the same.

Because that was what was best.

Nothing but pain existed if she allowed him any closer and she refused to risk it. She could not go through that again. Love and lose everything. Watch someone she cared about be destroyed in an instant.

"Aye, a strong lass in need of protecting," Adlin confirmed. His eyes narrowed on Conall. "Just like you're a strong lad in need of protecting." His eyes went between Conall and Lindsay, his tone leaving no room for debate. "And I expect you both to work together because I not only suspect at this point but *know* you're this country's only hope." He shook his head. "There cannae be any doubt. You two must defeat this warlock if Scotland is to move forward."

"That means working as a team," Grant added. "In case you dinnae quite ken."

Lindsay could not imagine working as a team with Conall, let alone getting along with him, but this seemed to be her destined path. Or so said the two most powerful wizards in Scotland. Her eyes fell to her ring. Oh yes, and then there was this.

It remained as black as night.

"Only for now, lass," Grant murmured as he took her hand and studied it. "Whilst its color is most certainly daunting, I truly believe if you and Conall work together, you can conquer this warlock as readily as Adlin and Milly did theirs."

Both Lindsay and Conall frowned at that. Because it almost sounded like Grant and Adlin had manipulated them into the idea that if they worked together, love would conquer all.

"Aren't you the least bit worried that the last thing I enchanted was a warlock?" Lindsay asked everyone. "And isn't anyone worried that he might show up again at any time?"

"Nay, not right away," Adlin said. "He wasnae prepared for the likes of Grant and me. He will lick his wounds for a bit but will be back." Quickly repressed worry flashed in his eyes. "Might we be there when he does."

"It will be at the next battle," Lindsay whispered before she could stop herself. Yet her tongue seemed to have a will of its own. "And he will bring down the wrath of God himself."

When everyone looked at her, she blinked, confused, before murmuring, "Sorry." She shook her head and swallowed hard. "I'm not sure where that came from."

"It came from your enchantment," Grant informed. "You will feel the aftereffects of luring him, but he cannae touch you. Not yet." He gave Conall a pointed look before his eyes returned to hers. "Especially if you learn how to hone your craft." Before Lindsay had a chance to mention it was a craft Conall knew nothing about, Grant continued. "And remember, lass, a creature not of God can *never* bring down His wrath. So see that first and foremost as the warlock's weakness. He lies to frighten you more. He uses something you believe in against you."

Lindsay said nothing to that and remained close-lipped. Her religious beliefs were her own.

As if she sensed Lindsay was about maxed out, Milly stood. "I think it might be time for everyone to crash." She looked at Adlin. "It's been a long night, and I could use some rest." Her eyes met Lindsay's. "We all could."

She nodded and stood alongside everyone else when William spoke up. "Lindsay, might ye stay for a moment or two, lass? I've missed yer company and could use the conversation."

Though Adlin and Grant shot him a look and Conall downright argued the idea, she knew what William wanted to talk about. What they had no chance to speak of until now. Whatever information she might have gleaned that he would find useful since that day seven years ago.

Or at least seven years ago for him.

"I'll stay," she agreed, frowning at them all before her eyes reluctantly met Conall's. "Then you can protect and teach me, okay?"

Conall's narrowed eyes never left hers, yet she saw his internal battle. This might just be his way out of the commitment they had just made to Adlin and Grant. Wallace might be the reason he could not keep his promise. So, despite his tense jaw, he nodded and backed out of the tent.

"I'm not sure if I have much to tell you," she said as she turned back to William, but he shook his head, ceasing her talk as he urged her to sit with him in front of the fire.

She really wasn't surprised by what he said next because the enchantment she had cast on him when they spoke of spying was half-hearted at best. She had wanted to make sure he was in her corner at the time, but even then she must have suspected deep down she could trust the MacLomains. More so, Grant, and yes, though she was not quite ready to admit it, Conall.

"I no longer want to know what Adlin's up to." He shook his head. "I no longer want ye to spy for me." His eyes met hers. "Instead, I hope ye will do something else for me."

She cocked her head, curious but somewhat alarmed by the determination in his eyes. "I think that might depend on what it is."

"I want ye to help me steer this country in the direction it needs to go next."

"Okay," she replied slowly, not sure where he was going with this. "What do you need from me?"

"Help," he replied readily. "I have a plan but can only see it through with a lass the likes of ye."

"The likes of me?"

"Aye."

"How so?"

"Well..." He held her hand between his and gave her a look only William Wallace was capable of. Charm mixed with conviction. "I know yer going to Happrew next, and I know Robert the Bruce will be there. What I need ye to do should be simple enough." The corner of his mouth curled up. "I need ye to make him fall in love with ye, lass."

Chapter Eight

IT SEEMED CONALL'S silent vows meant absolutely nothing. Especially since he was waiting outside William Wallace's tent for a *third* time as he did God knows what with Lindsay. Despite the snow, he didn't seek shelter but stood just beyond the tent's flaps trying to catch wind of their conversation.

"'Tis beneath ye to hover like this, Cousin," Rona muttered from nearby. "Yer a bloody chieftain!" She gestured with disgust at the tent. "If she wishes to be with Wallace, let her be and good riddance."

Conall scowled, shook his head and whispered, "Go get some rest. 'Tis only a matter of time before we leave this place."

"Aye," she agreed. "And ye've got to decide if yer leaving having been made a fool of or with yer head held high."

Though tempted to snap at her, he knew this night had been hard. They could only assume the warlock had cast her, Bryce and Aðísla into that unnatural slumber yet still, she was furious. Nothing was worse for any of them than feeling like they had not been there for their kin. That they had somehow let them down.

"*We cannae control the likes of evil, Rona,*" he said into her mind. "*'Tis as simple as that. Ye arenae at fault.*"

"*Yet ye think to teach this twenty-first century lass how to control what even ye just admitted ye couldnae,*" she spat back. "*And for no other reason than to get betwixt her thighs.*"

"*Och, I'd rather have my cock cut off.*" A complete lie in more ways than one. "*She's a vixen but a necessary one.*"

"*Why?*" Rona frowned. "*What makes her necessary outside of Grant and Adlin saying so?*" She shook her head. "*She has caused

107

nothing but trouble for ye since she arrived, Cousin. Ye should turn away from this commitment ye've made."

He understood her reasoning.

She was trying to protect him.

"I dinnae turn away from my commitments," he responded, well aware both he and Lindsay had been swindled. Still. He had given his word and would see it through. *"Go rest, Cousin. I will see ye on the morrow."* When she hesitated, he gave her a look she knew all too well. He wanted time alone. *"Go now. I love ye, aye?"*

When she clenched her jaw and dampness made her eyes shimmer, he embraced her. She had been one of his best friends for as long as he could remember, so he knew how lost she felt. How truly frightened she was when post battle she woke from her slumber and thought she might have lost both him and Graham.

"Do ye really think yer da is out there?" she whispered against his chest. "Do ye think he's alive?"

He wasn't surprised in the least her mind dwelled on his father as well.

Though tempted to tell her what she wanted to hear, he wasn't that sort of man. "I think 'tis unlikely." Yet, he would offer her the glimmer of hope he was foolish enough to have allowed Grant to give him. "But there is always a chance, aye?"

"Aye," she murmured and hugged him a little tighter before she vanished into the night.

He sighed and turned back to the tent entrance as Lindsay stepped out. She pulled her hood up against the snow and met his eyes, almost as if she expected to find him there.

"Lead the way, *protector*," she murmured as she made a flourish with her hand. "Wherever you go, I am destined to follow."

Conall ignored her sarcasm and led her to his tent. Though a part of him had been determined to get her here from the moment he headed for Wallace's tent earlier, he wasn't prepared for her close proximity. He wasn't prepared for the way her sweet flowery scent filled the space moments after she entered.

He clenched his jaw and kept his thoughts as clinical as possible. Unlike the Lindsay of his dungeons, she was no longer playing a sultry creature but seemed of the opposite mind as she sat. "Where shall I sleep?"

She didn't ask with her eyes hidden behind her lashes or use a husky voice but simply seemed weary as her eyes rose to his. "If it's all the same to you, right here is fine."

Conall nodded and spread his fur cloak over her when she lay down.

"I don't need that," she argued even as she buried her nose in it and her eyes slid shut. "You're the one who is injured," she mumbled. "What will you use to keep warm?"

"I have another," he assured, ignoring his pain.

The tent was too small to light a fire, but he had used a miniscule amount of magic to warm a fist size stone in the corner. One that lent the space just enough dim light and heat. Or so he thought until he caught her shivering.

"Lindsay?" he whispered, testing to see if she slept. When she offered nothing but a sleepy moan, he knew she was out.

Though mildly tempted to yank her boots off and disturb her peaceful sleep because of her mysterious time with Wallace, he instead took great care. It had been a long time since he removed something as simple as a lass's shoes, or boots in this case. Her feet were slender, small and soft, barely the size of his entire hand.

He clenched his jaw as he held one, tempted to press his lips to her milky white ankle just to see how it tasted. Then he would run his tongue over her calf and then even higher. His eyes traveled up her body cozied beneath his fur. Though he could see little, the shape of her curvy figure was obvious enough. The slight rise of her thigh as it led to the soft slope of her hip then the sweep down into the valley that was her stomach.

"Just take the other shoe off already." She chuckled in her sleep. "I'll go to bed, I promise."

Conall frowned as he removed the second boot. Was she dreaming of something she had experienced with Cressingham or the Earl in the Sassenach encampment in Stirling? He ground his jaw, trying to suppress anger. Or perhaps what she had enjoyed at Wallace's hands afterward? That thought only made him grow more upset.

"I love you, Mom," she whispered. "You too, Dad."

Conall froze. It seemed he was wrong all the way around. So he set her foot down gently then sat as carefully as he could, trying not to disturb her. It appeared he didn't have to worry though because she was thoroughly entrenched in a dream.

"I promise I'll go to sleep." She pulled the fur down enough that he could see her face. A joyous smile curved her lips though her eyes were closed. "Maybe you'll get some chocolate while you're out? You can give some to the babysitter when you get back then I'll have the rest tomorrow."

Conall pulled off his boots slowly, all the while watching her. She was growing more and more distressed, her eyelids fluttering as she roamed her dream. He glanced at the ring. Though the gem remained dark, somehow he knew this had nothing to do with the warlock.

This was all Lindsay.

"Oh, no," she suddenly whimpered, shaking her head as tears leaked from the corners of her eyes. Despite his reservations about the two of them, nobody could stop him from giving a lass comfort. So he yanked off his tunic, lay beside her, and pulled her close.

Completely unaware, she kept whimpering before she cried out, "No, please no!"

Conall tucked her head against his chest, unsure what else to do, especially when her thoughts started brushing his. She had just opened a door. There were shelves lined with food and canned goods. Something he only recognized thanks to his twenty-first century kin.

Everything was silent until it got very loud and gunshots resounded. Conall jerked back, startled, as several people fell to the floor. Blood started to pool on the white tile as he heard Lindsay's breathing switch. As he almost felt her heart stop.

Two more people fell as gunshots continued to go off.

A man and woman, side by side.

Then Conall saw her, felt her, was terrified right alongside her as a little girl with white-blond hair screamed and went scrambling through the blood toward the couple.

Her parents.

Lindsay's parents.

Conall's eyes shot open not to the terrifying scene he had just witnessed but to Lindsay snuggled against him. Any unease she might have felt was completely gone as her cheek rested against his chest and her breathing evened. She was out of the nightmare now, but he was not.

He wasn't sure he ever would be.

This lass had witnessed unthinkable horror. She had watched her parents murdered in front of her eyes via her magic. He wrapped his fur more firmly around her, pulled her closer and simply held her. What he had just witnessed explained an awful lot.

The pain at the center of her.

The admirable strength.

Most would become a far different creature having seen what she did yet here she was, trying to save the day at every turn.

"Trying to save your parents," he whispered, seeing it all clearly now. Her need to fix what she could not before. Her need to make everything right.

Though she slept soundly, he barely slept a wink. He replayed what he had seen over and over in his mind as she must have been doing her entire life. In some ways, it reminded him of what he had endured on the battlefield when he connected eyes with Fraser one last time, but it was harsher. Much more unforgivable.

She had been so young and had seen something most adults would never get over let alone learn how to cope with. Yet she had. Somehow, by the grace of God, she had. Not only that, she had excelled in life. Doing so, he realized, by wearing any face but her own.

By escaping that dreadful day.

He made sure he was sitting up with some distance between them by the time she awoke the next morning. Though she had moaned a little in distress when he moved earlier, she settled back down. Now she sat there tousled and more bonnie than ever.

"Hello," she mumbled and yawned before she looked at him curiously. "Did you rest at all, Laird Hamilton?"

"Aye," he assured as he handed her a piece of fish he had Rona catch earlier, despite her grumblings. "Here, break your fast, lass."

"Thanks," she said softly, nibbling on it as she eyed him with uncertainty. "Are you sure you slept? You look exhausted."

He would imagine he did between the physical pain remaining from the battle and the psychological pain of knowing what she had gone through.

"I did," he assured again. "Once you are finished with the fish, we will return to the caves and begin your training."

"So soon?"

"The sooner, the better," he said. "'Tis likely only a matter of time before we end up at the next battle and the more you can prepare beforehand the better."

She nodded, her eyes still vaguely unsure about what he assumed were their sleeping arrangements last night. He suspected she would eventually realize that he had held her. It was bound to happen as their minds connected more. A connection he could not seem to control in the least despite his best efforts.

Silence settled between them but at least it didn't feel as strained as it had last night in Milly's tent before the battle. Likely because his perspective had changed dramatically. Nonetheless, he needed to remember that it was best for them to be separated. He had no desire to pull someone close only to lose them.

He set a skin of water beside her. "Once you are finished, join me outside, and we'll prepare to leave."

Lindsay nodded. "Okay."

As he exited, she called after him. "Thank you for breakfast."

He didn't respond but joined Rona and Bryce at the fire. Most were up and about, and many of the tents were already packed up. The snow had stopped yet the wind still howled. When his grandfather joined them, Conall addressed something he did not have the chance to talk about the night before.

"Lindsay repeated a word twice last night before the battle. Moments before it began snowing." His eyes met Grant's. "Geamhradh or winter." He frowned. "Why would she say such? Might it be related to her magic somehow?"

"Good morning to ye as well, Grandson," Grant muttered before he explained that something similar had happened with Milly. Except in her case, the word *foghar* was spoken into her mind which meant autumn. "Milly is convinced 'twas Iosbail who said it from beyond the grave. 'Tis our belief that Adlin's former foster sister was simply confirming that Milly was on the right path. That 'twas her time to come together with Adlin."

Conall mulled that over. "Yet Lindsay *said* her word, 'twas not whispered within her mind." He frowned. "Worse yet, she said it as she enchanted the warlock."

112

"Both times she said it?" Grant asked.

"Nay." Conall shook his head. "The first time was in the tent with Milly. 'Twas what alarmed me to the fact Lindsay had drifted off."

"Yet ye were right there." Grant frowned. "How was it that ye did not *see* her drift off first?"

Conall smoothly side-stepped the question. "Everything happened verra fast."

Grant considered him for a moment, clearly seeing beyond that vague statement, but left it alone. "If 'twas that word she said in the tent that alerted ye to trouble, then the same word came before a storm that aided us greatly in battle, I would say 'twas likely Iosbail at work again." He cocked his head. "Because is it not winter?"

"Not officially."

"Close enough." Grant arched his brows. "Not to mention the next battle we attend in Happrew 'twill verra much be during winter."

Conall grunted and turned his eyes to the fire, allowing the conversation with his grandfather to go stagnant. Was Adlin's sister truly helping from beyond the grave? If so, why not reach out to them somehow rather than use these seasonal words?

"I will watch over Graham as he recovers," Bryce said, breaking the uncomfortable silence. "Already, he wishes to be moving about whilst he heals."

Conall nodded and headed Graham's way, eager to escape Grant. He wondered if a day would ever come that he didn't grow frustrated with his grandfather. That he did not look at him and wonder how he could have lost his son so easily. On a level he was not ready to accept yet, he knew evil magic could swindle the best of them. He knew that even Grant and Adlin could be fooled.

Graham was awake as Conall ducked in, passing Rona as she exited. Though his tent was not all that much bigger than theirs, Wallace had insisted he have a cot. One that Graham sat on the edge of now as he argued with Aðísla to allow him to stand.

"Loki's cock," she muttered as she shook her head. "I might have healed you, but your body needs time to recover." She frowned. "You need rest."

"Bloody hell I do," Graham complained before his attention swung to Conall and he grinned. "'Tis good to see ye well, Cousin."

He gestured at Aðísla. "Tell the Viking I am well enough. That we Highlanders heal better with fresh air and a wee bit o' exercise."

"I'll tell her no such thing." Conall handed his skin to Graham. "But I will sit and enjoy a wee dram with ye for a few moments."

Aðísla muttered something about that not being the wisest way to keep a man down as she left the tent, saying over her shoulder, "I'll be guarding this exit so do not try to leave. I can wound even quicker than I can heal."

"Aye." Graham scowled before he took a hearty swig. "I do believe she can."

Conall sat in the chair Aðísla must have used overnight. "How fare ye, Cousin?" He looked him over. "Is the warlock's wound still hurting ye?"

"Nay, verra little." Graham's grateful eyes met his. "I'm sorry I wasnae able to help ye until the end. 'Twas shameful that I couldnae."

"Och." Conall shook his head. "Ye did verra well and helped me for as long as ye could. For that I am grateful."

Graham's eyes looked troubled but not for long as he studied his wound free stomach. "She's a pain in my arse, but 'tis bloody amazing what Aðísla can do."

He was about to say more when Lindsay ducked in only to widen her eyes on Graham then turn around. "Oh my goodness, you aren't wearing anything. I'll come back."

In truth, he had a fur covering his lower half.

"Nay, dinnae go, lass," Graham said as he pulled a blanket around his shoulders. "I wish to speak with ye."

Lindsay peeked over her shoulder before she smiled and headed his way. "I wanted to check in on you before I began my training."

When Graham patted the cot beside him, Conall stood and shook his head. "Nay, lass, sit here. I insist."

But it was too late. Graham had already pulled her down beside him and wrapped an arm around her shoulders, putting her right against the very nudity she had graciously tried to avoid. Conall scowled and sat, wondering what his cousin was up to.

"Though I dinnae fully ken how ye did it," Graham rumbled, emotion evident in his voice as he looked at her. "Ye've my eternal thanks for what ye did for me. Had ye not done such, that warlock might have verra well ended me."

"No need to thank me," she murmured. "You would've done the same for me, Graham." She gave him a pointed look. "In fact, if I remember correctly, you *did* do the same for me shortly after that."

"Och, 'twas nothing on my part." Graham gestured at Conall. "My cousin was yer true hero, aye?" He gave Conall a look that told him he should have seen what was coming. "'Tis clear he cares a *great* deal for ye, lass." His lips turned down, but he didn't seem all that broken up. "He willnae be easy to compete with for yer affections, I'm afraid."

Lindsay snorted, the first unladylike sound he had ever heard her make. "Oh, I highly doubt that." Her amused eyes met Conall's. "It's safe to say Laird Hamilton, and I have come to an understanding that works for us both."

Had they? The only thing he agreed to was training and protecting her. He scowled at his own thoughts. If she wanted to add lack of affection to that list, who was he to stop her? It suited him just fine.

"Have ye come to an understanding then?" Graham looked between them, his expression as amused as hers. "Because I would say the only understanding that will matter betwixt ye two has ye beneath the furs, aye?"

"Och, ye go one step too far, Cousin." Conall frowned at Graham's rudeness. "Apologize to the lass, aye?"

"*So* not necessary," Lindsay began as Graham's alarmed eyes shot to her and he said, "I didnae mean any disrespect, lass, just that ye find happiness. 'Twas wrong for me to have said it that way."

"It's fine." Lindsay patted his hand. "But rest assured, I don't need to be with any man to find happiness, *especially* not Laird Hamilton."

Surprisingly stung by her words, Conall lost his scowl and resumed a stern expression as he stood. "'Tis best that we see to training and let Graham rest."

Lindsay nodded and stood, smiling at Graham. "Get well soon, sweetheart."

"Aye, many thanks, lass," Graham called out as she and Conall exited.

Aðísla, naturally, ducked back in soon after, anticipating that Graham would not stay put.

"Warm yourself by the fire whilst I gather my weapons and pack up our tent," Conall said to Lindsay.

"I can help you know—" she started, but he shook his head, leaving no room for debate as he set to work. He knew Wallace was short men, so he ended up taking several down and packing them up before they left.

He and Lindsay said nothing as they made their way through the forest. After they arrived at the caves and he set up the tents with her help despite his protests, he looked around and frowned. He had hoped Milly or some of his kin would have joined them by now, but none were here.

"What is it?" Lindsay asked. "You look upset."

"'Tis nothing," he muttered.

The truth was he simply wanted to bathe. He had battled hard yesterday. Though he used magic to do away with the blood of his enemies and to keep his scent tolerable, he preferred to clean himself in a normal fashion.

"Oh," Lindsay murmured, evidently following his thoughts. That seemed to be happening far too often for his taste. "You want a bath, and you don't want to leave me alone."

"I willnae leave you alone," he corrected, debating his next move.

They eyed each other before Lindsay sighed, shook her head and gestured in the direction of the cave with the small pond. "I'm not a child, Laird Hamilton. I've seen men bathe before."

"Yet you averted your eyes when you saw Graham," he reminded.

"Okay, let me rephrase," she said. "I averted my eyes with Graham and will offer you the same courtesy."

Conall considered it for another moment before he nodded and headed that way. He really wasn't concerned whether she watched or not as he finally stripped down and headed into the water. As it turned out, however, there was something about being in this state with her so close that made it exceptionally uncomfortable. He might be ignoring her, but his cock was fully aware of her presence despite the cold water.

She sat on a rock with her back to him and never peeked once as he made quick work of washing. While a part of him was grateful she never looked, another grew frustrated. Mainly his cock. He frowned as he waded out, more conflicted than he ought to be at the disagreement between his mind and body. He had always been strong when it came to lasses. He could easily turn them away if he wanted to.

"Och, *enough* already!" she suddenly declared. "If ye want him just take him!"

He stopped short as Lindsay stood abruptly and turned his way. Had she just spoken with a brogue? Her appreciative eyes raked over him as she sauntered his way. His jaw dropped at the sultry look on her face. The way she licked her full lips. The lust in her large eyes. What truly caught his attention though?

She wasn't acting in the least.

So what was she doing? Better yet why wasn't he getting dressed? Why wasn't he turning from her as he had back at the beginning? Instead, he stood there unmoving as she stopped in front of him, her bold eyes again taking in everything before they lingered on his cock. "Oh, my," she whispered, her lips curling up ever-so-slightly before her eyes roamed up his body followed by a hand that brazenly grazed his manhood before she touched more.

He barely breathed as her soft fingers followed the v above his cock to the muscles of his abdomen before she sauntered around him. "Just look at ye."

There it was again. That brogue. Yet he was frozen in place, eager for the next touch, for more of the way she was looking at him.

"Laird Hamilton," she whispered before she came around again, stood on her tip-toes and pulled his lips down to hers. It didn't matter that something was off. Not when their mouths connected.

Suddenly it felt like they were right back at Stirling Bridge, and then in his dungeons. The same passion flared. Strong, unrelenting, it made turning her away impossible. So he yanked her against him before his tongue began exploring. Tasting. Like before, they were perfectly matched, their tongues swirling, and tempting. Teasing. He dug his fingers into her warm, silky hair and tilted her head to deepen the kiss further.

Lindsay groaned and pressed against him, her hand still exploring as he lifted her, and settled her on a waist-high rock. She spread her legs, welcoming, tempting even more. His cock throbbed almost painfully he wanted her so badly.

He needed to finally have what she so willingly offered.

Hungry, desperate for more, he continued to dip his tongue in and out of her mouth as he started to push up her skirts. He knew he should stop, that this was a very bad idea, but he was beyond reason, his desire for her far too great.

"Lindsay," he groaned seconds before Milly exclaimed from the entrance, "I *knew* we shouldn't have come this way! Didn't I tell you, Adlin?"

Conall and Lindsay froze as their eyes shot Milly's way only to see her and Adlin backing away. His cousin called out, "Sorry then!" not looking sorry in the least before they vanished altogether.

"Oh my God," Lindsay whispered as her wide, confused eyes turned his way. "*What* just happened?" She frowned and pressed against his chest. "And *how* did we end up here?"

Chapter Nine

LINDSAY FROZE WITH her hand on Conall's hard chest and simply stared into his gorgeous, very startled eyes. What had just happened? What did she *do*?

"I—" she started and shook her head, not sure what to say she was so thrown off balance and wildly aroused. He was completely nude and pressed against her. She bit her lower lip at the feel of him between her thighs. His heavy erection had nothing but a bit of material keeping it from going where she *so* wanted it to go right now.

"Och, I'm sorry," he muttered and pulled back so abruptly, she almost fell right off the rock. Instead, her eyes fell down his body, again drinking in the sight of him. He was built like a damn mythological god with his strong legs, slim hips, washboard abs, broad shoulders and muscular arms. Yet her eyes kept getting drawn back to the admirable thickness between his legs. For shit's sake, never mind being a butt double, he could *easily* hold his own in a pornographic movie.

"Bloody hell," he grunted before he muttered a chant and turned away, leaving her with a fully clothed backside to admire. She tore her eyes away from him, shook her head and came to her feet, still trying to make sense of what just happened.

"That wasn't me," she blurted then swallowed hard when his eyes met hers again. "At least not at first."

"I know," he ground out, clearly more aggravated with himself than her as he raked a hand through his wet hair. His brogue was far thicker than normal, his R's rolling. "Ye were possessed, and I took advantage of ye." He frowned and looked at her with disappointment in his eyes, his breathing just as heavy as hers. "I am truly sorry, lass." He shook his head. "I knew ye werenae yerself yet I…"

When he trailed off, angry with himself, she debated how much to tell him. While yes, she had felt controlled by another as she sauntered his way and touched him, the feeling had fled the moment he kissed her.

Then she was just lost but very much herself until Milly and Adlin showed up.

Lindsay pressed her lips together and shook her head. If they had not appeared, she would have eagerly and very willingly had sex with Conall. And, *oh*, she knew it was going to feel unbelievable. She had never been so aroused and ready in her life.

"It's okay," she managed, deciding against telling him the truth. If she did, she would be admitting her interest in him, and that was the last thing she should do. Or so she kept telling herself as he crouched at the pool's edge and splashed water on his face. He might have just bathed, but she suspected he wanted to submerge his whole body in the frigid water again. Or so said his raging erection.

"Tell me about what possessed you," he finally said as he stood and faced her. His brogue seemed under control again. "Did it feel evil? Do you believe it might have been the warlock?"

"No." She shook her head. "Not at all on both counts." She cleared her throat. "It felt…" Seductive. Teasing. Practiced. Powerful. "It felt like a woman."

"A lass?" He frowned. "Are you sure she didnae feel evil? Warlocks can be lasses too."

"I'm sure," she murmured and shook her head. "No, she definitely wasn't evil." She pondered it as she absently twirled her ring. "If anything, she felt familiar."

He crossed his arms over his chest. "How so?"

"I'm not sure but…" Her words died away as her eyes fell to her ring. "It's changed colors again, Conall."

"You used my name," he said unintentionally based on his expression before he redirected his focus to her gem. "I dinnae recognize that shade of blue."

She shook her head. "Me either."

"'Twould have to match the eyes of whoever you might have become, aye?" he murmured as he took her hand and peered at it.

Her breath caught at the physical contact. At how the roaring need between her legs that had barely dulled fired right back to life.

Clearly sensing it, his eyes shot to hers before he released her hand and stepped back. But not before she saw the flash of fear. Not before she saw far more than he likely wanted her to. Losing both his father and Fraser had truly damaged him. Maybe beyond repair. It didn't matter that it had not been the loss of a woman he loved, it had been family members he loved and it cut deep.

It was easier for him to remain adrift than to make connections and she well understood. Milly, Christina, and Jessie were a fluke. Growing close to them had been strangely unavoidable, but they were the only ones since her parents had died. And, as she eyed Conall warily, they were more than enough. She didn't need something deeper.

She did not need to fall in love.

"Whilst we are both likely ready to return to the others," he said. "'Twould be wise to begin training as soon as possible." His eyes didn't quite meet hers. "Now, preferably…unless you need time to gather yourself."

She feared she was long past gathering herself, especially when it came to him, but dutifully tried to pretend otherwise.

"No, I'm fine. And I agree." She really did though she understood his need to remove himself from any possible intimacy. "Where do we begin…Laird Hamilton?"

His jaw tightened at her use of his title, but he nodded once as if agreeing with her decision to call him that again. At least, for the moment, they were no longer bickering. Rather, since they woke up, he seemed different somehow. The way he spoke and looked at her had changed.

Her thoughts went to the night before. Flashes of nightmares from her childhood, then peace. A sort of peace and warmth she had never felt before. Or had she? For a moment upon waking, she related that peace with snippets from the night Conall had taken her out of Grant's arms and away from Stirling Bridge. Flashes of how he had held and comforted her.

When she opened her eyes this morning she was *almost* surprised she wasn't in his arms. That he was not holding her like he had that night. But no, he was sitting there, stoic as ever looking like he hadn't slept in ages. If anything, his eyes appeared haunted.

So what happened? Because he had treated her oddly since. Yes, he still kept his distance but he wasn't quite so brash. While she could chalk it up to him learning about her gift to enchant rather than blindly seducing men, she sensed it was more.

Then again, she sensed stranger and stranger things from him. Or more so his thoughts. Especially the hairless faery in the tree. She wished she hadn't heard those thoughts because they were bizarrely relatable. If for no other reason, than that she had been bald at one point in her life.

"Though we both know I dinnae ken your particular gift, I do ken magic verra well," he began as he leaned against the rock opposite her. "The place to start when learning about your gift is at the verra beginning. The first time you used it and what caused it to happen."

As if she would tell him that anytime this century.

"'Tis doubtful you are ready to share as much yet though so I'll share my first time," he provided, evidently seeing the reluctant look on her face. "I was nearly nine winters old." A wry grin tugged at his lips. "A late bloomer, my kin said."

"So you were eight," she murmured, stating the obvious as a chill went through her.

"Aye." He nodded. "I was at MacLomain Castle with Adlin. Not surprising in retrospect."

"Why?" She relaxed as he did, caught by the sudden light in his eyes. A side of him she had never seen.

"Well, Adlin was who he was, but a mess at it." He chuckled. Actually *chuckled*. "He had a bad habit of thinking he was all-powerful from a verra young age, and though he was stronger than most with magic, he was, as a rule, overambitious."

She couldn't stop a small smile at Conall's nostalgia. "How so?"

"'Twas the tree outside his castle," he began. "A magical bonnie tree born of many. A MacLomain and Broun tree if ever there was one."

"Really?"

"Aye." He nodded. "It has a long history. One I'll share someday mayhap."

No sooner did the words leave his mouth then his posture tensed. She didn't blame him. His words skirted too close to hinting that they might know each other far into the future. She inhaled deeply and almost shook her head as her own shoulders grew tight. Not, she was shocked to realize, because of a potential *someday* that existed between them, but because there might not be.

As if eager to relieve the sudden tension, he continued. "Adlin doesnae have just one element like the rest of us. Instead, he controls all and at that age, was rather proud of it."

"Oh no," she murmured, biting back a small smile. "What did he do?"

"'Twas more about what he did *not* do." He shook his head, that same small smile curling his lips again. "He boasted that the tree and all its creatures were his to command. That every last leaf would blow in the wind if he commanded it. That every last creature would sleep if he willed it. None were so powerful as he."

She flinched. "It sounds like he was playing God."

"Aye." He nodded. "He's said the same many times since and regrets it." He shrugged. "Yet he got his comeuppance in a way most unfortunate considering the trail of wee lassies following him."

Lindsay met his smirk. "How old was he?"

"Only a few winters older than I."

"And girls were following him?"

"Aye." He looked confused. "Werenae lads following you around at that age?"

Something about the way his words grew softer alarmed her. Almost as if he had an inkling of her at that age. Lindsay simply shook her head in response and urged him to continue.

"So, showing off for the lasses, Adlin cast this great magical spell on the tree," he said. "One, by all accounts, that worked. It appeared the entire tree slumbered. No leaves moved, the air grew stagnant, and even a squirrel or two plunked peacefully to the ground sound asleep."

Lindsay barely breathed as he continued.

"Unfortunately for him, something in that tree didnae rest and made him a bit of a laughing stock for some time," Conall said, his tone changed, fonder almost. "Because whatever it was made the branches shake, and whipped acorns at him."

Breathe Lindsay, she whispered internally. This is just pure coincidence. Nothing more.

"Then what?" she managed. "How was this the first time you used your gift?"

"I apologized to the tree for Adlin's behavior," he stated simply. "Then I flung my arms in the air, chanted, and finally did what I had been trying so long to do. I manipulated the air and allowed the tree to return to normal."

"You *allowed* it?" she whispered, remembering all too well a day like this. Or maybe it had been a dream.

"Aye." He nodded. "I thanked the tree for being patient with Adlin then I used my magic and freed it to resume its normal routine. Being part of life." Conall shook his head. "What happened that day set me on the path to embracing my gift fully."

"I see," she whispered and did her best to keep an even expression, praying all the while he would not sense her thoughts as he seemed quick to do lately. "Fascinating."

Their conversation was beginning to take on a surreal feel. As though she was awakening from something she always thought was a dream but really wasn't. As if perhaps those long days spent alone healing really weren't a figment of her imagination. That they might have, somehow, actually happened.

"The point of my story is that I came into my gift," he continued. "When I did, I understood what was at the root of it."

"And what was that?" she asked softly, wondering perhaps if he really *was* at the root of it. Or could it have been the faery in the tree helping him?

"Lack of fear," he stated simply. "Acceptance that I possessed something that could help that tree. That I could help, period." He gave her a telling look. "Much like you blindly do for others. That is why 'twould be best to go back to the first time you used your gift so that we can better establish the reasons it became active within you."

"I was young," she said absently if not a bit breathlessly. "I can hardly remember."

"You are lying," he stated calmly.

"I am not," she responded just as calmly.

They crossed their arms over their chest at the same time as they continued.

"Mayhap if you arenae ready to share those details," he said, "you would begin by telling me what you did when you used magic for the first time."

"I can't remember."

"Then mayhap where you were."

124

"I can't recall."

"Then mayhap," his eyes narrowed, "how using your gift for the first time made you feel."

"Confused," she said before she could stop herself. But something about the way he was looking at her, the genuine help he tried to offer, made her able to share. That part of the memory at least.

"Aye, 'tis confusing for many of us the first time we use our gift." That same semi-amused look was back in his eyes as, she realized, he attempted to lighten the mood. "But imagine being able to put the likes of Adlin MacLomain in his place when you do it."

"That must have been something," she acknowledged, smiling. "I can only imagine."

And she truly could. Far more than he knew, she feared.

"Did you feel anything else but confusion?" he asked.

"Yes," she murmured. "Fear." Her voice grew softer, yet her eyes stayed with his. "Terrible fear."

"'Tis normal, lass." Conall never looked away but shifted closer, his arms still firmly locked over his chest as he considered her and his gaze softened. "There isnae anything like that first moment when you know you've controlled something else. That you've manipulated your surroundings in a way most humans could never imagine." His eyes held hers as he paused, his voice gentler than ever. "'Tis a verra lonely feeling in some ways."

Their eyes held for a moment before she finally found her voice. "Yet you had family who used magic. Which gave you so many people to talk to about it. Some, even, that controlled air just like you."

"Aye," he agreed. "I was verra lucky." He moved even closer, not in a sensual way by any means. No, she sensed he wanted to be there for her and truly help her. "Yet here you are, Lindsay, a full grown adult using your gift in such an admirable way. Aye, you need training and 'tis to be expected given you had no one to help you along the way, but you are by no means flailing, lass."

He cocked his head, considered her and continued. "You truly are verra powerful, and I'm impressed you've managed to keep as much control over your magic as you have. That said, I hope you will allow me to help you redirect it a wee bit." His voice remained soft, his eyes more intense. "I hope you will allow me to help you bring to life your oak without losing your own life in the meantime."

Lindsay might have found Conall all naked and sexy threatening enough to her senses, but she could fight that. She could, with great effort, look away. But *this* version of him? This genuine, caring, open version of him? She was utterly defenseless.

Hell if her knees didn't weaken just staring into his eyes right now.

Pull yourself together, Lindsay, she preached to herself. Do not let him get too close.

"I was a pre-teen when it happened," she blurted out the lie. "Someone was being bullied in school, and I wanted to protect them." Lindsay rubbed her lips together, summoned just the right amount of moisture in her eyes and whispered, "I didn't know what to do. I was too much of a coward." She swallowed hard and released a shaky sigh. "The next thing I knew I was seeing through the eyes of the girl getting teased and standing up for myself." She narrowed her eyes. "I was telling those bullies where to go, and it felt great."

That had actually happened…just at a much later date.

Conall, meanwhile, watched her with a detached eye. His lips thinned, and his brow furrowed more and more through her tiny tale. Afterward, he just contemplated her.

"What?" she murmured, still acting the part of a broken woman sharing her deepest secret.

He eyed her for another long moment before he shook his head and stepped back. "I think 'twill take more time than anticipated to teach you."

She frowned. "Why? I'm a quick learner."

"You are also a quick liar."

When she narrowed her eyes, he shrugged in return, uncrossed his arms, and again leaned against the rock opposite her. "Mayhap we should move on to something I can at least attest to. Something I was there for. What happened last night with the warlock."

"Right." Lindsay uncrossed her arms as well, braced her hands against the rock behind her, leaned forward a little and narrowed her eyes. "How was it again that you saw me with that warlock? Because it almost sounds like you may have used *your* magic against *my* will."

"I cannae in all honesty explain how I followed you last night, lass," he relented, taking the high road it seemed as his level eyes held hers. Gorgeous, piercing eyes that had a way of constantly making her feel off-kilter.

"What I *can* say," he continued. "Was that you couldnae hold that warlock's attention as long as you thought. And there was fear in your eyes when you realized it."

Lindsay worked to keep her breathing even as she remembered it all too clearly. First seeing out of Graham's eyes and feeling what he felt. The horror. The need to protect his kin then being paralyzed and speared by something unnatural.

"I couldn't get it away from Graham fast enough," she whispered as her eyes held Conall's. "It was going to destroy him before Adlin or anyone had a chance to stop it." Lindsay straightened her shoulders and locked her jaw against the pure power, the pure terror that had come at Graham. Most of which she took with her when she no longer saw through his eyes. He had been wounded and didn't need that evil to corrupt not only his mind but his body. "So I lured it away." She shrugged. "I looked into its eyes and did what I do best. Enchanted."

There was no missing the struggle in Conall's eyes as he tried to navigate how to educate her in this. It was clear he was concerned for her but was trying to accept that she had handled it. Though she had put her life on the line, she had survived and saved Graham in the process.

"How are you so sure of your gift?" he said softly. "How do you even know how to somewhat control it without guidance? Without help somewhere along the way?"

There had been help. Advice. But she wasn't sure he was ready for that yet.

Caught by his own curiosity it seemed, he closed the distance and stood a foot or so away. The look in his eyes mixed confusion with, if she were not mistaken, fear for her. He was raw right now. Not concerned in the least how he presented himself. He wanted answers. Ones that he could understand.

But did she have them to give?

As their eyes held, she realized she was not just talking to Conall or Laird Hamilton, but the wizard within. The very creature that had not only created but protected her the night before from razor sharp ice.

A man with eyes she was starting to recognize.

Eyes that had been tucked away in her mind for far too long.

She pulled her gaze away, terrified at the thought. Terrified that she might already care for him.

"Lindsay," he whispered, suddenly way too close as his strong fingers tilted her chin until their eyes met again. She swore this was the moment. Would he recognize her? Was she right about him? "Ye cannae do that again, aye? Ye cannae lure pure evil without knowing ye are fully in control of yer gift. He could have killed ye."

"I know," she whispered because she thought for sure he might be connecting the dots as readily as her. She licked her lips and tried to keep a steady voice. "That's why you're teaching me, right?"

His eyes fell to her lips as he whispered, "Aye."

Blood started pounding through her veins as his gaze lingered, as she became overly aware of the heat of his fingers. Then the path left in their wake as they trailed over her chin, down her neck then spanned her collarbone.

Their breathing became choppier as he continued to touch her, watching his hand as though it had a mind of its own. He trailed two fingers down until they hooked loosely over the material between her breasts.

He struggled. She could see it in the way his pupils flared, and his hand trembled slightly against her skin. He didn't want to desire her any more than she did him.

Yet here they were.

Not teaching and learning but drowning in desire again.

He wasn't stepping back, startled and polite or overly uptight. Instead, he remained close, the heat of his body melting through her dress despite the six inches or so between them. Though she knew very well what was likely coming, he didn't shrug off his fur cloak or the tunic beneath.

Her chest tightened, and she all but stopped breathing as he slowly cupped her breast and brushed the pad of his thumb over her nipple. He weighed it and continued to caress it as his eyes returned to hers.

The man looking at her now was not entirely Conall but a bit of everything inside. A chieftain *and* a wizard. More than that, a man filled with lust he wasn't, for the first time, trying all that hard to fight. Somewhere in there, she knew he knew he should stop...yet he didn't.

Her breathing grew more ragged as his eyes stayed with hers, he smoothly undid the ties on the front of her dress, and then scooped his hand beneath the material. She flattened her palms against the cool rock as sensations rolled through her.

Though tempted to give in and close her eyes, she kept them locked with his.

Because if she was not mistaken...he was daring her to.

Yet as he pebbled her nipple between his thumb and forefinger while simultaneously caressing her breast, her head fell back, and her eyes drifted shut. The moment they did, his free hand slipped around the back of her neck, and his lips were on hers.

This was always where she lost herself.

When he kissed her.

Now was no different as he continued to manipulate her breast in unthinkably creative ways as his mouth closed more firmly over hers. As he grew hungry and demanded more.

But he wasn't alone.

She was demanding more too.

Overly aware of his touch, his very proximity, she moaned, curled her fingers into the fur at his shoulders and pulled him closer. His large body caged her in but at the same time made her feel safe and free...wild.

Their kisses intensified and deepened as he left her breast and cupped the sides of her neck, his fingers caressing and warm. Then one hand traveled until he grabbed her ass and squeezed. She groaned and spread her legs, grinding against him as desperately as he was her.

She should stop.

He should as well.

Yet neither did as their kisses only grew more passionate and the heat between them blazed. The ache between her thighs had grown painful, and her whispered groans between kisses a desperate plea.

"We shouldnae," he said softly against her lips somewhere in there, but it got lost in a need that was already way out of control. He pushed her skirts up while she yanked at the strings on his trousers.

"Conall...Laird Hamilton," she whispered, not sure what to call him, then no longer caring as he hoisted her against the rock, shoved her skirts up the rest of the way, spread her thighs and pressed into her.

She gasped at his girth then flinched as he pressed deeper then downright groaned in pleasure as he kept going. Lindsay held onto the fur at his shoulders for dear life as he thrust deeper and deeper. Little lightning bolts of pleasure began to tingle and spread throughout her body as he moved.

As he filled her.

Their eyes met and held as long as they were able to before desire, and near frenzy took over. They were barely undressed, barely stable on the uneven rock at her back, but it didn't matter. He kept one strong hand clenched over her ass, rolled his hips and thrust with more vigor than she anticipated.

"Ohhh," she half moaned, half whispered as he drove into her. His hot, harsh breath was close to her ear, and his warm body created head-spinning friction against hers.

Nothing had ever felt like this.

Nothing made her feel so much.

There was no acting needed. She couldn't even if she wanted to.

Her hands cramped she gripped his fur so tightly, but she felt nothing beyond the sensual fire blazing between them. The pulse of her heart slamming in her throat. The harsh bursts of his breath as he thrust hard and deep, drilling her against the rock but at the same time pulling her so much closer to him emotionally.

It was impossible to describe.

All it took was him whispering her name on a low, lusty groan to spike an orgasm straight through her entire body. She locked up and belted out a wail before she swore the ground dropped right out from beneath them. Half a heartbeat later, he pressed deep, let out a ragged groan of pleasure and shuddered.

A thousand colors swirled around them, and it became impossible to breathe.

She felt weightless.

All she could do was feel, connect, be a part of the experience. It was far beyond anything she had ever felt. Beyond anything she had even pretended to feel. For all her long hours training to become an actress, she never once imagined it feeling like this.

Nothing could compare.

Nothing could touch it.

Her body trembled and shook as her insides quaked. Endless ripples of pleasure fanned through her in steady bursts.

"Who goes there?" came a deep voice, ripping her from her reverie. "What are ye doing to that lass?"

It seemed Conall already knew there was a problem because he had pulled free and lowered her skirts while supporting her, so she didn't crumple to the ground.

The sound of a blade sliding free from its scabbard echoed through the cave followed by the masculine voice. "Did ye hear me?"

Conall's eyes met hers, and he shook his head a fraction as he adjusted his pants.

"I guess ye didnae then," came the same voice seconds before a dagger came around Conall's neck and he was forced backward away from her.

Eyes wide, her body still quivering and trembling with the aftershocks of what he had made her feel, she tried to adjust herself and figure out what was happening. Only one thing snapped into focus though.

A pair of royal blue eyes she would never forget.

"Are ye well lass? Answer fast, or this man dies," he growled, his blade already cutting into Conall's neck as he awaited her response. Though she should have said a great number of things, most of which would preserve Conall's life, she instead whispered three small words.

"Who are you?"

Though he hesitated a moment as though remiss to share as much, he ended up being far more honest then she anticipated.

"I am the Earl of Carrick." His blade never budged. "Robert the Bruce."

That could only mean one thing.

They had traveled through time again.

Chapter Ten

Happrew, Scotland
Near Peebles on the Scottish Border
February 1304

CONALL HAD SPENT his entire life deeply revering and respecting Robert the Bruce only to find himself instantly disliked by the man. While he should have been solely focused on that fact, all he could do was stare at Lindsay.

All he could *think* about was how it had felt to be with her moments ago.

More than that, how much he wanted to be with her again.

While some might say it was part of her enchantment, he knew better. Whatever that had been, whatever they just shared, went *far* beyond mere enchantment. Far beyond what he needed in his life right now. It was terrifying, dangerous, and perfect. Everything that could break his heart all over again but a thousand times worse.

Yet he wanted more.

Right here, right now, despite the blade to his neck and the famous king at his back, he wanted to have that kind of passion again. To let himself go and bury himself in her tight heat. To not care. That's when it occurred to him how erratic and undisciplined his thinking was.

Worse than that, what he had just let happen between him and Lindsay.

"He didn't hurt me," Lindsay said, her voice a weak, hoarse squeak before she cleared her throat and shook her head. "Laird

133

Hamilton is innocent." Her eyes stayed with the Bruce's. "I swear it."

Robert's blade only dug deeper as he contemplated.

If Conall wanted to, he could have already taken down Robert, but he thought too highly of him. At least so long as he didn't swipe the blade he supposed.

"*Are you serious?*" Lindsay said, speaking telepathically without realizing it as her eyes flickered between Conall and Robert. "*You would let him kill you here and now for something you didn't do because you think so highly of him?*"

The feel of her in his mind nearly had his cock at attention once again.

Rather than respond to her, telepathically or otherwise, he murmured, "My name is Conall Hamilton, son of Darach Hamilton, grandson to Grant Hamilton. I come on behalf of Adlin MacLomain to aid ye in yer upcoming battle. My blade is yers, Earl."

Though he felt Robert's hesitation, the Bruce didn't budge until he had further confirmation from Lindsay. "So he wasnae raping ye, lass, or hurting ye in any way?"

"No." She shook her head. "He was just trying to steal a kiss is all."

A kiss, was it? But he appreciated her vagueness.

"Was he then?" Robert murmured before he, at last, pulled the blade away but kept a wary eye on Conall. Though several inches shorter, he was a formidable man with enough weapons to have easily taken down the average man.

"Ye claim to know some verra important men." Robert's eyes narrowed on Conall. "And by all accounts, ye do bear a striking resemblance to the Grant I once knew. More so, Darach." He shook his head. "Though 'twas a long time ago, indeed, that I saw either of them."

"Aye." Conall kept a close eye on Lindsay though he spoke to the Bruce. "So ye havenae come across any of them yet? I am the first to arrive?"

"Aye," came another voice before William appeared, grinning at Conall and Lindsay. "'Tis good to see ye both again! It has been a bloody long time." He looked from one to the other. "And still kissing I see?"

Conall and Lindsay glanced at one another before they greeted William. It was odd having seen Wallace hours ago though he had no memory of it. How could he? The battle they had just fought together would not happen for another six months or so.

"'Tis clear ye know these two, Wallace," Robert said, sheathing his blade as his attention returned to Lindsay. Though some might question that kissing comment, it was clear the Bruce was very confident and already enamored with her. Blatant admiration lit his eyes as he held out the crook of his elbow. "Come, lass, let us all go talk where 'tis warmer, aye?"

"Why thank you," she said softly, back to the lass he knew all too well as she smiled warmly at Robert and took his arm. "My name is Lindsay by the way."

What had he expected of her anyway? That she would say no and run into Conall's arms because they had just been together? Because as much as he had thoroughly enjoyed it and wanted more, it should never have happened.

They should not happen.

So he did his best to swallow his jealousy as he joined Wallace and they followed.

William, of course, was curious how everyone had fared since the Battle of Stirling Bridge. It was a bloody odd conversation, but Conall navigated it to the best of his ability, careful not to mention the Skirmish at Earnside.

Skirmish, his arse. That was a full out battle.

"Well, 'tis good to know ye will all be amongst us again." William's eyes narrowed on Robert's back. "We only just reconnected a few days ago, and 'tis clear he's as proud to be him as he ever was. Though 'twas welcoming to see he wasnae as determined to capture me as I figured he would be."

Robert the Bruce would not become king for two more years and certainly not beloved by the Scots. No, he had a ways to go before that happened. In fact... "Is the Bruce not here with the Sassenach to capture ye and Sir Simon Fraser?" A man he knew had once fought alongside Andrew Moray but now fought with Wallace. "Did the Bruce not arrive with a chevauchée of Sassenach knights led by Sir John Segrave?"

He could barely utter Segrave's name, knowing full well his ultimate role in William's fate. His part in Wallace's execution.

"Aye," William said gravely. "But what they dinnae know is that they've a traitor in their midst."

"That traitor being the Bruce. Fighting for Longshanks whilst helping the Scots. Or at least helping ye," Conall murmured. "So where are we heading now? How is he here and not with the Sassenach?"

"Stealth," Wallace muttered. "One of the Bruce's more questionable attributes but most welcome right now."

It was clear William and Robert had a strained relationship, but at least they had one. That, of course, was thanks to the actions of not only Grant, Adlin, and Conall's parents, but his aunts and uncles as well. Many years back, they helped bring these two men together as bairns so they could better understand and see who the other *really* was before Fate took over.

"So are ye set to battle the Sassenach then?" Conall asked. "Is it happening soon?"

"'Tis hard to know," William said. "We've got them going in circles right now." His chuckle sounded strained. "We're staying one step ahead of them thanks to Robert but 'tis only a matter of time before the battling begins."

Conall frowned as he considered that. "Where are ye hiding out then?"

"Here." Wallace gestured at a small encampment as they exited the cave. "'Tis close to the river and several abandoned cottages."

One of which they followed Robert and Lindsay into.

As always, she caused a stir everywhere she went. A lass the likes of her should not be here. His gut clenched. They were with Scottish rebels on the run. It was far too dangerous. Aye, that could be said about the last few places she had been, but something about this one gave him a very bad feeling.

Especially considering his kin had yet to arrive.

More so, that he really had no proof that Robert was truly a traitor to the Sassenach. History did not record it that way. Only Grant and Adlin did. While it seemed they might be right, it was hard to know, hard to trust anyone where Lindsay was concerned.

"Please sit, Lindsay." Robert escorted her to a crude chair near a crackling fire. "Would ye care for something to drink?"

"I would," she said, her voice soft and oh-so-feminine as she batted her lashes at him. "Thank you, Robert."

Conall frowned. Though she had just shared her body with him, it didn't seem to affect her in the least. Instead, she appeared to have moved on quite readily and far too easily in his opinion.

"Here, friend." Wallace handed him a mug of whisky as they all sat. "Though tempted to ask ye what to expect from the future, I know better." He slanted a look at Conall. "Unless, that is, ye are a different sort of man than Adlin."

"Oh, he's a different sort all right." Lindsay grinned and winked at him. "Isn't that right, Laird Hamilton?"

She could adjust to any situation, couldn't she?

"I am." He gave her a look no one could mistake. "You, more than anyone, know that, aye?"

Robert gave her a curious look. "Is he yer lad then, lass?"

"Oh, dear Lord, *no.*" She made a dismissive gesture with her hand and flashed one of those stunning smiles that lit up her face. "He, like most lads as you can imagine, likes to think he might be." She glanced at Conall, rolled her eyes then looked at Robert again. "But rest assured, he is the furthest thing from it."

Conall narrowed his eyes. The little vixen. He took a swig of whisky. Something he would normally never do under these circumstances.

"Actually," Conall mentioned. "I am Chieftain of Clan Hamilton and her sworn protector."

"Sworn protector, is it?" Bruce considered the two of them. "So is it normal where ye come from to try and kiss the lass yer sworn to protect?" He shook his head. "Because that doesnae sound like the best way to go about keeping her safe."

William chuckled but said nothing.

"She is *never* safer than she is with me." Conall frowned, took another sip of whisky and reiterated, "And, *aye,* I am her sworn protector."

Amusement lit Robert's eyes as they returned to Lindsay. "Is he then, lass?" His tone softened. "Must I go through him to get to know ye better?"

Conall took another swig of whisky as she appeared to contemplate that. When she answered, he was not sure what to make of it. "No, you do not need his permission. You can get to know me all you like." She frowned at Conall, her eyes resolved yet reluctant as they returned to Robert. "Though, for decency's sake, it would be best if I stayed with him in the evenings for protection of course."

Yet again, William chuckled but said nothing.

"Agreed." Robert leaned forward, took her hand and held her eyes. "Because despite this protection he offers in the evenings, ye will soon see that I can offer more." The corner of his mouth tilted up. "*Far* more."

A flicker of surprise lit Lindsay's eyes before her lips curved softly and she nodded. "That would not surprise me Earl Robert the Bruce."

The sultry way she said his name almost made Conall toss her over his shoulder, bring her anywhere but here, and remind her just how much more *he* had to offer than the Bruce.

Instead, he took another deep swig of whisky.

"So yer from the future then." Robert smiled and never let go of her hand as his eyes searched hers. "I met several lasses from the future when I was a bairn and though verra bonnie, none were quite so stunning as ye."

"One of those lasses happens to be my ma," Conall commented, not sure why he said it other than to possibly remind Robert how interconnected they really were. How he might want to be a bit more respectful.

William tossed him a look that told him he hoped for a lot.

"Was she then?" Robert nodded, clearly recollecting. "She could have only been Darach's, Jackie then." He finally tore his eyes from Lindsay and looked at Conall. "How are they? I liked them both verra much."

"Da's dead," he stated bluntly. "And Ma is coping."

While he might not be all that pleased with the Bruce right now, it was clear based on the look in Robert's eyes that the news truly troubled him.

"I am verra sorry to hear that, Laird Hamilton," he said softly. "Ye have my condolences."

Conall nodded, downed the last of his whisky and offered no response.

Lindsay, meanwhile, shot him a troubled look. Well, what was that all about? He said nothing wrong.

"I must admit to being quite exhausted from time traveling," Lindsay murmured, a charming yet apologetic look on her face as she once again drew Robert's attention her way. "Might we be given a place to rest?"

"Are ye sure?" Disappointment flashed in his eyes. "'Tis barely sundown and the last eve we might be able to enjoy a stroll before the next storm arrives."

"Is that so?" Her eyes went to the window and lingered. "A big storm then?"

"Big enough to prevent future strolls," Robert said. "And nothing would please me more than walking ye down to the River Tweed. 'Tis a bonnie sight at this hour."

Conall never took his eyes off of Lindsay and her antics as Wallace refilled his mug. While he thought for a moment she wanted to be alone with him it seemed he was wrong. He ground his jaw before he took another swig. If he knew what was good for him, he would approve her flirting with anyone but him. He would approve of those beautiful silver eyes enchanting any man but him. Yet it seemed he didn't know what was good for him when he stood and shook his head as Lindsay agreed to go with Robert.

"I will be all right," she assured Conall as Robert swung another fur around her shoulders. "Just a small walk then I'll join you to rest."

It was not a request but a statement.

"*I need to do this,*" she said into his mind. "*And you need to let me.*"

"*I need to do no such thing,*" he responded.

Her pupils flared a little, likely in response to hearing him speak so directly within her mind.

"*We never should have done what we did, Laird Hamilton, and we both know it.*" Her eyes met his, her expression firm, hard almost. "*I'm sorry, but I don't want to be with you. Not like that again and certainly not in a relationship.*"

Stung by harsh words that he should be grateful to hear, Conall clenched his mug and sank back into his chair. Robert offered him a small but very smug smile as he put a hand to the small of her back and they left.

"Och, lad," William muttered and shook his head, eying Conall. "Yer a better man than I letting the lass ye love leave with the Bruce like that."

"I dinnae love her." Conall frowned and kept at his whisky. "Nor will I ever."

William offered another annoying chuckle. "Then yer a bloody fool." He looked at Lindsay out the window. "She's a better lass than most."

While he might agree with William, he refused to admit it. Not right now. Not after she actually left with Robert the Bruce to woo him into what...her bed? Unexpected fury filled him at the thought. Anger, it seemed, Wallace saw clearly enough.

"'Tis obvious enough she cares for ye, Laird Hamilton," William said, his voice soft as his eyes met Conall's. "Yet 'tis also clear yer set to push her away as readily as she is ye." He cocked his head. "Why is that?"

Though he would normally end this conversation and retire, the drink was going straight to his head, so he responded. "Our losses are too great to risk more."

"Ah." William contemplated him. "So ye are both cowards."

"Aye," Conall whispered before another swig. "So it seems."

"'Tis foolish that," William murmured. "With all that is happening in our beloved country, all the strife and endless heartache, I would never turn from love if I caught a glimpse of it." He shook his head. "I would consider it a rare gift even if I knew I might verra well lose it the next day."

Though tempted to mutter something along the lines of William not understanding, he suspected Wallace knew more about self-sacrifice than most. In the end, the man beside him would give up everything for his country. So it made sense he would say that.

Yet as Conall contemplated it alone later in another small cottage, he understood that his statement applied to each and every one of them. Death could be a day away. A moment away.

Even so, he never moved from his chair in front of the fire. He never went after Lindsay, told her to be done wooing the Bruce, and shared how he really felt. But then, until this moment, staring into the flames contemplating William's words, he had not admitted it to himself.

He had not admitted that he was falling in love.

Worse yet, that he likely had been since the moment he laid eyes on her.

Not lust but *love*.

While that revelation should make him run after her and bring her back here, it did the opposite. Because, despite William's wise enough words, the fear he felt was too great. Near paralyzing actually. So he buried his errant thoughts in another swig of whisky and tried not to dwell. On her, how he felt, and most especially that she was with Robert the Bruce right now.

Though tempted to leap up and pull her into his arms when she finally entered sometime later, he did not. Rather he kept his eyes on the fire and took another swig of whisky. Though he hoped she would crawl onto the cot and rest, she sat in the chair next to him, held out her hand without looking at him and said, "Mind if I have a sip?"

Actually, he did. He might never drink but tonight…well, tonight he was, poor judgment or not. So he handed over a skin of whisky William had given him earlier instead of his mug.

Lindsay took a long swig then settled back before murmuring, "I'm sorry if I hurt you, Conall. It was not my intention."

"Laird Hamilton," he corrected, slipping into his brogue more and more. "And ye didnae hurt me. Ye did what ye should have, and ye were right. There isnae anything betwixt us but…a moment of weakness."

"That's right." She took another swig. "Weakness and sex that will *not* happen again."

"'Twould be unwise," he agreed, his eyes firmly on the flames as he said something he knew he would regret but needed to be said. "Ye are free to be with the Bruce if ye've taken a liking to him. I willnae stop ye but only caution ye to be careful. Though he might be a spy, he fights on behalf of the Sassenach right now. His loyalties are greatly marred by politics and though we both know someday that will change, 'twill be no time soon."

"Well, thank you for your permission, Laird Hamilton," she replied, her tone borderline sarcastic. "God only knows how I managed without it for so long."

Having thought he did a noble thing, Conall could not help but narrow his eyes on her. "Do ye not want to lay with him after having so soon laid with me?" He perked his brows. "I know enough about twenty-first century lasses to know ye might have thought I would be troubled by that." He frowned. "Or are ye such a different sort of creature from my ma and aunts?"

"Actually, I'm very much like them, and you damn well know it." Her eyes narrowed right back. "Because I guarantee if they were here right now, they'd think you a boorish beast."

"Boorish beast?" His brows slammed together. "Not once have I heard that phrase from them." He narrowed his eyes again. "Likely because ye are still acting the part ye just did with the Bruce. Pretending to be someone yer not and speaking with words that arenae yers but part of some screenplay or script."

Her brows flew up in surprise laced with aggravation. "And what do you know of screenplays and scripts?"

"I know 'tis a rare moment yer life is anything but," he shot back.

Having said far too much because of the whisky, Conall frowned, shook his head and redirected his eyes to the fire. Unfortunately, Lindsay was as bright as she was beautiful and it didn't take her long to figure it out. "You asked about me beforehand, didn't you? You asked about my profession?"

"It only made sense," he mumbled, quick to come up with a lie. "'Twas clear enough early on that you and I would need to work together."

"Work together," she mouthed. Her eyes narrowed further as she contemplated him for an uncomfortably long stretch before her voice grew soft. "More like you didn't just lust after me but were truly curious about *who* I was. What made me tick."

"Och, nay," he muttered and took another swig, remembering all too well questioning his grandmother about it at his castle. He knew nothing about acting, most especially about women the likes of Lindsay. While grandmum only knew so much about the craft or celebrities in general, she knew enough to share the basics.

"From what I've seen you are verra good at what you do, Lindsay." Though he knew he should leave this alone, his eyes turned to hers. "Do you miss acting in the twenty-first century? Will your fans miss you?"

"It's odd hearing you ask me that," she murmured, clearly caught off guard but not as confrontational as she had been moments before. "I like to think my fans will miss me..."

When she trailed off, he waited for her to say more. A few moments later, she did as her eyes drifted to the fire and her voice grew softer. "I just wish I missed *them* more. I wish I knew what was going on inside me."

His eyes went to the skin. How much had she drunk? Had she been drinking with Robert? Because it almost sounded like she wasn't eager to get back to the twenty-first century and that made no sense. Not with a lass like Lindsay. Not with a lass who had clearly loved what she did. Or so he thought.

"I never wanted to be laird," he murmured, not sure why he suddenly said that other than he could relate to her mixed emotions. The strange paths life led one down. "Graham did fiercely, but never me."

"Why not?" Her eyes met his, not all that surprised by his revelation it seemed. "You might be more uptight than most, but from what I saw at your castle, you're very good at what you do."

"What you saw at my castle?" He frowned and took another swig. "You mean when the Sassenach managed to get past my defenses, and my clan was slaughtered?"

"We both know that likely won't happen," she said, her voice firmer than expected as defiance flared in her eyes. "Not if we can help it."

"*We*," he muttered. "Something neither of us wants, but we ken it needs to happen in order to save the future?" He shook his head. "'Tis difficult to imagine."

Lindsay's jaw clenched, and her eyes whipped to the fire. If he wasn't mistaken, his words had stung her as readily as hers had him earlier. Good. Let them. Yet he found himself setting aside his drink, and leaning closer. "Why are ye back here, lass? Why are ye not in the Bruce's cottage where 'tis clear enough ye wanted to be?"

Her incredulous eyes turned his way. "You really are the biggest jackass I've—"

That's all she managed to get out before he moved fast and pulled her onto his lap.

"Oh, no," she began before he wrapped his hand into her hair, tilted her head, met her eyes, and repeated, "Why are ye not with the Bruce? Why are ye back here with me when ye know what will likely happen?"

"Because I just met Robert!" she sputtered, her eyes wide as she squirmed but didn't exactly try to get away. "I don't sleep with guys I just met."

143

"Ye've known me less than a week," he reminded, unable to lessen his brogue any. "Some would say ye *just met* me so to speak, aye?"

The motion of her arse on his lap had his cock rock solid. A fact she was well aware of based on the way she stilled and her cheeks grew flushed.

"I thought we both agreed that never happened," she whispered as the fire reflected and danced in her silver eyes.

"Did we?" he murmured, not quite recalling that. Blame it on the whisky. But then, it made sense because it should not have happened. Yet it had. This very day. "Mayhap we should begin on the morrow."

"Begin what?" she managed as he trailed a finger along her soft jawline.

"Agreeing that it never happened." He brushed the pad of his thumb over her plump lower lip. "Which leaves today open to interpretation."

"How so?" she whispered as the tip of her little pink tongue snuck out and licked his finger. Just a quick sample but enough to make his cock leap.

"We've a few hours left to this day," he murmured as the wind began to howl outside and snow started falling. "Mayhap today is a day of things that never happened. Of things that we can wake on the morrow and know are in our past." His eyes stayed with hers. "Things we vow now will never happen again."

"I'm intrigued," she said softly, her eyes half-mast but still somewhat coherent as he grazed his fingers down the side of her neck, barely touching. "So today doesn't count...doesn't exist. And none of this," she shifted her arse along his erection, her voice husky, "ever happened."

"'Twould be best, aye?" he murmured as he put his mouth where his fingers were and tasted her sweet softness. Her flawless skin.

"I think you're probably right," she whispered as her eyes slid shut.

Just like that they were done bickering and on to far more enjoyable things. While he knew he was taking them down a path harder and harder to turn from, he truly believed in his near drunken state, that they had come to a logical conclusion.

Be together now then end it on the morrow.

It made perfect sense and would assuage what was taken from them before. Though they had come together well and true, there had been little time to enjoy it. Especially when Robert's blade met his neck.

But that was behind them, at least for now, and Conall intended to enjoy *today* to its fullest.

That meant, before all else, getting her out of this bloody dress. A task he set to with great attention to detail and with more relish than he had ever felt when undressing a lass. But then, this was Lindsay, and she was, by far, the most bonnie creature he had ever laid eyes on. A fact that became more and more apparent as he set her back in her chair, knelt in front of her and began removing her clothes.

He took his time and started with her boots, remembering the sight of her delicate feet and calves the eve before. How he had wanted to run his hands over her snowy white flesh and memorize the dimensions of her slender, perfectly shaped legs.

Now he did, his eyes going from her legs as he removed the boots altogether then up higher as he slowly pushed her skirts up. She never said a word but watched him from beneath drowsy lids, her eyes as full of desire as his.

When she leaned forward and tugged at his tunic, clearly wanting it removed, he pulled it off and tossed it aside. Then he yanked her forward enough that she fell back and was once more at his mercy. Or so he liked to think as he ran his hands along her slender thighs, pushed her skirts all the way up and spread her legs.

"Ohhh," she whispered and arched as he licked and teased her center before he focused on the tiny nub that had her arching more and crying out. She tasted as sweet as he imagined she would.

A flavor made entirely for him.

He wrapped his arms around her waist and arse and held her in place as he continued enjoying her. He liked the way she groaned and squirmed then gyrated against him as he devoured her. Nothing pleased him more than how she buckled time and time again as he used his mouth and fingers to take her somewhere he sensed she rarely, if ever, went.

"Conall," she eventually groaned and whispered. "We're running out of today." Her eyes slid open just enough to meet his. "And I want more…"

He understood.

Though he could have remained there all night and been in bliss, his cock more than appreciated her impatience. He pulled her dress over her head, and drank in the sight of her full breasts and tiny waist. Bloody *hell* he wanted her. Eternally grateful the chair was the perfect height, and without arms, he was quick to take advantage.

"Oh, my," Lindsay gasped as he yanked down his breeches, pulled her forward to the edge of the chair, came between her quivering thighs and thrust deep.

She bit back a ragged groan as he grabbed the back of the chair to stabilize it, hooked an arm around her lower back to keep her in place, then kept moving. She gasped incoherent words as she wrapped her arms around his shoulders and let him take control.

He shook as he thrust, lost in the feel of her tight heat, lost in the feel of her soft, voluptuous body against his. Her pebbled nipples grazed his chest and her firm, silky thighs wrapped around him as he moved. First methodically then with longer strokes and casual but deep rolls of his hips.

"Conall," she half groaned, half whispered in a husky, broken voice as he increased his pace then slowed and stopped as she climaxed again. He had loved the way her release felt against his mouth but almost appreciated this more. The way she locked up tight, her body frozen against his, completely vulnerable, before she shuddered and began milking his cock.

As she drifted, he stood, never pulling free as he brought her down on the cot. Not willing to risk using magic, he peppered small kisses along her neck and collarbone as he yanked off his boots and trousers. All and all, he managed everything far more smoothly than he could have hoped considering the whisky he drank.

But then this was Lindsay and today was all they had.

A sobering fact that left no room for sloppy lovemaking.

"Conall," she whispered again, her eyes still closed as she reached for him.

He loved the sound of his name on her lips but needed the distance right now no matter how close he pulled her.

"Laird Hamilton," he corrected hoarsely as he kept her hands away from him by pulling them above her head and holding her wrists with one hand.

"Laird Hamilton," she whispered as her eyes opened a mere crack and she arched, her well-rounded breasts, an invitation he could not refuse. He pulled one nipple into his mouth as he began thrusting again.

Not quickly but very, very slowly.

As he twirled his tongue around her nipple, he rolled his hips and pressed deeper. It took everything he had to keep from letting go as he watched her. As he saw the bliss in her eyes as he continued to touch, taste and move. In its own way, pleasuring her gave him great strength. Endurance beyond reason.

When she cried out again and locked up against him, he wrapped his elbows beneath her knees and pulled her legs up high. The added depth and friction of him rubbing against her center had her clenching the cot and struggling for breath as he elongated her pleasure.

Though tempted to plunge into her and at last, release his seed, he paused as tears leaked from the corner of her closed eyes. Her thoughts swirled with his. This level of pleasure was new to her. Sexual pleasure with a partner. Then other things started to come through. Flashes that connected them more and more.

Exhausted from pleasure, Lindsay was drifting off to sleep, so he carefully settled her back, bypassed his own release and pulled her into his arms as she slumbered.

Yet still, the flashes came.

Her parents were gone, and she was broken until she found strength. Alone, living amongst strangers, she grew stronger. Images rippled through his mind of her looking in a mirror as she ran a razor through her hair and large clumps fell away.

As she did, her big silver eyes became clearer and clearer to him.

He *knew* those eyes.

He had *always* known those eyes.

Lindsay, somehow, some way, had been his faery in the tree.

Chapter Eleven

"**NO MORE**," LINDSAY whispered through clenched teeth into the mirror as she continued to shave off the last of her white blond hair and confronted the new her. The girl that would no longer be defined by her looks or her past but by this.

The person who stared back.

At least for now.

That was the day she climbed high into the tree in the backyard of her foster home and began planning a new life. One chapter was over, and it was time to start another. A chapter where she accepted that she was completely on her own now and *she* ruled her own destiny.

Nobody else.

Not the kids who teased her and certainly not the bizarre almost surreal things that had begun happening. The daunting ability to see through other people's eyes when they were going through something traumatic. Now would be the beginning of the end of all that. *Now*, starting today, she would embrace a new person. If this person didn't make life more tolerable, then she would embrace another and another, staying one step ahead of her past and the curse that was hers.

As she sat near the top of the tree that day, she suddenly felt free in a whole new way.

Nothing could touch her here. She was part of something bigger and better, more magical than anything she had ever experienced. So it wasn't really all that surprising when she looked down through the leaves twisting in the sunlight and saw a boy around her age staring back at her. She was about to call out, yelling over the wind that had kicked up, but jolted awake instead.

Confused, she blinked several times, trying to acclimate, only to find herself beneath furs on a cot and Conall sitting in a chair beside her. While it was clear he had set up camp to watch over her, he had dozed off. His chin rested on his chest, a dagger firmly in his grasp on his lap despite how soundly he slept.

She frowned and rubbed her forehead, confused as she glanced out the cottage window. It appeared to be pre-dawn and snowing quite heavily. When she shifted and felt the soreness mixed with pleasurable tenderness between her thighs, everything started coming back.

Conall and her.

What he had done to her…no, *for* her.

"Oh, *hell*," she whispered as she peeked beneath the fur. She was fully dressed minus the boots. Her eyes went to him again, remembering all too well his sinfully hot body pressed against hers in this very cottage. She licked her lips as she recalled how thorough he had been.

How relentless.

How downright talented.

"I, oh *no*," she whispered under her breath as she swung her legs over the side of the cot and kept staring at him. Per William's request, she was supposed to be doing her best to get Robert the Bruce to fall for her *not* fall all over Conall Hamilton the minute they were alone.

"Make the Bruce fall in love with ye," William had requested back in Strathearn. "And Fate will happen as it should. Scotland's history will be safe."

"How could you possibly know that when you don't even remember me being there?" She narrowed her eyes. "Or *do* you?"

"Och, nay." He frowned. "I dinnae recall ye but know without a doubt this is how it should be. How Grant and Adlin would want it."

"If that's the case, why would *you* request such a thing of me," she had pressed, "and not Grant or Adlin?"

"I dinnae know," he whispered, sudden confusion in his eyes. "Just that 'tis yer only hope, lass. Our only hope."

"You make no sense." She shook her head. "This makes no sense."

Yet she had left his tent that night somehow convinced of what she needed to do. Now, in retrospect, she wondered if she had been bewitched. Had the warlock somehow spoken through William? Was she playing right into its hands having flirted so brazenly with Robert last night?

Somehow, she didn't think so.

Why, she couldn't be sure, but she felt strongly something else was at work here.

As if in response to her thoughts, she swore the blue in her gem glowed for a moment. The same shade, of course, that it had been since she seduced Conall.

She rubbed her forehead again as she eyed him.

One way or another, she had been seducing him since they arrived here, hadn't she? And what had he done in return? Given her so many orgasms she couldn't count them. Powerful climaxes that had her toes curling and her insides twisting in pleasure just thinking about them.

Gone, it seemed, were the days of fake orgasms.

She closed her eyes and shook her head at her line of thinking. One that kept Conall between her thighs long into the future. She rubbed a hand over her face and nearly groaned. Thinking like this had to stop. Not only did she *not* want a man but he was…her pained eyes rose to him. He was exactly who she had started to suspect he was.

The boy standing at the base of the tree looking up.

"Oh, God," she whispered and braced her head in her hands. If he were truly that boy, then he knew so much more about her than she wanted anybody to know. He knew her better than anyone.

He knew the girl she had left behind so she could morph time and time again.

She shook her head and stared at him. That boy was only ever supposed to be part of her healing process, not an actual person she somehow connected with across time. Now that it was all starting to come back, she marveled that she hadn't put the pieces together right away when she saw his eyes. Those thickly lashed gorgeous eyes that no woman could forget regardless of their age. Because she *had* been very young when she met him.

Magic related or not, she was shocked that she hadn't figured out who he was far sooner. But again, since she left that tree behind it had all become dreamlike. As time went by and memories of him began to fade, she started to assume what happened was just part of her gift. A self defense mechanism that allowed her to heal and grow strong.

"Lindsay," he rumbled, not a boy at all, but a man as his eyes met hers. He had awoken and seemed fully alert. "'Tis early. Get more sleep."

As their eyes held, she zipped right past the boy of her past and suddenly remembered all too well what the man had done to her last night. Her eyes fell to his sensual lips. To a mouth that had made her head spin time and time again. Her eyes unwillingly trailed lower to his groin and all the wonders *that* had done.

"We were undressed but not anymore," she whispered as her eyes returned to his. "Why?"

"Because that was yesterday," he reminded, his voice back to being stern. "And today is today, aye?"

Right. Their pact that allowed them to enjoy more sex without feeling as if they were betraying themselves. Though tempted to dispute their agreement, she realized that might not be wise for two reasons. The first, her promise to Wallace to flirt with Robert. The second, her vow to keep Conall at a distance. To protect her heart.

She finally managed to nod her agreement about today being a new day as she contemplated him. Yet her stubborn thoughts kept drifting. How he had been as selfless a lover as he was a warrior. How he filled her and made her whole world explode. But he never reached his own fulfillment, did he?

What sort of man did that?

What sort of man didn't ultimately take what he needed when she was so very willing? When she would have welcomed the feel of him throbbing deep inside her and finding release?

She swallowed hard, fought lust and met his steady eyes. Tired eyes that likely got about as much sleep last night as the night before. "Come," she whispered as she laid back, curled onto her side and patted the cot. "Come get some sleep, Laird Hamilton."

Though she would have preferred to call him Conall, she could tell by the guarded look in his eyes that remaining formal was the better choice. When he hesitated, she patted the cot again then closed her eyes, hoping he was simply exhausted enough not to overthink things.

Unfortunately, it seemed he wasn't because he never joined her. Or so she thought until she awoke several hours later to find herself beneath the furs wrapped in his arms. Her back was to his front, and as far as she could tell based on his heavy breathing, he was out like a light. She closed her eyes and breathed deeply, overly aware of his spicy scent, and the feel of his hard body touching every inch of hers.

She meant to get up, but as the wind whistled outside much like it did through the tree of her youth, she cozied in, relishing the safety. The choice to be herself before she became so many. Something she had done all on her own so long ago with the help of a boy from far below.

"You're gonna have to tell him soon, honey," came an unmistakable southern accent. "You're gonna have to tell him you've gone and fallen in love with him."

Christina?

She opened her eyes and bolted upright only to find Conall gone and it much lighter outside. How long had she slept? She glanced around, confused. It had sounded like Christina was *right* here. *Right* beside her.

Almost as if he sensed she was awake, the door opened, and Conall brushed snow from his fur-clad shoulders before entering. Back to being as stiff and formal as ever, he nodded hello. "I've brought salmon to eat and water."

She nodded and hid her disappointment that she hadn't woken sooner. She wanted to talk after what they shared last night. Perhaps explore the idea that what they experienced together would not truly vanish because of a pact about todays and tomorrows.

"'Tis fresh salmon from River Tweed," he said as he handed her a plate. "I caught it myself."

She was taken aback by the rush of raw emotion that washed over her. He might be a hard-to-read hands-down jackass on a rather consistent basis, but he also had a sweet side that could cripple her on occasion.

"Thank you," she murmured, trying to keep her eyes off him as he set a mug beside her. She tried to forget the things he had done to her. How intimate they had been. How unbelievable he had made her feel.

Her eyes flickered over him despite her best efforts to do otherwise. As tired as he must be, he still looked more handsome than ever. Dressed in brown linen breeches, a dark tunic, and black boots, he had more tiny braids in his hair than usual.

It was strange watching him become an entirely different man. Better yet the one he had been before. Especially considering how creative and ambitious he could be between the sheets.

Her eyes flickered across the room.

Or creative and ambitious on a chair.

As if following her thoughts, Conall cleared his throat, set the chair in the corner as though it had already caused enough harm then focused on the fire. He remained silent at first until he finally said what she should have seen coming.

"I had too much whisky last night, and for that I am sorry." He cleared his throat again, his eyes on the fire as he stoked it. "The Bruce eagerly awaits your company when you are ready."

"*Really*, Conall?" she nearly said. "When it's taking everything inside you not to bend me over this cot and have me again?"

Naturally, she kept quiet, yet she didn't miss the tightening of his posture. One that seemed far too coincidental, so she called him on it. "You're reading my thoughts, aren't you?"

"'Tis unavoidable sometimes," he grunted, his eyes still trained on the fire. "Especially when they are so…graphic."

She twisted her lips and repressed a smirk. They *had* been that.

"Well, that's neither here nor there," she said, trying to make her tone sound as light as possible. "Because today's a new day, right?"

"Aye," he said softly as his eyes finally turned her way. "As you likely gathered yesterday, we willnae be staying in one place overly long. Many have already packed up and traveled. You should eat so that we can follow."

Lindsay nodded and nibbled on her fish as he went to the window and kept an eye out. It was clear he was tense about their situation as his eyes stayed trained on their surroundings and his hand rested on the hilt of his sheathed blade.

"So no sign of anyone else yet?" She frowned. "Not even Adlin or your grandfather?"

"Nay." He sighed and shook his head. "Right now, I am the only wizard here."

She sipped her water and considered that. "But not the only one with magic."

His eyes met hers. "Which is why we should continue working on your training." His expression grew sterner yet she swore his eyes softened. "Something that would go far better if I knew what first sparked your gift."

He was about to say more when several taps came at the door before William entered. He looked more disgruntled than ever as he made a flippant gesture. "The Bruce is gone but will try to catch up with us later."

"Gone back to the Sassenach?" Conall frowned. "Is that not what he needs to do?"

"Aye," William muttered as he shook his head. "But I dinnae like it." He scowled. "Something feels off."

"You dinnae trust him after all then?" Conall invited William to sit, but he shook his head. "Did something happen?"

William clenched his jaw, clearly debating how much he wanted to share. "He just wasnae himself." He glanced at Lindsay. "Different in a way that is hard to explain."

Conall's frown grew heavier as he began strapping on weapons. "Nonetheless, explain the best you can, aye?"

"He was acting…bewitched this morn, for lack of a better word." William's eyes returned to Lindsay. "And 'twas not yer name on his lips, lass."

She could not help but be genuinely surprised. He had seemed quite smitten.

"Whose name was it then?" Conall asked.

"Christina," William murmured as his eyes narrowed on Lindsay. "A most unusual name in these parts."

She stood abruptly and shook her head, remembering all too well Christina's voice in her dreams before waking. "You must be mistaken."

William shook his head. "Nay."

"There's more, isn't there?" Conall said softly, his astute gaze on William.

"Aye." William looked from Lindsay to Conall. "The Bruce's eyes werenae quite right…they werenae quite his."

Tension knotted her shoulders. "What does that mean?"

Deep down she knew. Suspected.

"They were darker than they should have been," he stated. "So dark that superstition has several of my men scattering."

"How many?" Conall asked.

"More than I would like," he replied. "Mayhap a quarter so far."

Conall frowned, more concerned, it seemed by a possessed Robert returning to the English. "Do you suspect he returns to the Sassenach to tell them of your location?"

"I think 'tis best to assume that, aye?" William said. "As such, we will be breaking off into smaller bands to confuse them."

Conall nodded, evidently in agreement as his eyes went to Lindsay. Though he masked it quickly, she didn't miss his concern as he ripped a strip of material off the bottom of his tunic and headed her way.

Her eyes widened as he stopped in front of her. "Am I to play prisoner again then?"

"Nay, but 'twould be wise to look less like you," he murmured as he tied her hair back so swiftly, she would swear he had done it countless times. He stood close enough that she could feel the heat coming off of him and see the tiny mint flecks in his rich green eyes.

His gaze never quite met hers as he finished with her hair then wrapped a fur cloak around her shoulders before he pulled on her hood. Yet all the while, she knew he wanted to meet her eyes. That he was as aware of her as she was of him.

"There, that's a bit better," he said, his voice deeper and huskier than usual before he stepped back and looked her over. "Have you a spare pair of trousers, Wallace?"

Lindsay frowned. "You can't be serious." Her eyes went to William. "He's got to be almost ten inches taller than me." Her eyes returned to his. "Just like you."

"'Tis but fabric that can be adjusted." He glanced over his shoulder. "Have you then, William?"

"I'm afraid not." William gave Conall a pointed look. "And whilst I ken yer trying to make her look more like a lad, with a lass like Lindsay, 'tis wasted effort, aye?" He winked at Lindsay. "She's the bonnie sort that is unmistakably a lass no matter how much ye try to hide it."

Conall's gaze flickered down her body so quickly she barely caught it, but what she did see told her he was in complete agreement.

"'Twould probably be best if ye didnae travel with me," William said as he opened the door. "They'll be tracking me before all else."

"Mayhap," Conall murmured, clearly not all that convinced as his eyes swept over Lindsay again. "Whilst mayhap some of the Sassenach will, I suspect their warlock has but one target."

"Or two," Lindsay said, her eyes firmly on Conall as he took it upon himself to sit her down and put her boots on. "You tend to think I need all the protecting when you do as well."

He offered no response but tied her boots with the same swift precision he had her hair. Meanwhile, William left, saying he would see them again soon if that's what fate intended. Once they were alone, she put a hand on Conall's shoulder before he could stand.

Though she meant to say a great number of things when she touched him, as his eyes met hers, she said something unanticipated but surprisingly true.

"While today is a new day and things shouldn't progress like they have been," she murmured. "I would like things to change between us. Not sexually..." She shook her head. "I mean yes, things need to change sexually." Not really. Not at *all*. Lord, get your words straight, Linds. "What I mean is...I'd like to try to get along better...maybe be friends."

Conall considered her for a moment, his expression unreadable before he finished lacing up her boot and stood.

"So is that a yes?" she asked as she stood as well.

"I think we both know we're past that," he grumbled as he doused the fire. His eyes finally met hers again and lingered before he said the last thing she expected "After all, we've known each other since we were bairns, aye?"

Chapter Twelve

CONALL DIDN'T GIVE Lindsay a chance to respond but opened the door to thick drifts of snow and urged her to follow. The day had dawned cold and windy. Though it was no longer snowing, it would be again by nightfall.

"We've one horse to spare," came a deep voice as a man with dark auburn hair came alongside with a dappled gray. "He's sturdy enough for ye both if ye dinnae push him too hard."

Conall nodded. "Thank you, friend."

"The name's Simon Fraser." He swung up onto his own mount. "Wallace wishes ye to travel with me."

Though Conall didn't recall Simon from the Battle of Stirling Bridge, he knew he had fought well and stood by Moray until the end. In all honesty, he had a great deal of respect for Simon's role in all of this. How much he had been willing to sacrifice for Scotland.

Lindsay smiled and introduced herself. "Nice to meet you, Simon."

Like all men, Simon's eyes lingered on her face for a moment before he nodded firmly then trotted on ahead.

"My goodness," she murmured as Conall mounted then pulled her up in front of him. "I think I finally just met a man who can't be enchanted...outside of you that is."

"Och, there were bound to be one or two of us about," he muttered, not so sure about that. Maybe when it came to Simon but not Conall. He was beginning to think he wasn't immune to Lindsay's charms in the least. Not based on the smitten and protective way he always felt around her.

Before she could speak again, he entered her mind. *"From here on out 'twould be best to speak within the mind. The wind can too easily carry our voices."*

He didn't miss the slight tremble of her body in response. One directly related to the sound of his voice in her mind. She said nothing for some time as they followed Simon's men, single file into the forest. When she finally did speak, he sensed rather than heard how careful she was with her words.

"So you finally figured out who I am," she said. *"You figured out I was the girl in the tree."*

"Aye," he responded, softening his internal voice the best he could. *"You were..."* How should he phrase this? Truthfully, he supposed. *"A welcome addition to my life, lass."*

"How did it happen?" Her voice was distant, soft, though he sensed great emotion in it. *"How did we connect across time so long ago?"*

"That was something I believe we were somewhat curious about back then too, aye?" It took all he had not to wrap his arm around her mid-section. To pull close a lass who had meant so much to him.

"We did talk about it back then," she conceded, shaking her head. *"But as you can imagine, I thought you were, in some ways, make believe."* Humor laced her words. *"I was proud of my Scottish ancestry, so creating a Scottish boy at the base of a tree wasn't all that far-fetched."*

"You created a lot of things back then if I recall correctly," he commented, unable to stop a small smile. *"I remember meeting several versions of you. All of which always became the girl I knew from the beginning. The girl who eventually vanished."*

"You mean your friend." She glanced over her shoulder into his eyes. *"We were friends, Conall, and we can be again."*

Their eyes lingered on one another's before she looked forward again.

Could they be friends now after so much time had passed? Could they be friends after the intimacy they had shared?

"Of course we can," she whispered into his mind, following his thoughts far too readily. *"We got along pretty well if I recall. We had fun."* She grinned and jested. *"Come on now, it isn't every little girl who stands up to a wizard as powerful as Adlin."*

160

"That's right. You helped spark my magic, aye?" A small grin tugged at his lips. *"'Twas you who embarrassed Adlin in front of the lassies that day at the oak tree."*

"Like you said," she replied. *"He was awfully full of himself."*

"Even then, you were coming into your magic," he remarked. *"Shaking the tree like that then whipping acorns. 'Twas a good way to make Adlin's spell appear as though it hadnae worked."*

"I always thought so," she agreed, a smile in her internal voice. *"Something you found out much later."* She glanced over her shoulder with amusement. *"So why tell me that was your first time using magic when technically it wasn't?"*

"Because I always felt it was in its own way, and I told you as much back then," he reminded. *"I might not have initially known it was you in the tree that day, but everything I said when teaching you was true. I felt my magic had ignited and that's all it took. I released my fear and embraced my gift."* He shrugged. *"Technicalities dinnae matter."*

"Some could say technicalities very much matter when it comes to magic." She smirked, her eyes all-knowing because she was absolutely correct. *"But you always did like that story, so I'll let you get away with it."* She chuckled and faced forward again. *"I definitely think it might be good for us to try to find what we once had rather than bickering so much."*

"What we once had was a kinship betwixt bairns," he pointed out. *"'Twas easier."*

"Maybe..." she replied, her internal voice trailing off.

Conall debated his next words, remembering all too well the difficulties she had shared. Her upbringing had been hard. More so than he ever realized. Though she had told him a lot, she never divulged how she ended up where she did. She never shared the violent death of her parents.

That event, he imagined, first triggered her magic.

Yet how was he ever going to get her to talk about it? How, when she had not even told him way back then, were they going to bridge that gap?

Then he realized the answer was staring him right in the face. She had even suggested it.

"We will try." He nodded though she could not see him. *"At friendship...again."*

When she flashed a bonnie smile at him over her shoulder, he remembered well why this was a bad idea. Especially when his cock stirred, not interested in mere friendship in the least.

"*Good,*" she replied. "*Though your father said otherwise, did your family ever know about me? Did you ever tell any of them?*"

"*Nay, only Da,*" he began before stopping.

"*Right,*" she responded, her voice soft and distant again. "*You told him you would only marry the faery in the tree.*"

He offered no response because he truly had no idea what to say other than he very much meant it at the time. She was his closest friend, so it made perfect sense. What he never could have imagined, however, was that hairless lass growing up into the woman in front of him now.

"Why did you cry that last time?" he whispered aloud before he could stop himself. Based on her lack of response, he assumed his question was carried away by the wind.

Until that is, she replied at last.

"*Because I was leaving,*" she said, her eyes still dead ahead. "*That tree had given me a great deal of solace. You had. But I had to leave. I needed to start my life.*"

"*You were still fairly young though, aye?*"

"*I was,*" she conceded. "*But I looked old enough to pave a path for myself that wasn't part of that world anymore. I stayed strong, made friends in the right places, started making money and forged my way to where I am now.*" A wry grin tugged at her lips as she turned her head just enough that he could see her. "*And where I am now seems to be right back where I began in some ways...but better.*"

Conall didn't realize he had slipped his arm around her waist until her hand rested over his.

They did not speak for some time after that but bore down against the inclement weather. Where he suspected Wallace would travel north some, he had sent out three groups going in every other direction. Including one brave lot across the river.

Though it was barely audible on the wind, Conall didn't miss the low whistle Simon suddenly released. Trouble was afoot. Though men were both ahead and behind them, it was hard to see anyone through the wind-driven snow, so he acted purely on instinct.

"Remain silent," he said into Lindsay's mind as he swung down then pulled her after him. He had just enough time to pull her around a heavy cluster of evergreens and urge her to crouch before he heard voices.

"Dinnae move," he whispered before he nudged her further back into the bushes, pressed a dagger into her hand then carefully unsheathed his sword. He met her eyes, put a finger to his lips to remind her to remain silent then slowly edged along the bushes as cries rang out just ahead.

They were under attack.

While tempted to go fight and defend the men they traveled with, his first concern must be Lindsay. So he stayed close but not too close. If he did and were cut down, he would have accomplished nothing but leading the enemy right to her.

So he remained vigilant and took down anyone who thought to head in her direction. First, a thin lad with an ugly sneer and haphazard armor. It was easy enough to slip his blade past the poorly kept chainmail before he put a hand over the enemy's mouth to silence him and slit his throat. Next came a slightly larger Sassenach with a limp but a mean swing. Conall ducked beneath the blade, drove his dagger into the man's windpipe then cracked his neck.

All the while, Lindsay remained perfectly silent, her calm eyes watching his every move. More so, watching the blood that stained the snow not all that far from her. He realized as he fought another that she would not go into hysterics or even shock. If anything, what had happened to her parents had transformed her into something else entirely.

A lass, as it happened, who was very good at keeping a level head in battle as she tossed him her blade when he struggled with not one but two foes. Though he managed to drive one through with his sword, the behemoth behind him was another story. The brute gave him more of a challenge than anticipated before heading in Lindsay's direction.

Rare was the day he came across a man taller than him, not to mention one with such a daunting girth. Typically, Conall was good at stabbing men where he could easily pull his weapon free, but it didn't go that smoothly with the last man so he had naught but Lindsay's dagger now. A dagger he used with expertise as he slashed the huge warrior again and again. Unfortunately, that didn't slow him in the least. If anything, he seemed to be a rabid bear with nothing but Lindsay in his sights.

To make matters worse, it appeared she had nothing but the rabid bear in her sights as well.

"Bloody hell." Conall shook his head as she slowly but confidently stood and locked eyes with the Sassenach warrior barreling her way.

"It's okay," she said into Conall's mind. *"Let me do this. Let me help."*

Asking him to allow the enemy anywhere near her was downright impossible, so he kept at the warrior only to run into a hard fist. He staggered back, stunned. The monster of a man had turned fast and punched him. The shocking part? The Sassenach had been defending Lindsay before he fell to one knee in front of her and lowered his head.

When Conall started toward them, her words were sharp within his mind. *"Let me do this, Laird Hamilton."* Jaw clenched, her eyes didn't meet his but remained on the warrior kneeling at her feet. *"Let me protect you like you protected me."*

It went against every grain in him to allow a vulnerable lass with no battle skills so close to a seasoned warrior, never mind that it was Lindsay.

"Please," she repeated, her eyes firmly on the warrior as she shifted her hip seductively. *"I can do this, Conall. You have to trust me."*

Trust her? It wasn't about trust in the least. It was about her losing her life in an instant. Never uttering another word. More than that, him never hearing her voice again.

"Hello, there, *darling*," she purred as she tilted the warrior's chin up until their eyes met. "'Tis so nice to meet you in the midst of all this violence." She batted her lashes, a mysterious but promising look in her eyes. "Have you come to keep me safe until my friend over there saves me?"

The warrior nodded without looking Conall's way.

"I thought so," she whispered, pleased. "Thank you."

The man offered a wide clueless crooked-toothed smile.

"Do you mind if I ask you a few questions before my friend saves me?" she said softly as she lowered her hood and released her hair. "Would that be all right?"

Wide-eyed, he nodded avidly.

"Good. Thank you." She ran a finger down the side of his chainmail covered head. "Where is your leader? Is he close?"

Though in awe of what she was doing, Conall remained braced to attack.

"He is not as close as he would like to be," the warrior replied obediently.

"So he's having trouble finding William Wallace," she murmured as she cupped his cheek. "As is Earl Robert the Bruce?"

"Yes." The man nodded. "Both are being outwitted."

"*Are* they?" Her curious eyes never left his. "Did you see the Bruce this morn? Did he have any new information?"

"None." He shook his head. "But 'twas his idea to head in this direction."

"Was it then?" she said softly, still stroking his cheek. "Did he say why?"

"Just that if we went south," he reported, "we would find what we were looking for."

"And the Bruce is still with you, aye?" she asked, focused and alluring. "He helps you find the Scots rebels?"

"He does," the man confirmed. "He is trusted well enough."

"Well enough?" She cocked her head, still stroking his cheek. "What does that mean?"

"He's Scottish so hard to trust to begin with." A sneer curled his lips despite the worshiping way he looked at her. "'Twill only be a matter of time before this cursed country falls altogether."

Lindsay nodded, feigning agreement before she stepped back, apparently finished. "Don't kill him, Conall. He's just a—"

He didn't wait for the rest of her request but came up behind the Sassenach, ripped off the chainmail, pulled his head back and sliced his throat open. Not sorry in this least, his eyes met Lindsay's, his brogue thick. "He's just a bloody Sassenach who would have raped and murdered ye had ye no' enchanted him." He kicked him face first into the snow. "May the buzzards finish him off."

He wiped his blade and sheathed it, watching her closely.

Some might say it was poor of him to have done something like this in front of her. That it could have triggered sensitive memories. Those he needed her to share with him so that he could properly train her. But as he surmised earlier, a scene like this did not make her weaker but stronger.

His grandfather was right. Lindsay was very special. Hardened in ways he never would have guessed. Talented in ways he had just seen firsthand. Which made him think back to Stirling and what had happened to her in the Sassenach encampment. The things he had accused her of when it came to Hugh de Cressingham and the Earl of Surrey. Two powerful men she should never have survived but did.

Now he knew why.

Though he had seen it with her and the warlock, this presented a much clearer picture.

"Come." He took her hand and pulled her after him, scanning their surroundings for more of the enemy before they reached their horse. As far as he could tell, those who had attacked were cut down quickly, and their group was on the move again. So Conall swung Lindsay up, joined her, and they continued on.

A strained silence settled between them as the day wore on. One he had trouble figuring out but knew had to do with the Sassenach he had killed. As far as he could tell, her thoughts were swirling not just with anger but something else. A level of disappointment he could not understand.

Though the wind had settled some, snow began falling again by the time Simon Fraser fell in beside them. He pointed north-northwest through the trees. "Just over the landing, there will be low but habitable caves to seek shelter in for the eve." His eyes went to Conall. "If yer able to hunt, 'twould be most appreciated. We have wounded men."

Conall nodded before Simon trotted ahead.

"I can't believe we still haven't heard from anyone," Lindsay muttered once they arrived. Thankfully, there was enough tree coverage and overhang from the caves for the horses, but not all that much. Wary of using magic, all he could offer his horse was a pat down and his own fur.

Now to figure out how to hunt and keep Lindsay safe at the same time.

"You just saw what I was capable of, Laird Hamilton," she said softly as her eyes met his. "So you know I'll be okay if you go hunting."

Though he wanted her to call him Conall, something back there had put renewed distance between them. Though he should be grateful, he wasn't. It was best that they got along if he wanted her to open up to him about her gift. So he tried to understand her by bluntly stating the obvious. "I upset you."

"Yes," she stated just as bluntly, her eyes searching his. "But I can see you have no idea how so and that, I'm afraid, is not the best way to start off a friendship."

"Then we will try again," he said logically.

"Honestly, I'm not so sure I want to." Her troubled eyes stayed with his. "Because I have a feeling a friendship with you is going to be too much work."

What was that supposed to mean? As a rule, his friendship had always been valued by those he gave it to, and none had ever said it was too much work. Surprised by how much her words upset him but not about to let her know, he focused on what needed to be done.

Hunting.

As she had said, she could take care of herself. And God knew she would have no trouble finding more friends around here if she needed one. Friendships she might not end before they had a chance to begin.

"I willnae go far, lass." He gave her his dagger. "Settle in and help where you can, aye?"

He didn't wait for a response but headed out. For the first time since he met Lindsay, he officially took his eyes off of her. Now that he knew what she was capable of, he had faith she could protect herself. Or so he kept telling himself as he hunted.

The truth was he remained confused.

In the beginning, it had been simple. He knew he wanted nothing to do with her. Nothing sexual that was. Or even this friendship she sought then ripped away. Yet he realized as he tromped back to the cave later with fresh game that her friendship could not be so easily taken away.

That it had been his for a very long time.

Though unsure how he intended to phrase it, he planned on presenting it just that way when he saw her again. That aye, though he agreed romance was out of the question, friendship had always been and would always be theirs. Hard work or not.

"Where did my lass go?" he asked Simon as he tossed down his carcasses, doing his best to remain calm when he didn't see her right away.

"Lindsay?" Simon gestured at the cave entrance. "Gone with the Bruce."

Conall frowned. "The Bruce?"

"Aye." Simon's eyes met Conall's. "She said you knew she'd go with him when he returned."

"Do I look like the sort of lad that would let my lass go off with the likes of Robert the Bruce?" he growled, doing his best to repress his rage.

Simon shrugged. "To be honest, I didnae get the impression she was all that much yer lass when she left."

If he was not so important to Scotland's history, Conall might have strangled Simon right then and there, but he had bigger things to worry about. Had the Bruce somehow been possessed by the warlock that morn? If so, did that mean the warlock now had Lindsay?

He pushed aside panic, made sure his weapons were intact and headed outside again. If she had been taken, he would find her. He would get her back no matter what.

"*Lindsay*," he said telepathically, trying to feel her mind against his. His blood roared. His heart hammered. She *had* to be all right. *"Can you hear me, lass? Where are you?"*

No response.

Nothing.

Then he saw her. Not with a knife to her throat because the Bruce was possessed but standing beside his horse as he embraced her. Conall never slowed but strode their way, ripped Lindsay out of his arms and held Robert at sword point with narrowed eyes.

Amusement flickered in the Bruce's eyes as his hands rose slowly. "So good to see ye again, Laird Hamilton." His eyes flickered to Lindsay. "Did he not know that *ye* came willingly with *me*, lassie?" He gestured over his shoulder. "So I could see to my horse."

"Did you come alone then?" Conall's eyes never left Robert. "Or can we expect more?"

"Aye, mayhap a few." The Bruce grinned. "But I imagine ye'll like the lot."

"Grant!" Lindsay exclaimed as his grandfather appeared out of the falling snow and she embraced him. Soon after came his cousins.

Conall nodded and embraced first Rona before clapping Graham and Bryce on the back. He scanned the area and frowned. "Where are Adlin and Milly? Aðísla?"

Grant shook his head. "Not with us, I'm afraid."

"Where did you last see them?" He did his best to ignore the enthusiastic embraces Graham and Bryce gave Lindsay.

"In the caves we last saw ye, Cousin," Rona reported as she looked him over and frowned. "How did ye travel back?"

He met her frown. "How did *you* travel back?"

She gestured at Grant. "This time, with help from yer grandfather."

When Conall looked at Grant, it was to find his grandfather's eyes trained on Lindsay's ring with a bemused expression.

"What is it?" Conall repositioned himself between Lindsay and the Bruce.

"'Tis the color of her gem," Grant said softly as he took her hand and studied it with a whimsical smile. "'Tis a color that is hard to forget." When Conall and Lindsay continued to look confused, he murmured, "'Tis the verra color of Adlin's foster sister's eyes in another life...Iosbail Broun's."

Chapter Thirteen

LINDSAY DID HER best *not* to look at Conall the remainder of the evening. As it turned out, there was a very good chance she had initiated their first sexual encounter because she was possessed by Iosbail Broun, or MacLomain, depending on who you asked.

So she had been someone else.

Or at least she allowed everyone to believe that, including Conall, as they sat around a small campfire later. They had convened in one of several caves with exceptionally low ceilings. Wind carrying random snowflakes gusted, creating a spooky sound as it whistled through the tunnel-like caves.

Robert removed his fur and wrapped it around her shoulders. He had remained by her side since he arrived, his attention as much on her as it was on Grant. The two had known each other before so they had a lot of catching up to do. Bryce sat on her other side with Graham beside him. Conall and Rona sat across the fire, talking softly for the greater part of an hour.

As far as she could tell, Conall was back to being his old distant self, and quite frankly, she felt it was for the best. She might have hoped to renew the friendship they once shared, but when he so callously disregarded her wishes earlier in the woods, she realized there was no hope. She had asked him not to kill the Englishman, yet he did.

That, unfortunately, had been the beginning of the end for them.

He had made her feel like an accomplice to that man's death.

Much like she had felt at one time in regards to her parent's death. Though she knew better now, it took a long time to figure out that there was no way she could have saved them. That asking for chocolate that night, which in turn put them in that convenience store during a robbery, was not her fault. Better yet, that she had not really been there, so her gift wasn't somehow responsible.

After that, she spent her entire life changing herself and growing stronger so that she could look in the mirror without shame. So that she could finally see herself as someone to be proud of. Someone Conall had at one time understood even if only to a degree. He had been her friend and confidant when that sort of thing wasn't possible. When, outside of him, that sort of person just didn't exist.

"Yet they do now and always have," Graham declared softly as he leaned over and winked at her.

Lindsay frowned, confused. What was he talking about?

"The determination of the Scots willing to rise up," Bryce informed, filling her in on something that seemingly had nothing to do with what she had been thinking. "They may be dispersing now, but Wallace is talking about one last battle in Strathearn later this year near River Earn." His knowing eyes met hers. "One final stance before he might have to vanish for good."

Lindsay continued to frown as she nodded, not sure what to say because she didn't know Scottish history nearly as well as Milly. What she did know, however, was that William Wallace's days were numbered and that truly saddened her.

"Though I cannae say much about that battle," Robert murmured, almost consoling her without realizing it. "I *can* say that hope for this country doesnae wane but sparks through these darkened nights." His eyes drifted to the men at nearby fires, wounded and otherwise. "Those that continue to come to random skirmishes such as what lay on the horizon." His eyes went to each and every one of them, a glimpse of the king he would someday become in his eyes. "Those that come to the aid of men such as Wallace and Fraser because they believe in hope."

Simon Fraser did not sit with them but moved amongst his men offering words of encouragement.

"Aye," everyone agreed, some raising their skins in salute.

Meanwhile, Lindsay sipped her whisky and did her best to keep her undivided attention on Robert as William had requested. Though she seemingly flirted for all she was worth, she found herself doing something else as well.

Watching his eyes and looking for the darkness William had warned them about.

Had it been the warlock? What else could it be?

"Whilst we cannae stroll outside this eve," Robert murmured close to her ear. "One of these caves has a slightly higher ceiling and a sight ye might find worthy of seeing."

Though she knew Robert would likely make a move on her, she saw an opportunity to find out what he had been up to all day. Was he possessed by a warlock? Or was he perhaps a spy for the English?

She slanted her head just enough to appear demure and met Robert's eyes beneath lowered lashes. "I would very much like a stroll." She kept her voice soft and just shy of sultry. "Whether or not beneath the stars this time."

"Och, you play a dangerous game all things considered, aye, lass?" Conall said into her mind.

"All things considered, I think somebody needs to find out if Robert has a warlock lurking around in him," Lindsay responded though she should have ignored him. She smiled widely, her sole focus on Robert as he pulled her after him. He was looking for Christina this morning, and she needed to know why.

"We are all curious about his behavior earlier," Conall grumbled into her mind, his brogue thickening with aggravation. *"Yet ye dinnae see us wandering off into a dark cave with him."*

Lindsay ignored Conall this time and followed Robert deeper into the cave. As promised, it opened up slightly, its walls round and sweeping as snow fell from openings above. He lit several torches before he urged her to sit on a rock beside him to enjoy the view. It was rather magical as snowflakes danced and twirled then caught in the wind and whipped along the walls before racing into the other caves.

"Something happened this morn, did it not?" he asked, his voice soft as he tucked her fur more firmly around her. "Something that has many distrusting me now."

Lindsay glanced at him, surprised though she probably should not be. This was Robert the Bruce. A man that would go on to do great things someday. Nevertheless, she was curious by the look in his eyes considering how enthralled she thought she had him. How very level he seemed and not all that enchanted...at least not by her.

Which made her wonder.

When she narrowed her eyes, thinking he may very well be the warlock after all, his eyes narrowed in return. "What is it, lass?" His hand slid into hers in reassurance. "What has ye so wary of me when just last eve ye were quite taken?" He winked. "As much as ye could be, that is, desiring the Hamilton as ye do."

Her eyes widened in surprise before she could stop herself. Mainly because she had used her gift of enchantment on Robert yesterday. An enchantment designed specifically to convince a man that she only had eyes for him.

Yet it seemed he had seen right through it.

"I don't desire Laird Hamilton," she led out carefully. "Rather, I was truly hoping you and I—"

"Och, nay," he whispered and shook his head. "Though yer truly bonnie, it can never be, lass…well, not when we are alone that is."

She *so* hoped Conall wasn't following her thoughts right now.

"It can't?" she whispered, truly perplexed and curious as she peered at him. "Why not?"

"Because another is promised to me," he informed. "And I to her."

"Oh." Lindsay rounded her lips and nodded. "I see."

"Aye?" Robert smiled. "I so hoped ye would." He squeezed her hand. "More so, I hoped ye'd play yer part until I find her."

What part?

"Ye know." He brought the back of her hand to his lips, his eyes charming. "Wooing me as I do the same to ye when we are around others." His brows perked. "Mayhap continuing such a thing will also help ye put off Laird Hamilton until yer ready for him."

Her mouth must have been hanging open in a most unladylike fashion because she involuntarily snapped it shut. Had Robert the Bruce just asked her to pretend to be…together?

He pulled her closer and cupped her cheek.

"Something has happened, lass," he whispered. "Something that has steered me in this verra direction. That has made it much easier to support Wallace when at times I am tempted to cut him down and give him to the Sassenach."

"And what is that?" she whispered back.

"Ye," he said vehemently before he shook his head. "Or the likes of ye." His eyes rounded. "The future and a lass I couldnae describe if I wanted to." He sighed. "So verra bonnie."

174

Oh, goodness. Please don't let it be Christina or Jessie. Yet had he not been looking for Christina earlier today?

Up for his game of discretion but needing to know more, she murmured, "So she was from the future like me? What did she look like?"

"So bloody bonnie, she was..." he began before the whisper died on his lips.

Lindsay pulled back and frowned at the blade that had slipped around his neck then the man holding it. Conall ignored her, leaned forward and whispered in Robert's ear. "Please go on, Earl, I would verra much like to know about this bonnie wee lass, aye?"

"Yer looking right at her," Robert murmured, his amused eyes on hers despite the blade cutting into his skin. "Lindsay."

"I dinnae know if I mentioned it," Conall never removed his blade, "but I took an oath to protect Lindsay."

"Aye." Not daunted in the least, Robert squeezed her hand in reassurance. "A job ye take quite seriously, aye, Laird Hamilton?"

"Never more so." Conall finally pulled the blade away but not before he murmured in Robert's ear, "Play yer part with Lindsay but dinnae think to pull her so close again, aye?"

Lindsay made to respond, mainly to tell him he had no say in who pulled her close, but it was too late. Conall vanished further into the cave.

"Ugh," she muttered under her breath, squinting into the darkness after him. "He's the worst sort of pain in the ass."

Robert chuckled. "Though I cannae help but wonder with wariness what other type of pain in the arse ye've experienced by comparison, I *can* agree ye've yer hands full with the Hamilton." Pleased, he peered into the darkness after Conall as well. "He is a good protector, lass." His eyes returned to hers. "But not one we'll fool it seems."

Lindsay sighed and shook her head, trying not to be disappointed. Where had her acting skills gone? She thought she had done a rather stellar job, but Conall had seen right through it. Yes, granted, he could read her mind, but still, she sensed this last bit had nothing to do with that.

"I think he knows I want him," she whispered with narrowed eyes.

"Do ye then?" Robert chuckled and shook his head. "Normally, I would congratulate ye, but I dinnae think the likes of Hamilton will be a prize easily won."

What? She blinked several times and stared at him before she shook her head and stuttered, "Won? By me?" Lindsay shook her head again. "Oh, *hell*, no." She stood so abruptly, she would have hit her head on the slanted ceiling if Robert didn't lurch to his feet and protect her. "I have *no* desire to be with Conall, and he feels the same." She shook her head and started back the way they had come. "We can't even manage friends never mind *more*."

"Are ye no longer curious about the lass I was talking about then?" he asked, quick on her heels.

"I'm curious about medieval Scotsmen who appear out of thin air after I haven't seen them for nearly half my life," she muttered. "I'm curious about friends who can't even prove they're my friend by *not* killing an Englishman when I ask them not to."

"Why would ye not want to kill the enemy?" Robert began, but she shook her head and kept on muttering.

"He was my *best* friend," she spat as she walked. "Can you believe that?"

"Laird Hamilton?" Robert asked, truly curious.

Lindsay only nodded, too caught up in thought and how frustrated she was with Conall to realize that her mutterings had suddenly fallen on deaf ears. That is until she heard a voice that made her stop dead.

"Outside of my da, Conall was my best friend too, lass."

She turned slowly, knowing full well who was behind her.

"Darach," she murmured. "I wasn't sure if I would see you again."

Robert the Bruce seemed to have vanished.

"Aye, I wasnae sure I would see you again, either," Darach said. Much like his son and most likely how Grant had been in his younger years, Darach had an imposing way about him as he looked down at her. "Did you give the message to my kin? They know not to search for me?"

"I did," she confirmed, eying him. "But they're worried. They need to know you're okay."

"It doesnae matter how I am." His pained eyes stayed with hers. "Tell Jackie she's right and that I am never far from her side."

Lindsay frowned, saddened by his expression, saddened by the wall he felt he lived behind. More than that, by all those that mourned him and the divide it had created in his family.

"I'm sorry to ask but I must," she said softly. "Are you dead, Darach?" She tilted her head in question. "Did someone kill you?"

He offered no response other than to shake his head as his gaze shifted to her ring. "Follow the gem." His eyes met hers again. "Move beyond all the faces you're willing to wear and follow the gem."

Baffled, she shook her head and attempted to ask him more, but he faded when a harsh wind whipped through the cave. She twirled, confused, only to find Conall standing there. He clasped her upper arms and frowned. "Who were you talking to?" He glanced over her shoulder before his eyes returned to hers. "The Bruce says you were mumbling incoherently."

She frowned and looked around. "Where did he go?"

He scowled. "I sent him back to the others."

Though tempted to tell Conall she had just seen his father again, she decided against it. He was too unpredictable at the moment. Always *there* though she never saw him coming. She would speak with Grant when she had the chance. That made the most sense. He would give her much needed advice.

"You should get some rest," Conall said softly.

She was surprised by the look in his eyes. Far gentler than she expected. But why?

"I *will* get some rest," she agreed as she pulled away and strode back toward their small group only for his hand to clamp around her upper arm and stop her.

"Rest there." He pointed toward a tent braced against the wall in the far corner. "There's a fire inside that will keep you warm against the wind and elements."

Her eyes shot to his. "I can only assume you think you'll be joining me."

"Nay," he murmured, his gaze again doing that not-quite-meeting-her-eyes thing. "I put it together for Grandfather, and he wishes that you enjoy its shelter as well."

Chilled to the bone in more ways than one after seeing his father's ghostly spirit, she nodded. "Are you sure?" Her eyes went to the others. "Aren't you all going to freeze to death out here?"

"Och, nay," Rona said, joining them. "We're Scots wizards with more magic in our wee finger than ye've got in yer—"

"Rest, lass," Conall interrupted and gestured toward the tent. "We'll see ye in the morn, aye?"

Her eyes lingered on his before they went to the inviting tent and she nodded. "If you're sure."

Conall put his hand on her lower back and escorted her over before he pulled back the tent flap and gestured inside. "Sleep well, lass."

Her eyes met his one last time, remembering all too well how he had ensured her sound sleep the night before not to mention other things. Things she put firmly to the back of her mind as she entered the tent and joined his grandfather.

"Lindsay." Grant smiled and gestured at a spot in front of the fire. "Please sit."

"It's roomier than I thought it would be in here," she mentioned as she smiled and sat. "Much more."

"Aye." Grant grinned, shook his head and handed her a skin. "'Tis a verra wee trick o' magic I felt it safe enough for Conall to use. The ability to make spaces appear larger than they actually are." He winked. "In truth, one more could comfortably fit in here with us, but my grandson is worried he might be that one, so claims 'tis just big enough for the two of us."

"It sounds like he makes things more difficult than they need to be," she muttered before she thanked him for the skin.

"Aye," Grant agreed as he leaned back and stoked the small fire between them. "To say the least." Then something sparked in his eyes, nostalgia she supposed as he stared into the flames. "I'm sure you well know Conall wasnae always so difficult." His eyes rose to hers. "That he used to be quick to laughter and even quicker to joke alongside Adlin."

"No, I didn't know that." She barely believed it. "That must have been something."

"'Twas," Grant whispered as his eyes drifted back to the fire. "Conall did nothing but think life and his future responsibilities were a joke where his cousin Graham thought the verra opposite." He stoked the flames some more. "Now look at them. Conall so stern and Graham so carefree."

Lindsay frowned, not sure where he was going with this. "Well, Conall's been through a lot losing his father and Fraser so it makes sense he might be running a little dry." She cocked her head and narrowed her eyes. "As to Graham, shouldn't we be happy he's how he is now rather than, no offense, being like your grandson?"

"Aye, mayhap," he conceded softly as his eyes met hers and his brogue thickened. "Would it not be safe enough to say yer as eager as me to help Conall break free from his overly disciplined nature and mayhap embrace the lad he once was?"

"Of course, I want to see Conall happy," she said carefully. "Though I'm not sure I'm the one to do it."

Grant eyed her for a moment with that all-knowing look of his before he pressed his lips together, nodded grimly and settled back.

Well, what did that mean?

"Wallace wanted you to pursue the Bruce, did he not?" Grant's eyes were locked on the flames again. "He likely said as much in Strathearn."

When Lindsay didn't answer, not sure how to respond, Grant continued. "He was wrong." His eyes went to hers. "You should not pursue the Bruce but Wallace himself."

"To what purpose?" She crossed her arms over her chest, having had just about enough of these cryptic requests.

"Toward the same purpose that Wallace told you to pursue the Bruce," Grant said. "To get things where they need to go next. To ensure Scotland's history."

"Is that right." She narrowed her eyes, catching on a little too late but at least catching on. "Why is it that me pursuing a man will save the day? Could it be because it drives Conall nuts?" She shook her head and frowned. "I'm by no means doing it on purpose, but it's pretty clear Conall has a thing for me."

"Aye." His knowing eyes held hers. "Just like *you* have a thing for *him*."

"I do not," she started before Grant shook his head and closed his eyes, murmuring, "Dinnae lie to me lass. I like you far too much to abide fibbing from you." He sighed. "Far too much."

"Let's put it this way then," she murmured. "Though there's clearly an attraction between Conall and me, we've agreed that it's best not to pursue it."

"I see." Grant arched a brow as a small grin ghosted his face. "So what will you do if Iosbail possesses that gem again somehow?"

She was about to tell him Iosbail never really had that much control, but she sensed by the humor in his eyes, that Grant already knew.

So, instead, she took a swig of whisky and redirected the conversation. "Something just happened out there, Grant." Her eyes stayed with his. "I saw Darach again."

"Aye, I imagined something like that might happen." Emotion flickered in his eyes. "What did he say this time, lass?"

She told him then shook her head. "Why do you think I'm the only one he's reaching out to?" Her eyes fell to the gem. "And outside of the obvious, what do you think he meant when he told me to move beyond all the faces I wear and follow this?"

"First off, I think him being able to contact you must have something to do with your gift," he said. "As to your gem, I think 'tis not outside the obvious at all but verra much about your acting abilities. Better yet, not implementing them at every turn." There was a smidge of challenge in his eyes as they stayed with hers. "He wants you to embrace the *real* you, not one of your many personas."

"Well, not to point out what you've likely already figured out," she said, "but my gift goes hand in hand with my multiple personas."

"Aye, and is the real you not amongst those personas?" He eyed her with curiosity. "Personas you created to protect yourself, but when fueled by your gift, instead protect others."

Lindsay tensed. Why did it sound like he knew more about her than he should?

"When you do things such as what you did the night Graham was attacked," he continued. "When you transported so easily then lured the beast away, I believe you walked a line between good and evil, life and death, to get where you needed to go. To do what you needed to do."

She frowned and shook her head. "That sounds so sinister."

"Nay." He shook his head as well. "There is nothing sinister about what you were able to do to save Bryce in the Sassenach encampment. And there's certainly nothing sinister about saving Graham's life." His wizened eyes never left hers. "Something verra traumatic happened to you, lass. When it did, your gift ignited. A gift meant to sway men and monsters alike so that you can protect those you feel need protecting."

Before she could respond, he gestured at her ring. "Outside of Iosbail, who likes to play her games every bit as much as Adlin ever did, that ring's gem has been turning verra specific shades." His brows inched up. "Has it not been turning the color of whose eyes you look through then ultimately protect?" His gaze was compassionate, his brogue thickening with his emotions. "I think what my son was trying to say is that if ye embrace who ye really are and remember who Conall once was, the gem will lead ye where ye need to go."

"What does that mean?" she said softly, her eyes narrowed. Because it almost sounded like Grant knew that she was Conall's childhood faery.

"It means what it sounds like it means, lassie." When Grant settled back, she swore she saw a twinkle in his eyes. "Did I say *remember* who Conall once was?" He shook his head. "I meant pull forth who Conall once was. Be friends if nothing else, aye, and see if ye cannae give me back my grandson."

"I'm sorry, but I think you're asking the wrong person," she began but ended it on a sigh when she saw Grant's eyelids slide shut. Moments later his breathing turned heavy. Goodness, he could fall asleep quickly. But then, maybe wizards had shut-off valves when it came to evasive, cryptic conversations.

Lindsay took a hearty swig from her skin, pulled a fur over herself and lay back. She supposed in the long run, she didn't so much mind Grant knowing about her childhood. In fact, out of everyone, including Conall, she trusted him the most to keep her secrets.

Her thoughts churned as she listened to the wind howl through the cave. There were so many unanswered questions. So much she needed to understand.

"It seems pretty simple to me, sweet pea," came a soft southern accent. "Just be you so Conall can be him."

Lindsay's eyes shot to the corner of the tent.

This time she wasn't dreaming in the least.

Christina stood there clear as day.

Chapter Fourteen

"**W**HAT DO YE mean Lindsay wasnae in yer tent when ye awoke?" Conall growled, his eyes narrowed on Grant.

"She was there when I drifted off. We were talking." His grandfather seemed genuinely distressed as he frowned. "Then she was gone when I woke."

By gone, he truly meant gone.

No one in the immediate vicinity could sense her.

"Ye lost my da." Conall glared at Grant. "Now ye've gone and lost my lass."

Before Simon Fraser could pipe up and say something again about Lindsay and him not being together, he shot him a ferocious look. Eyes narrowed, his infuriated gaze finally settled on Robert the Bruce. "What did ye do to her last night?" He pointed a finger at him and roared, "She had that strange episode when she was with *ye*." His eyes widened. "Now she's bloody well gone and not a soul saw or felt her leave!"

That included himself, which set him on edge and made him feel fear like never before. Had he grown weaker when he needed to be at his strongest? He didn't question his magic but his heart. What if the things he felt for her were clouding his ability to protect her? What if the warlock was somehow using that to his advantage?

"I sat outside her tent the entire night," he groused as he raked a hand through his hair and eyed the men present, especially the Bruce. "Never once did I sleep and never once did she leave."

"Ye must calm yerself," Rona insisted as she tried to hand him a skin of whisky. "Acting as ye are isnae helping matters."

Conall dismissed the whisky and sighed. She was right. Acting this way would get him nowhere. But he felt helpless. Directionless. Fearful.

"We *will* find her," Bryce said through clenched teeth, fire sparking in his eyes as his dragon tried to surface. "I will see it no other way."

"I agree." Graham nodded, fury in his eyes as they met Conall's. "We will find her, Cousin. She means too much to all of us."

Grant, as usual, was not overly fazed by Conall's anger at him but instead seemed to be contemplating the tent.

"What is it?" Conall followed his line of vision. "Do ye think the warlock got her somehow?"

His eyes narrowed on the Bruce again though he said nothing. After talking with his kin yesterday, they all felt it was best to monitor Robert rather than confront him about his unusual eyes the day before. If, as they suspected, the warlock worked through him somehow, it was best not to tip it off.

"I didnae go anywhere near her last eve, Laird Hamilton," the Bruce vowed. "Not after ye tucked her away to rest."

"The lad tells the truth," Grant said absently as he headed for the tent with an intent, curious look on his face.

"What is it?" Conall repeated as he strode after him, well aware of how his grandfather got when his magic was taking over. "What are ye sensing?"

"Something I didnae sense before," he murmured as he ducked into the tent and Conall followed. Once inside, Grant looked around and frowned before he shook his head and said under his breath, "Nay, we need more to see correctly," then stuck his head back out.

"Join us, Bryce and Graham." His eyes went to Rona. "Ye too, lassie."

They looked at each other curiously before they joined them. Only when Bryce, the largest of them all, stepped in, did Conall begin to sense what Grant already had. How bloody tight it became when moments before Conall's magic had made it appear larger.

"That might just do the trick," Grant whispered before they heard Robert exclaim, "Och, there ye are, lass!"

Conall flew out of the tent only to find Lindsay in the Bruce's arms. He had never felt so much relief mixed with anger. Relief because she was clearly all right. Anger because he had not been the one to pull her into his arms when she reappeared.

Because she *had* simply reappeared, hadn't she?

"There she is," Robert suddenly whispered, as his eyes shot to the tent. "There's my lass…the one I'm promised to."

Bryce and Grant had already exited but slowed as a woman appeared behind them. Lovely but transparent, she stared wide-eyed at them all. A second later, she spun and appeared to sprint into the tent though it was hard to tell because Graham ducked out at that very moment. For all intents and purposes, she almost appeared to vanish right inside of him.

"Christina!" Lindsay cried as she stepped away from the Bruce.

Graham stopped short, and his brows slammed together as he evidently saw *Christina* running at him. Then she was gone, and his cousin seemed stunned.

In the meantime, Lindsay flew past him into the tent with Conall right behind her.

"Damn it, where'd she go?" She spun and looked around. "I told her she was here and not there, but she didn't believe me."

"Where have ye *been*, lass," he managed, his voice hoarser than intended. He seized her upper arms gently, hoping she would look at him though she kept gazing around. "What happened to ye, Lindsay?"

"I was right here," she whispered and blinked several times before her eyes finally met his. "I never left…not really."

"But ye did," he insisted, unable to control his thickening brogue as he searched her eyes. "When Grandfather woke, ye were gone. Vanished!" He shook his head. "And I never saw ye leave."

She went perfectly still as their eyes held, as she likely finally heard how upset he was.

"I'm here now, Conall," she said softly. "And I'm okay."

He started at the use of his name. More so, the gentle way she said it. As though she liked the way it felt in her mouth. That mouth. Beautiful, full, perfectly shaped lips he should not be staring at right now. Yet he was as he reeled her closer. As he did what he swore he would not do again and kissed her. Just a small kiss, he figured. One meant to relieve his angst over having thought he had lost her. That she might have been stolen by the warlock or worse yet, dead.

He should have known a small kiss would be impossible based on the way her lips felt beneath his. The way they softened as he wrapped his hand around the back of her neck, tilted his head and deepened the exchange. Their tongues had only just touched when she managed to find the strength he could not and pulled away.

Though her breathing had grown heavy and her eyes dewy, she swallowed hard and shook her head. "We shouldn't." Her voice dropped to a whisper. "And you know it, Laird Hamilton."

He clenched his jaw and nodded.

She was right.

But that knowledge did not make the moment any easier as they stared at each other. As he imagined bringing her to the ground and showing her just how much losing her had affected him. How bloody foolish they were for thinking they were capable of anything but what already existed between them.

He shook his head at his own thoughts.

How quickly he was letting this progress in his mind despite her pulling free from the kiss. As their eyes held and emotions fluctuated between them, he knew what they felt was going to be very difficult to ignore never mind turn away from.

"Ah," Grant murmured as he entered and looked around. "So Christina really *did* vanish, aye?"

"She did," Lindsay said softly as her eyes finally left Conall's and she looked at Grant. "How was Christina even here to begin with?" She shook her head. "And don't tell me that wasn't her because I know it was."

"Aye, 'twas a lass from the future and nothing but," Grant assured. "Though I dinnae know Christina enough to say if 'twas her, I'll take your word for it."

"It was." Worry knit Lindsay's brows as she looked around again then ducked out of the tent, saying over her shoulder, "I don't understand. Where did she go? And again, how did she even get here?"

They followed to find her looking around the outside of the tent alongside Graham and Robert. Both of whom seemed desperate to locate Christina.

"That was her," Robert exclaimed as he looked at Lindsay. "The lass I was promised to."

Perplexed, Graham glanced at Robert before his eyes went to Lindsay as well. "Who is she, lass? Who is Christina?"

"The lass intended for me," Robert offered before Grant shook his head sharply and gestured at Conall. "You need to remove your magic from this tent lad then we'll take it down altogether."

Conall frowned. "Are we leaving already?"

"Likely," Simon said, eying them all with a great deal of interest.

"Och, nay," Grant muttered before his eyes met Simon's, he murmured a chant then said, "See to yer men, aye? 'Twould probably be best to head out soon and reconnect with Wallace."

Caught in Grant's magic, Simon blinked several times before he nodded. Based on his less-than-curious expression, he seemed to have forgotten everything he just saw. His next statement confirmed it.

"Ready yerselves soon because we leave to find Wallace," Simon said then left.

Grant's attention swung back to Conall. "Please just do as I asked, aye, lad?"

"Mayhap if you explain why," he responded.

"Though I didnae see it at first, 'tis rather simple really," Grant replied. His eyes swept from the tent to Lindsay before landing on Conall again. "You used your magic, manifesting air and its dimensions, to allow Lindsay and me to have a spacious sleeping area. Or so it appeared. And 'twas kind of you." His eyes returned to Lindsay. "But what none of us took into consideration, lass, is that you almost seem to create anomalies within Conall's magic."

She shook her head, seemingly as confused as the rest of them. "What does that mean?"

"Whilst mayhap Iosbail has played a part in directing you through time," Grant explained. "I think 'tis your gift combined with Conall's that gives it that extra oomph."

Her brows shot up. *Oomph?*

Conall would call the intimacies they had shared when time traveling a wee bit more than that.

"Aye." Grant nodded. "Like his da, Conall's magic is entirely wrapped up in the manipulation of air and yours, Lindsay, is that of enchanting and protecting."

Lindsay shook her head again. "What does any of that have to do with...whatever you're getting at?"

"I think, somehow, when you two come together, most especially in a passionate manner," Grant said, twisting his lips in amusement. "Conall's air becomes enchanted by you."

"While I'm tempted to jest a fair bit about this," Robert said as he winked at Lindsay. "What does that have to do with Conall needing to take down the tent? Or my promised lass?"

As a whole, Conall was surprised by the sense of humor lurking beneath the surface of Robert the Bruce. It was something he never would have imagined the man having. But then, such a personality trait might be necessary to buffer the endless stress of being a supposed traitor to the Scots.

Grant directed the answers to Robert's questions to Conall.

"For starters, you seem to move through time often when intimate, aye, lad?" Grant looked between Conall and Lindsay. "I think, in a way, it's happening because Lindsay is subconsciously keeping you safe. She's enchanting you to follow her to safety, and your magic is making sure you both get there."

Conall frowned. "So Iosbail has nothing to do with the time traveling?"

"'Tis hard to know." Grant shrugged. "Truthfully, I think mayhap you and Lindsay are controlling this entire journey. I think you put us at the Skirmish at Earnside then one way or another, here." He again looked between them. "And I think 'tis because Lindsay, on some level, sensed the evil intent to harm Conall the moment a Claddagh ring appeared on her finger. That alone could verra well have amplified her need to protect you, Grandson." He nodded, clearly pleased with his theory. "Hence her magic paved a path through time that would best prepare you both to face this warlock."

"You make me sound so...powerful," she said softly.

"Aye." Grant's eyes whipped to hers. "Because you *are*, lass. You always have been. You have a verra specific magic about you and 'tis, as you know, verra much that of an enchantress. 'Tis known as many things to different cultures. A Selkie of sorts within Irish, Scottish, Faroese and Icelandic folklore. A Circe or Siren amongst the Greeks. Even a Nymph to some degree."

"Most of those creatures are water related," she murmured, grateful it seemed as he caught snippets of her thoughts, that Grant had not said *succubus*.

"Aye," Grant said. "But they are just examples of the sort of power you possess, lass. The ability to lure and enchant men." Respect lit his eyes. "The ability, as daunting as it sounds, to enchant evil."

Putting voice to what she had just been thinking, Lindsay flinched. "Like a succubus might be able to do."

"Bloody hell, lass," Grant said, his brogue thickening as he shook his head. "Ye arenae a demon." His eyes widened. "Do ye think I'd let ye anywhere near my kin let alone into my grandson's bed if I thought ye'd suck the life out of him?"

She nearly had in a *very* good way, but Conall kept that thought to himself.

Or so he thought until her eyes sparked with amusement as they flickered to his.

"So where did my lass go?" Robert interjected.

"And ye never did finish explaining why the tent needed to come down," Bryce reminded.

"Or how it all might relate to why Graham is acting like a bloody fool," Rona added.

"Och, one thing at a time," Grant muttered as his stern eyes landed on Conall again. "Because of the magic you used within the tent, Lindsay's magic mixed with yours and allowed her to enchant others more readily than usual."

When everyone frowned, Grant continued. "Your air unknowingly expanded her gift so she could connect with whoever she was most concerned about at the moment." His eyes went to Lindsay. "I take it that was your friend Christina, aye?"

"Not at the particular moment she appeared," she said, her voice soft and surprised. "But in general, since that morning, yes, Christina."

"And who is she again?" Graham asked, his voice deeper than normal as he eyed the ceiling with wonder, acting, as Rona had said, very strangely.

"My lass," Robert reminded, scowling at him.

"She's nobody's *lass*." Lindsay frowned at Robert. "I'm sorry, but she's not."

189

"Anyway," Grant said. "Once we filled the tent with enough bodies to reset its perception so that it was small again, it was enough to pull Lindsay back to this side."

Conall frowned. "What side was she on before?"

"Somewhere she can go while she's enchanting," Grant explained. "Like she could be with that warlock, and wherever she is when she sees your da. Then wherever she was just now…here but not here."

Why did it sound like she had seen his father more than once?

"So where is Da?" He shifted closer to Lindsay out of instinct, not pleased in the least that she could simply vanish at will. "What extra space is he in right now?"

What he did not do was come out and ask the question everyone knew he wanted to. Though he had come to terms with his father's death years ago, having just seen Christina gave him a spark of hope. She had appeared transparent here but was alive somewhere else. Perhaps the same went for his da.

"Your father's somewhere he doesn't want any of you to go," Lindsay reminded, worry in her eyes as they met his. "He was very serious about that, Conall."

"He would be," Conall ground out and shook his head. "But I will go there." He closed the distance and clasped her shoulders. "Tell me where you think he is, and I will go."

She shook her head, her eyes truly pained as she whispered, "I'm sorry, but I just don't know."

Conall held her eyes for a long moment before he ground his jaw, nodded and stepped away. He believed her. He truly did.

"You need to get that tent down and dispel the magic attached to it, Conall," Grant said softly, his voice overly compassionate. "Right now 'tis a conduit that is more confusing than naught for Lindsay and I imagine Christina."

"I would say," Lindsay whispered.

"Who is Christina again?" Graham said before he blinked several times and almost seemed confused by his surroundings.

"You just saw her, didn't you?" Lindsay headed his way. "You saw Christina."

"I did," he agreed as he stood, clearly not sure how he ended up on his knees. "First right outside the tent then…somewhere else."

"Not caves but man-made rock formations, right?" she asked. "Ones in a forest?"

"Aye." His eyes met hers. "Where was that?"

"Stonehenge at Mystery Hill in the twenty-first century," she replied. "Where I just was with Christina before I...*we* ended up back here." She shook her head. "Though I don't think I ever really left."

Conall frowned and glanced at his grandfather who nodded and said, "Aye, that makes sense. You traveled to her time, and she traveled to yours...sort of."

Graham's brows perked. "Sort of?"

"Aye," Grant said. "You didnae technically travel through time...not really." He shook his head. "'Twas more like you shared a glimpse of one another's surroundings."

"Interesting," Lindsay murmured as she contemplated that. "Mystery Hill is close to Milly's house. Christina had been out for a morning jog. That's when we somehow connected."

"Aye, I know the area." He nodded. "It has enough power to easily connect you two when combined with yours and Conall's magic."

"Ah," she said softly, clearly contemplating something before her eyes turned to Robert. "I know we discussed secrecy but in light of recent circumstances, may I ask how you knew of Christina ahead of time?"

"I saw her," he replied. "And talked to her."

"Where?" She shook her head and frowned. "When?"

"After I left Wallace yesterday...or mayhap whilst I was still there..." He frowned and shook his head. "I spoke with her. She was so bonnie, and I knew our fates were intertwined. That we were destined to be together..."

Almost as if he realized how foolish he sounded, Robert's words trailed off. In fact, he suddenly seemed downright baffled.

"Aye, then." Grant put a comforting hand on his shoulder. "As it was for Sir Richard Lundie, a Scots knight who joined the Sassenach for a wee bit, it seems ye might have been ensorcelled by a warlock."

Robert frowned at him. "I dinnae ken."

"Nay and I wish it could stay that way but as ye well know, though none of us much like the Sassenach," Grant reminded. "There are far darker creatures out there. True evil."

"So she was..." Robert shook his head and looked from Lindsay to Grant. "The lass I came across wasnae real?"

"Nay." Grant shook his head and was about to continue when Lindsay cut him off.

"I'm not so sure about that." She frowned. "Christina said she dreamt about a man claiming to be Robert the Bruce. She even remembers making a promise, but she can't remember if it was to him or someone else."

"There ye have it." The Bruce's eyes widened, and he nodded. "The promise was to me. We are to be together."

"How do we know it was really the Bruce though?" Rona frowned, ever the cynic. "What made her so sure?"

"Well, her description of him for starters."

Lindsay purposefully kept her eyes from Conall, and he soon learned why.

"In the twenty-first century, we have a certain perception of Robert the Bruce thanks to Hollywood cinematics. While certain movies portrayed him to be handsome enough," she cleared her throat, "they didn't *quite* get it right." Her eyes stayed with Rona's. "Christina described Robert as an extremely handsome man around six feet tall, maybe six-foot-one with a," she cleared her throat again, "a 'hot *damn*' body and a sexy-as-hell presence you just don't forget."

Robert chuckled and nodded. "She's an observant lass, aye?"

"She's scared." Lindsay frowned at him. At all of them. "Jim and Blair are there in the twenty-first century with her. They've filled her in on everything that's happened." She gestured at their surroundings. "And now *this* is happening, her seeing me when I'm not really there." She shook her head. "She's staying at Milly's house and has had to all but tie Jessie down, so she doesn't leave."

Conall knew Jessie was the fourth Broun lass and from what little he had heard about her, was considerably different than the others. A hermit of sorts that lived alone in the forest. A witchy type by the sounds of it. His eyes found Lindsay's. But then they were all witches, weren't they?

"You know what I find curious," Bryce said, frowning. "If this warlock is becoming more and more involved and may have even influenced Robert, then would it not stand to reason that he knows the Bruce secretly stands with the Scots?" His eyes met Grant's. "And if that's the case, why not simply tell the Sassenach? Would that in itself not likely change Scotland's history?"

"Aye," Grant said. "But then we dinnae know what games this warlock is playing." He frowned. "And we've no real proof the Sassenach even knew he was amongst them in Strathearn. For all we know the warlock might be Scottish and not affiliated with the English at all."

"That would be so sad," Lindsay whispered.

It bloody hell would be.

"Grandson." Grant made a gesture with his hand. "The tent?"

"Aye." Conall nodded and murmured a chant, dispelling its magic before he began taking it down. He probably should not have used magic to begin with but it had been such a small amount, he wasn't overly worried. Nor was his grandfather. Yet now, in light of what happened, he had to wonder. Had he drawn the warlock's attention?

Likely catching some of his thoughts or thinking along the same lines, Grant joined him as he finished up with the tent.

"Though I wasnae overly concerned before and knew your heart was in the right place," he said softly. "I think 'twould be best if ye didnae use your magic again unless necessary, aye?"

"Aye," Conall agreed and nodded.

Though determined to leave this alone until he had further proof, his eyes drifted to Grant. "Do ye think Lindsay is really connecting with Da?" He did his best to keep his expression tight and emotion out of his voice. "Do ye think there's a chance he lives?" He shook his head. "Or is this just the warlock playing tricks?"

"I think, mayhap, 'tis a bit of both," Grant replied, more honest than Conall expected when this was the perfect opportunity to sugar-coat things and mayhap win his grandson back.

Conall nodded, grateful for his straightforward answer. "We will hope for the best then."

"Aye." Grant nodded as well as they headed back toward the main cave. "I think if he's to be found, Lindsay will lead us to him."

His voice softened. "I'm glad she's taken a liking to ye lad. She's a good lass. Yer grandmum, and I like her verra much."

That did not surprise him. Gift of enchantment aside, she was quite likable when she wanted to be. As to her having taken a liking to him, he wasn't so sure. They seemed at odds more often than not.

"Because ye keep each other at odds," Grant muttered. "Convincing yerselves that there's nothing but heartache ahead if ye get too close."

When Conall frowned at him, his grandfather shrugged. "Ye think such strong thoughts about her 'tis a wonder yer kin back home dinnae hear such." He shook his head. "Then again, nobody needs to read yer thoughts to come to the same conclusion I have."

Instead of continuing the conversation, Conall veered off and headed for his horse. He found Lindsay not that far off. She had her fur wrapped tightly around her shoulders as she stared into the forest, her gaze faraway. Neither said a word at first as he prepared their horse for travel.

Eventually, she spoke, her voice whisper soft. "I used to love the outdoors, especially the woods and the solace it offered."

"But you dinnae anymore?" he ventured, without meeting her eyes. "'Tis now a place of bad memories?"

"No, quite the opposite." She shook her head, her eyes still trained on the trees, her voice quiet. "It reminds me of how far I've come and how strong I am."

Not of all their long talks? Not of the friendship they once shared?

It was that, the things she did not voice, that suddenly made everything crystal clear. She had connected with him and nobody else when they were bairns. They were there for each other then and could be now.

Or at least for their kin.

"I think we are being selfish and 'tis time to put an end to it," he stated as he stood beside her, crossed his arms over his chest and knew he had come to a sound conclusion. "'Tis time we accept we are doomed to be together, announce it to everyone then lay together as often as possible so we can harness the power of the gem and defeat the enemy."

Chapter Fifteen

IF NOTHING ELSE could be said about Conall Hamilton, it was that he had the unique ability, one way or another, to consistently render her speechless.

"Come, then." He plunked her on the horse and swung up behind her before she could formulate a thought, never mind the biting response he had coming.

"The Bruce will return to the Sassenach for a bit," he continued as though he hadn't just said *those* words. "Meanwhile, we will reconnect with Wallace."

As they fell in behind the other horses and he began speaking again, she tensed, shook her head and cut him off. "It would be in your best interest to stop talking, Laird Hamilton."

When he began to anyway, she narrowed her eyes over her shoulder, shook her head sharply, and bit out, "Like I said, it would be in your best interest to stop talking."

When he was foolish enough to do it again, she raised her voice and called out, "Graham, I could use your help."

Conall's brows slammed together, and he frowned as Graham trotted up alongside them.

"May I ride with you, Graham?" She smiled at him seductively to aggravate Conall. "I find my current company presumptuous, rude and most definitely *doomed*, but not for the reasons he thinks."

"Doomed is it?" Graham smirked at Conall as he steered his horse closer.

"Doomed, to say the least," she concurred, using the insulting word Conall had just spoken.

"*Och, ye dinnae want to take my lass,*" Conall said into Graham's mind thinking she didn't follow every word.

"For starters, I'm not your lass, Laird Hamilton," she spat as she leaned over enough that Graham could scoop her off and plunk her down in front of him. Lindsay narrowed her eyes at Conall. "Secondly, I have no further need of your training or protection." She glanced over her shoulder at Graham and mouthed, "This is when you spur your horse and leave him behind."

"Aye, then." He nodded, shot Conall an apologetic look and pulled out ahead of him.

Calling on Graham, of course, served two purposes. It put distance between her and Conall and allowed her to question Graham further.

"Thank you," she murmured as she settled in and ignored how different he felt at her back than Conall. "Your cousin drives me crazy."

"Aye," he replied. "Yer not alone, lass."

She nodded, knowing full well she was not.

"So, now that we have time alone," she continued. "Do you mind if we talk about what happened in the caves?" She met his eyes over her shoulder. "What happened after you first saw Christina?"

"Aye." He winked. "I figured ye had called on me for a verra specific reason."

"Two very specific reasons," she reminded, glancing beyond Graham's shoulder to Conall's moody countenance. "One of which appears to be working perfectly."

"I imagine 'tis," he replied, his suddenly serious eyes catching hers before she turned back. "I know his behavior is hard to tolerate on occasion, but ye've got to remember that he's been through an awful lot." His voice softened. "I couldnae imagine losing my best friend then my da so soon after."

"I know," she said softly as she looked forward again. "And while I feel for him, I really do, it doesn't give him the right to continually treat people poorly."

"Does he then?" Graham murmured. "Treat *everyone* so poorly? You?"

She thought of the magically spacious tent last night and how concerned he seemed that she stayed warm and sheltered.

"Let's talk about you and what happened," she said, not in the mood to further explore the riot of emotions Conall could too easily invoke. "You saw Christina run toward the tent. Then what?"

"Then…" He cleared his throat, clearly feeling strongly about something. "Then I was there at Mystery Hill. She stopped running and turned around after she passed through me somehow."

"So she *did* pass through you?"

"Aye, I suppose," he murmured. "'Twas a feeling unlike anything I've ever felt before."

"What sort of feeling?" She glanced over her shoulder into his dark eyes. Eyes, she realized, that were smoldering with something undefinable. Interest, confusion…lust? "Happiness, sadness, anger?"

"More like…recognition."

Her brows shot up. "Recognition?"

Could they have shared a childhood friendship like she and Conall had?

"Aye," he replied. "'Twas as if I had seen her before."

"Okay." She nodded and faced forward again. "That makes sense considering everything that's going on with all of us. The rings and their gems."

"Och, nay, 'twas not like that," he said so softly she barely caught it. "'Twas as if I remember her as an important historical figure."

Lindsay frowned. "I don't understand."

"Nor do I," he admitted. "I think she thought I would be the Bruce when she turned back. There was hope in her eyes."

She shook her head. "But we figured out that Robert was under the influence of dark magic."

"Aye," Graham said. "But what of Christina's dream? Was it not of the Bruce? And is he not one of the most important figures in Scottish history?"

She looked at him again, still frowning. "Why do I almost get the feeling you're saying you think Christina is going to become part of Scotland's history? That she might very well end up with Robert the Bruce?"

He shrugged, but she didn't miss the troubled tone of his voice. "Are we not all to become part of Scotland's history?"

"Yes, well, some of us," she conceded. "But it sounds like you're talking about actual *recorded* history."

Because all of them on these quests to save Scotland, MacLomains and Brouns alike, would never be part of recorded history. Or so she had been told.

"All I know is 'tis likely she'll be traveling back in time," Graham continued softly. "And that she will play a verra important role when she does."

She nodded as she turned her eyes to the path ahead. Of course, Christina would be traveling back in time as would Jessie. She didn't doubt that in the least. No more than she assumed Graham and Bryce would be their matches.

Not for the first time, she mulled that over. For some reason, she had pictured Christina with Bryce. Likely because it was a stretch envisioning the largest of the MacLomains with the smallest of the Brouns.

"Such a size difference didnae stop my great Aunt Torra MacLomain from ending up with my Great Uncle Colin MacLeod," Conall muttered into her mind. *"Against all odds, be it physical or mental, connections that are meant to be will be."*

If she knew what was good for her, she would ignore him.

"When I got off your horse and freed you from both training and protecting me," she replied, *"that meant staying out of my mind as well."*

"You know I cannae do that," he said. *"And you know why."*

"Think what you want, Laird Hamilton, but I do not have to commit to you." She rounded her eyes though he couldn't see them. *"And I most certainly will not sleep with you until we harness the power of my ring."*

"Lying together is logical," he replied, clearly stuck in utter-jackass-mode. *"And 'tis no hardship for you, aye?"*

Did he *really* just say that? Was he *truly* that arrogant? Yet as she fumed, deep down she knew he was right. At least about the lack of hardship on her part. And maybe even all the rest. But that didn't make his continual lack of tact any easier to swallow. Rather than respond, she clenched her teeth and kept fuming. Nobody needed to see her aggravation. Least of all Conall.

"He is going about this the only way he knows how, lass," Graham said sometime later after she had cooled down.

"You followed all that back there, eh?" she murmured. Snow had started spitting, and the wind had grown more gusty. Thankfully, Graham had his fur around her as well, so she was warm enough.

"'Tis verra likely all of us caught yer telepathic exchange 'twas so heated," he replied. "But I meant what I said. Like ye, Conall is struggling but 'tis obvious to all, he's come far in a verra short time. Since he met ye, lass."

"Then I can only imagine him beforehand," she muttered.

"Can ye truly?" Graham said. "Can ye imagine what he was like before all the loss and heartache?"

The truth was she could because she had met that Conall. She remembered the carefree boy. His smiling eyes. How he made her laugh when she never thought she would again. They had shared a unique, uplifting connection. Uncomplicated. So much so that they, ironically enough, had never even bothered exchanging names. It never seemed necessary.

"No, I can't imagine how he was," she lied. "It's hard to envision him any other way."

"He used to be much like me," he informed, the devil in his voice. "Somewhat."

"Somewhat?"

"Aye." He chuckled. "But for all his flirting, he never took a lass for long. Days at a time at most."

"Why?" She hated that her breath caught as she waited for his response.

"We always thought he was waiting for someone…looking for someone," Graham murmured, the tone of his voice a little too all-knowing. "No lass, despite how bonnie or even-tempered, held his attention for long."

"That sounds sort of sad," she remarked.

"Aye, mayhap," Graham said. "But he was never down. Nay, quite the opposite. As though he knew whoever he was waiting for, would someday come." He squeezed her shoulder gently. "I think he was waiting for ye, Lindsay. And I think, in some way, yer a gift from the gods for him…especially now."

She bit her lip against unexpected tears. At one time, Conall had done the same for her. He gave her a glimpse of happiness. While she couldn't say with any certainty she had offered that to him in return, they had gotten along well. Especially considering they never saw the whole of one another and their conversations took place while she was perched in a tree.

"A magical tree," a familiar voice reminded as Darach suddenly appeared striding alongside them.

"Oh, my goodness," she whispered. "How are you here...again?"

"What is that?" Graham asked.

"I...um...nothing," she whispered, still seeing Darach clear as day as he said, "Remember lass, move beyond all the faces you're willing to wear and follow the gem. The more you do, the easier 'twill be for me to reach out to you."

She nodded, not sure what she was agreeing to. Or so she tried to convince herself as she glanced back at Conall. He had remained right behind them, his vigilant eyes still firmly locked on her. It was obvious he intended to remain her protector, whether she liked it or not.

By the time she turned back, Darach had vanished once more.

Yet, not surprisingly, Grant trotted up alongside them, his eyes alert as they met hers. "Is all well, lass?"

"Yes, thank you." She smiled. "Graham has been taking good care of me."

While she knew Grant could not see his son, she was beginning to think he sensed when Darach was around.

"Aye, good then." His eyes met Graham's. "'Tis time to walk your horse. We veer off soon down an embankment that brings us closer to the river. 'Twill be slick."

Graham nodded and stopped the horse as did many others before he swung down and helped her after him. Her feet had no sooner hit the ground when Conall was there, his tone tight and his eyes sterner than ever. "You will continue with me, lass. 'Twill be a dangerous decline."

"I'll be just fine with Graham—" she began before Graham interrupted her. "Nay, lass, go with Conall. Bryce and I will lead the horses down. Ye shouldnae be near the beasties whilst they make the descent." He shook his head. "Especially not in this weather."

She nodded, not about to argue when she didn't know the land. As it turned out, the way was rather steep considering they weren't in an overly mountainous area. Conall took her hand and led the way. "Watch my every step and mimic it."

So she did, suddenly remembering a day when it mysteriously snowed in her tree. Not weather from where she lived, but where he was. While there were always variants between their temperatures, this day had been notable. It had gone from warm to blustery and cold in an instant.

In fact, it had been the first time she saw snow.

It was also the first time Conall became determined to climb up and finally find her…meet her face to face.

"There has *got* to be a way up," he muttered trying over and over to climb or find other inventive ways up, but always failing.

"Maybe I can come down," she replied, her eyes wide with wonder as she watched the snow falling. "Maybe this is a sign. The snow is here and will somehow help."

"If anything 'twill only make it slicker." She could hear the frown in his voice. "Dinnae risk it, lass. We will try another day."

"But what if there isn't another day?" she argued. "We have no control over when and if we'll see each other again."

"Och, we'll see each other again," he vowed, worry in his voice. "But mayhap not if ye try to get down this tree, aye?"

"I'll be fine," she assured as she eyed the branches and tried to determine which ones might best lead her down. "Trust me, I'm a master tree-climber."

"Not in snow, yer not," he grumbled.

"I'm coming down," she declared. "So be ready to catch me if I fall."

"If yer so determined then listen to me carefully, aye?" he called up. "Follow my every direction, so ye dinnae slip and fall to yer bloody death."

"All right but you better talk fast," she replied as she started to edge along a thick branch. "Because I'm ready!"

Unfortunately, her first mistake was not listening to him because seconds later, she started to slide on the slick branch until she went ass-over-teakettle and started falling. She remembered feeling sheer panic then a strange sort of peace because she knew no matter how high up, he would catch her.

He would be there.

Almost as if her thoughts of the past manifested in the present, she started to slip only for Conall to brace his body and stop her. Whereas before she never landed and he vanished, this time he was right there. When his eyes met hers, however, his words were not heroic-like in the least.

"This isnae the past, lass," he grunted with a frown. "Pay attention, aye?"

"Yes, sir," she answered his stiff attitude in kind then met his frown. "I got this. Let's go."

Her breath caught when his eyes lingered on hers for a second longer than she anticipated. How did he *do* that? How could she be so irritated with him, yet he could turn up the sexual heat simmering between them with one look. A look that could be one of many dismal, stoic expressions. She could hardly imagine what it would be like if he started smiling, flirting and maybe even laughing.

"I remember a day you knew how to flirt," she muttered under her breath, unaware she had spoken aloud as she carefully followed his every step down.

"And I remember being grateful I had someone to practice on," he muttered back. "But then you made it easy."

"We were just kids," she scoffed.

Suddenly, Conall stopped short and braced himself against a tree to keep them both from sliding. She was surprised by the turbulence in his eyes as they met hers and he murmured, "We werenae bairns near the end, lass."

"I was fourteen," she said softly. "And you weren't that much older."

"I was old enough." He allowed her to slide until she was against him. Until his lips were so close their breath intermingled. So close his brogue thickened along with other things. "Old enough to know I wanted ye…that I would catch ye when you fell and never let ye go."

"Aye," came a roar she thought might have been her inner voice she was so caught in the moment. "I told ye we'd find them."

Seconds later, an arrow hit the tree less than a foot above Conall's head.

202

Chapter Sixteen

RIPPED FROM SOMEPLACE he had no intention of going with Lindsay, Conall soon found himself somewhere far worse. The Sassenach were everywhere, and as the bloody bastards likely planned, the Scots were at a disadvantage on the slick slope. It was hard to know how many were coming at them but he would say double their numbers.

"*'Tis Robert de Clifford up there,*" Grant said into his mind. "*We willnae be able to kill him, but we may be able to evade him then attack.*"

He knew who the man was. One of several traveling with Robert the Bruce.

Robert de Clifford was the first Baron de Clifford of Appleby Castle, Westmorland, amongst other things including feudal baron of Appleby and feudal baron of Skipton in Yorkshire. He would become well known in history as the first Lord Warden of the Marches, responsible for defending the English border against Scotland.

"*What should we do?*" he replied to Grant, taking in their surroundings. As far as the eye could see there were nothing but trees, an icy slope and endless arrows raining down. "*We are in a poor place, indeed.*"

Several Scots had already been taken down by arrows as they made a run for it.

"*Can we use magic?*" he asked his grandfather.

"*Nay, I wouldnae,*" he replied. "*I dinnae sense evil about, and dinnae want to attract it unless necessary.*"

"Like Grant said," Lindsay whispered. "You need to evade then attack."

Though he was not surprised she had followed their conversation, he wondered at her meaning. Or at least he did for a second or two as his eyes met hers.

"Nay." He shook his head. "I willnae allow it."

"You will not allow it?" Her brows whipped together, and her voice grew tight. "At some point here soon, you need to realize you don't control me, Conall." She shook her head. "I'm offering to help you and give the Scots a chance not only to survive but to possibly defeat the men trying to slaughter them." She stood up straighter and notched her chin, not *acting* in the least but very much the *real* Lindsay. "If you don't let me do this, you're risking the lives of everyone you care about."

"But if I let you do this," he countered. "I risk losing *you*."

Their eyes held, and she swallowed hard. "I'll be okay."

Would she? How could he be sure?

"When did your gift first ignite, lass?" he said softly as more arrows slammed into nearby trunks. Arrows he would deflect if any got close to her. "Tell me what sparked your gift so I know you can control it."

Unsure, her pained eyes stayed with his, and she started to speak but stopped.

"No," she whispered and shook her head, renewed determination in her gaze. "Outside of a warlock being present which Grant just said wasn't the case, I know how to control my gift. I have for a long time, Laird Hamilton." She sounded steady and strong. "You saw what I did with the English warrior in the woods and defied my request not to kill him." She narrowed her eyes. "Will you do the same now? Will you defy my request when I have a plan that can save everyone here?"

Though tempted, he did not mention that she didn't seem in control when the Sassenach raided his castle. Nor did he share that he had heard her thoughts about why she grew so upset with him when he killed the Sassenach warrior yesterday. That, above all, he intended to address. Just not right now. Not in the midst of chaos.

"*I believe in her*," Graham said into his mind.

"*As do I*," Bryce concurred. "*She is a strong and talented witch, and we're running out of time, Cousin.*"

He had lived through few moments as difficult as this. Few as trying as looking into her eyes then letting her go. Yet he knew this was a test he could not fail. He had not handled things correctly with the Sassenach warrior yesterday, and now she was giving him a second chance. Yet it went against his every instinct.

"*I need ye, Grandson,*" Grant murmured, his mental voice pained. "*I need ye to trust Lindsay and come defend me.*"

His blood chilled, and time seemed to slow as he scanned the slope and finally locked eyes on Grant. He had taken an arrow to the shoulder and leaned against a tree. Blood blossomed on his tunic far too quickly. If Grant were twenty years younger, Conall might not be so worried.

Torn, his eyes whipped between Grant and Lindsay. What sort of cruel trick was this?

More arrows kept flying as the Sassenach released a war cry.

They were coming.

"Go." Lindsay pressed a fist against his chest in a sign of strength and said through clenched teeth, "I can turn this in your favor very quickly if you just let me." Her eyes pleaded with his. "If you just *trust* that I know full well how to use my gift, Conall. I'll get them to the bottom without all this fighting. All you need to do is be ready to ambush them, okay?"

She was right, and he knew it. He had to trust her.

No, he *did* trust her.

He nodded and meant to say a hundred things, but nothing came out as she shoved at him. "Then go." Her eyes rounded. "Go save your grandfather and these men, all right?"

Though he wanted to yank her into his arms and kiss her one last time, he knew better. It might be seen. So though it was the most difficult thing he had ever done, he left her and raced down to Grant. While his grandfather appeared weakened, he also seemed relieved and maybe a little embarrassed as Conall scooped him up into his arms and kept moving.

"I have two feet," Grant muttered.

"Aye." Conall did his best on the slippery ground. "Two feet that willnae work once ye've lost enough blood."

He skidded when he hit a patch of ice but got his bearings, all the while trying not to jostle his grandfather.

"There used to be a day when an arrow wouldnae dream of coming near me," Grant grumbled as he wrapped his arm tighter around Conall's neck. "Bloody changin' times."

Though tempted to pull the arrow out, he knew better. He would set his grandfather down somewhere safe, defeat the Sassenach, and then find a doctor in the nearby village. Assuming, that is, all went as planned and Lindsay did not get herself killed beforehand.

"She willnae get herself killed, lad," Grant murmured. "She has too much to live for."

Conall said nothing because he knew that his grandfather was referring to him.

Once he reached the bottom, he carefully sat his grandfather against a tree, pulled off his own tunic and tied it around Grant's wound to stop the blood flow. Concerned, he tried to sense Lindsay's thoughts, but she was closed off.

"She does that so ye willnae worry, lad," Grant murmured, his half-mast, tired eyes on Conall. "And so that ye willnae distract her."

Conall nodded as he looked up the hill and frowned. Everything had grown very quiet, and he had no idea what to make of it.

"It means she's doing what she told ye she could." Grant squeezed his hand. "She willnae let any of us down, lad. More so, she willnae let *ye* down."

He met his grandfather's eyes and frowned. "Ye put too much faith in what we share."

"Nay." Grant shook his head, clearly weak. "I put *everything* in what ye share."

"*There's movement*," Graham said into his mind. "*They're coming, Cousin.*"

"How many?" He scanned his surroundings. "And from which direction?"

"Just beyond those trees," Grant whispered, his eyes narrowed as he followed the telepathic conversation. "Seventy or so. All the Sassenach in this particular band."

"And Lindsay?" he whispered, almost afraid to hear the answer.

"The verra reason they're about to be where ye can best attack them."

He met his grandfather's eyes as both hope and relief washed over him. "Aye?"

Grant smiled and squeezed his hand again. "Aye."

Their eyes held in a moment of connection they had not shared for a very long time before Grant murmured, "She's done her part, Grandson. Time to do yers."

"I dinnae think I should leave ye," he began before Rona fell in beside him. Blood streaked her cheek, and her hair was disheveled, but she seemed unharmed as her eyes met his. "'Tis a bloody good ambush she's setting up, Cousin. Go fight, and I'll see to Grant, aye?"

Conall's eyes returned to Grant, torn. It was not easy choosing between protecting his wounded grandfather and his vulnerable lass.

"There ye have it, lad," Grant murmured, clearly following his thoughts. "Ye've done nothing but call her yer lass these past few days, as ye should because she *is*." He nodded. "Go help her as she just so readily helped us, aye?"

He was right. More than Conall realized until that moment.

When his eyes met Rona's, she nodded.

"Go, Cousin," she replied to his unspoken question. "I might not like anyone who can bruise yer heart more, but she's brave and deserves our protection." She sighed, her next words clearly hard to say but at last, said. "She deserves yer love if that's what yer aimin' for, aye?"

Their eyes remained locked in a moment of mutual understanding and acceptance before he drew his blade and made his way through the forest. What he saw as he fell in beside Bryce and Graham behind thick shrubbery, made his heart leap into his throat.

Lindsay limped into a small clearing, supported by none other than Robert de Clifford. Like his cousins with their superior hearing, Conall could follow her flustered, whisper-soft words.

"I tried to get away," she whimpered as she clutched her side but still managed to swing her hips just enough to turn men's heads. "But they wouldn't let me…" Her voice grew breathy and hoarse as she turned her big, silver eyes to Robert. "I am *so* lucky you came when you did."

He nodded, seemingly quite concerned as he helped her to a rock so she could lean against it and gather her strength.

"M'lord, we should not be here," one of his men bit out as he scanned his surroundings. "We killed some but not nearly enough. The Scots rebels could be anywhere."

Lindsay pouted and tossed her hair over her shoulder as her eyes stayed with Robert's. "But they are not, are they?" She shook her head and hid behind her long, thick lashes. "The minute they saw you coming, they ran…" She touched his bicep, appearing shy as she blushed. "How else could it be with a man like you chasing after them?"

Though his cousins grinned at each other because of her cunning, Conall's eyes remained trained on her, his weapon at the ready. If Robert made a single threatening move toward her, he would close the distance with his magic and end him.

"'Tis true," Robert de Clifford murmured, enchanted as he stared into her eyes then made a random gesture before saying to his man, "The rebels are gone. We will track them down later."

"Are you sure?" his man began before Robert cut him off. "Have them group here as Lindsay suggested. Away from any direction she knew the rebels were heading."

"How would she know what direction they were heading?" the man countered before Robert turned furious eyes on him and roared, "Have them group *now,* or I will cut you down where you stand!"

The man nodded briskly and left as Robert redirected his attention to Lindsay. He crouched in front of her and began touching her leg here and there, asking where it hurt.

Conall narrowed his eyes and scowled. His logical side might understand what was happening, but his emotional side was a blade whip away from taking the man down for simply touching her. Following his thoughts, Bryce put a comforting hand on Conall's shoulder and shook his head.

"*Is everyone in position?*" he said into Bryce's mind.

"*Aye, all are ready to attack on yer orders,*" he responded. "*Graham and I saw to it.*"

He nodded, grateful that they had managed to convince Simon Fraser never mind his men to attack when Conall said so.

"I will be all right," Lindsay murmured, then flinched when Robert touched her knee.

He shook his head, scooped her up and leaned back against the rock. "You will stay off this until we have found you somewhere to rest."

"Oh, that is not necessary," she said softly, her voice and eyes equally demure as she blushed. "But thank you for seeing to me, m'lord."

"How could I not?" There was nothing but worship in his eyes. "When you were treated so poorly by the rebels."

More and more warriors joined them. Almost all by the looks of it. Every last one of them with wary, confused eyes. But an order was an order, and they were stalwart soldiers all. His biggest concern now was getting to Lindsay once the fighting started. She might have lured the Sassenach but what of her once war broke out?

"We'll help ye every step of the way, Cousin," Graham vowed.

"Aye," Bryce agreed. *"Run straight for her, and we'll see none stand in yer way."*

He nodded his thanks as the last few Sassenach joined Robert.

This was it.

There was no more time to waste.

So he gave the signal, drew his blade and raced forward as his countrymen poured out of the forest and attacked. With nothing but Lindsay in his sights, his quick dash was as promised, well protected by his cousins as they cut down any who came too close.

In the meantime, Robert was wide-eyed as he tried to hold Lindsay while gripping his blade. Unfortunately, he was unable to accomplish both, and she plunked to the ground. Still, Robert took up arms in front of her, and he and Conall ended up crossing blades right over her head.

"Oh, goodness," she whispered, her eyes wide as she scrambled back a few inches until she was against the rock.

"Can you disenchant him, lass?" Conall said telepathically as he did his best to steer Robert away but was met with a force he suspected was much like his. Passion meant to protect the one he loved.

So it was a vicious battle nearly on top of her.

"I don't know," she responded. *"I've never tried."*

Conall thrust his sword at Robert, but he leapt to the side before leaping back. Robert swung his blade at Conall, but he blocked it. Then it turned into a fast, vicious swordfight without moving their position in the least. A fast paced feat made more extraordinarily difficult because they had to find absolute balance or Lindsay could get hurt.

Though it was clear his cousins tried to help, they were far too busy fighting off those trying to come to Robert's aid.

"*As ye've always suspected, Lindsay,*" Grant whispered into her mind, words that Conall heard as well. "*'Tis your eyes and hair that lend to the enchantment. Hide them both and Robert should be released.*"

Lindsay swiftly covered her head with her fur then sank down lower. Seconds later, confusion flashed in Robert's eyes, and he paused just long enough for Conall to gain the upper hand and kick him backwards.

Robert plunked down on his arse and scrambled back as Conall came at him. He knew full well he couldn't kill this man. Not now. Not when he played an important part in Sassenach history and in effect, Scottish history. Though sorely tempted to end his life regardless for what he would do against Scotland, staying close to Lindsay and protecting her took precedence.

Without the advantage they had before, the Sassenach fell quickly beneath the blades of their infuriated opponents. Caught in a trap with nowhere to run, the slaughter was quicker than Conall expected considering the Sassenach were more seasoned warriors. Yet when given a chance to finally take retribution and fulfill their bloodlust, it was amazing what a ragged bunch of Scots could do. Aye, many knew how to fight, but it was clear some had likely joined the rebel's cause right off their farms.

As he knew they would do, his cousin's cut down the men protecting Robert in such a way and in such a direction that Robert alone managed to scramble into the bushes and get away. They all knew it had to happen though none were pleased about it. Letting such a powerful enemy go was not easy. Not at all.

Conall fought very few before the vast majority had fallen and he was able to turn his attention to Lindsay. She remained buried under her fur with her knees pulled up to her chest. Though she was very still, he sensed it wasn't out of fear but determination.

"Lass," he murmured as he crouched. He pulled the fabric back enough so he could tilt his head and see her face. "All is well." He smiled. "You did it. You saved us."

Her wide eyes met his and the corner of her mouth tilted up. "Yeah?"

"Aye." Despite how strange it felt to do so, he couldn't stop smiling. "Thank you, Lindsay."

"You're welcome, Laird Hamilton," she whispered.

"Nay." He shook his head, pulled the fur away altogether and cupped her cheek, so damn grateful she was still alive. "'Tis past time you call me Conall, lass."

Their eyes held, lingered, before she nodded and whispered, "All right then, Conall."

"*I hate to interrupt the moment, lad,*" came a strained whisper in his mind. "*But...*"

"Bloody hell." He frowned and pulled Lindsay after him. "Grandfather's hurt."

By the time he made it back to Grant, he was in rough shape. He picked him up and started for the nearby village, muttering, "What ever happened to Aðísla?"

They needed their Viking ancestor and her ability to heal.

"I dinnae know," Grant managed, weakened. "Any more than I know what happened to Adlin and Milly."

Conall nodded and kept moving alongside his cousins as they headed for the village. It was small and far too close to the English border, but with any luck, they would find help. As if his prayers were answered, a large bearded madman with a mass of long curly hair partially covering his face came out of nowhere.

"Och, there ye are," he boomed as he put a finger to his lips and approached. "I heard a rumor there was fighting about." He shook his head and winked. "Are ye friend or foe?"

Conall and his cousins frowned.

"We're friends," Lindsay called out, a small smile on her face. "You can approach."

Before Conall could say a word, she smirked at him. "That's William Wallace."

He couldn't help a chuckle as Wallace approached. But of course it was, and well disguised at that.

"Let me have him," Wallace said as he came alongside. "The village ahead has a good healer and is full of nothing but Scots sympathizers."

"Many thanks." Conall nodded and handed Grant off to William. "We will be right behind you."

211

"Thank you, William," Lindsay murmured, a pretty smile on her face as she looked up at him. "You came right in the nick of time."

He nodded and winked. "I tend to do that."

Conall frowned and looked between them. What was this?

He had no chance to further analyze it before Wallace spurred his horse and started through the forest. Soon after, Simon Fraser joined him, his hard eyes pleased no doubt because of their success.

"Once we have settled in the village, my cousins and I will help bury the dead," Conall said softly. "They were brave men, all. We are sorry for your loss."

"Aye, they were," Simon agreed, eyeing all of them before he held out his hand to Conall. "Thank ye for yer offer, but as I suspected, yer far too important to risk being out in the woodland after dark. I've men that will see they're properly buried." His brows rose. "Mayhap just a toast later to those lost, aye?"

"Aye." Conall clasped his arm, hand to elbow, and nodded. "'Twould be our honor."

"Though none but I caught it..." Simon kept his grip, his eyes astute. "Ye fought to let Robert de Clifford go." His jaw clenched. "Ye let a bloody bad man go. Why?"

"To send a message," Conall said firmly, having expected this. "To let the Sassenach know what we are capable of if they continue forward. If they keep looking for Wallace."

"Would carnage have not been enough?" Simon said softly, watching him closely. "And what would an arrogant leader the likes of Robert de Clifford say when he returns without his men? Would it not reflect poorly on him to tell the truth? That he was defeated by a band of rebels?"

"Actually," Conall said. "If I were him, I would see it as the perfect opportunity to boast about how valiantly I fought."

"They will see him as a coward," Simon Fraser countered. "They will see him as having abandoned his men."

"They will see him as a survivor caught in the midst of foolish council on his first-in-command's part," Conall said. "Because that is how he will tell it. He will use the weather, and foolery to his advantage then he will spin a decorated tale telling how much he learned about us in that short time. He will turn their doubt to awe as he recounts our every move and how such will help the English be better prepared next time." He perked his eyebrow. "Because did he not see yer men at their verra best? Did he not see them fight with a passion that might verra well bespeak well-trained warriors?"

Simon frowned. "That will make them come at us harder."

"Aye, mayhap," Conall conceded. "But 'twill also make them remain wary." He considered him as though impressed by how Simon himself must have somehow planned all this. "Ye and yer men proved yerselves today in this forest. Rumor will travel now that ye are spirited beasties that come out of nowhere. Ye blindside warriors without them ever knowing yer coming." He shook his head. "Ye created something fierce here today. Rumors that ye can manipulate if ye have yer men say the right things this eve in the village." He winked. "To the barkeep, whores, stablemen, and what not."

Simon eyed him for a long moment, and though it was clear he was not entirely convinced, he shook Conall's hand again and finally pulled away. His eyes went to Lindsay. "Are ye well then, lass?"

"I am." She nodded and offered a soft smile. "It was frightening at first, but I could not be more thankful for the help of you and your men."

"Our pleasure." His eyes stayed with hers for a moment before he nodded briskly. "I will see ye in the village."

She had no chance to respond before he strode away.

They had just continued walking when his grandfather mentally cried out, and his magical distress nearly made Conall double over.

"We have to go, lass," he managed as he pulled her after him.

"Why?"

"Because." He clenched his teeth against the pain. "Something is verra, verra wrong."

Chapter Seventeen

LINDSAY FELT CONALL'S distress down to her bones, so she never said another word. By the time they made it into the village, through the tavern and up to the rooms above, Grant was sleeping but did not appear to be in trouble.

"What happened?" Conall frowned and looked between the young woman who was evidently the healer and Grant. "Is he dying?"

"Goodness, no, he will be just fine. 'Twas a bit of pain for him but he will heal," she said softly. "He is verra strong." Her large, dark eyes remained surprisingly calm even as Graham and Bryce walked in, both dwarfing the small room and covered in blood.

Though Lindsay was as worried about Grant as the rest of them, she found it hard to look away from the woman. She seemed familiar somehow.

"Take some time with him, then allow him to rest," the healer murmured before she took a bowl of bloodied water and sidled past them. "I will check in on him later."

If she wasn't mistaken, the woman's eyes lingered on Bryce.

"Thank ye," Conall murmured to the healer as he sat beside Grant, his eyes glued to his face. His cousins clasped his shoulders and offered comfort but did not stay long. They knew he needed this time. Lindsay was about to leave as well when Conall whispered, "Nay, lass. Stay. Please."

So she did.

When Conall spoke again, she was surprised by the raw emotion in his voice. "I've been verra angry at him since Da left." He shook his head, his eyes never leaving Grant. "'Twas an awful waste of time, aye?"

Strange how at this moment she remembered all the conversations they had as children. How he had asked her advice often in just this fashion. Not quite directly.

"You needed someone to blame, and he understood that," she said softly as she rested her hand on his shoulder. "I remember you talking about him when we were children. How you looked up to him but also feared him."

"Aye," he whispered, emotion thickening his voice. "'Tis no small thing having Grant Hamilton as yer grandfather."

"I know." Lindsay smiled. "You said so many times." She squeezed his shoulder. "But you also said having him as your grandfather made you want to try harder and be better." She shook her head. "You knew you would never be as powerful as him, but at least if you learned to use your magic to the best of your ability, and defended those you loved, you would make him proud."

"I did say that," he whispered as his eyes turned to hers. "How could you remember all that and not say as much the minute you met him in this century?"

"You never used his name," she reminded and shrugged. "But then, I imagine all of what we shared back then was controlled by some greater magic. The tree maybe. And that meant everything happening in due time *if* it was meant to happen at all between us."

She could have sworn, for a split second, as his eyes lingered on hers, that she saw moisture in his gaze, but it vanished as quickly as it came.

"'Twas verra likely controlled by the tree's magic," he murmured as his eyes returned to Grant. "And mayhap ours too."

Lindsay nodded but said nothing to that. He was reconnecting and by the looks of it, finally forgiving Grant for his role in Darach's disappearance. Something he had no part in but Conall was only now accepting.

They stayed that way for some time, Conall holding Grant's hand and watching him while Lindsay remained by his side. Eventually, he stood. "He needs his rest."

She nodded and remained respectfully quiet as he tucked the blankets around his grandfather, whispered, "I love ye, Grandda, and I'm sorry…" in Grant's ear then pulled away.

As they left, Rona entered, clearly the first to keep watch over Grant.

Things were somewhat jovial in the tavern as men celebrated a battle won yet at the same time said goodbye to those who had fallen. Though they mourned their deaths, they also toasted to their happy journey into the afterlife.

"There ye are," Bryce said as he met them at the bottom of the stairs with a bundle of clothing, some plaids and a crude bar of soap. "Go bathe out back in the stream then join us for a wee bit of food and good company, aye?"

As usual, Bryce wore his MacLeod tartan, yet he wasn't alone in representing a clan. Graham now wore a plaid boasting the MacLomain colors. How was that possible? Not only the tartans being available but clean at that.

Conall greeted them. "Where did the healer go? I would like to thank her again."

"I havenae seen her since she provided us with our new clothes." Bryce shrugged, his eyes a little too curious as he looked around. "But she couldnae have gone that far."

"If you see her, let her know I was looking for her," Conall replied before he and Lindsay headed for the door with Graham's chuckled words following them. "Not even yer lust will keep ye warm out there for long so hurry back!"

As it turned out, Graham wasn't kidding. Though it was no longer snowing, wind still gusted, and it was pretty damn cold. Conall handed her the bar of soap and offered an apologetic look. "If I could use magic, I would warm the water for you, but I cannae risk it."

"I'll be fine," she assured as she set aside the soap and began to strip down. "While it wasn't quite like this, I had plenty of icy showers as a kid."

He nodded, likely recalling her telling him as much. "Do you remember what I told you then?"

"Yes. You didn't tell me to visualize someplace warm but picture something that made me angry." She smiled through chattering teeth as she took a cloth, knelt by the edge of the stream and washed up the best she could. "And I remember how wrong I thought you were, but it turns out you were right."

"Aye, I know. You told me." She heard the smile in his voice as he cleaned up beside her. "Anger tends to heat a person up faster than most anything else."

"Most?" she murmured, knowing full well she should leave it alone but he *was* nude. And no matter how frigid the weather, Conall was *always* worth admiring.

"I'm sorry I upset you with the Sassenach warrior yesterday, Lindsay," he said softly, catching her unaware. "Betwixt Fraser's death, my da going missing and the endless harm I've seen done to my countrymen, my hatred of the Sassenach runs deep. And whilst I would certainly try to do otherwise for the sake of our friendship, I cannae guarantee that I wouldnae do the same again if we found ourselves in a similar situation."

Lindsay tensed, wondering if he might have heard her thoughts about this. Why she grew so upset, to begin with. While tempted to ask, she wasn't ready to hear the answer, so instead, she focused on what he had said and took his viewpoint into consideration. An exceptionally valid one. Even if he *had* heard her thoughts and knew her reasoning, she respected his honesty.

"It's all right." She met his eyes. "The truth is I didn't give much thought to your reasoning at the time or your past, and that was unfair. So I'm sorry too."

He nodded, grateful it seemed that they understood each other, before he urged her to finish up and get dressed. She grinned, curious at their attire. Hers was a simple dress with a plaid to wrap over her shoulders and his, not pants anymore, but a plaid to go with a white tunic and tall, black boots.

"The Hamilton plaid," she murmured as she eyed him, far more turned on by his appearance than she would admit.

"Aye." He strapped on his weapons, gathered up their dirty clothes and pulled her after him. "'Tis an odd thing all of our clothing is so readily available. All of our colors."

"Will people wonder about it?" she asked. "Seeing how nobody wears their plaids in this fashion here?"

He shrugged. "I'm not overly concerned." Then he winked over his shoulder and said something incredibly un-Conall-like. "Mayhap we'll start a trend, aye? It might take a century or two but people talk and who knows." He shook his head as he held the door open for her and grinned. "Anything is possible."

Everyone had their mugs raised in the air ready to toast, but Simon Fraser asked that they wait a moment as the barkeep slid two mugs Conall and Lindsay's way.

"Here's to a sound defeat," he continued, proud as he looked around, his eyes meeting Wallace's for a split second before moving on. As it stood, William was a wanted man, so for tonight, he wasn't William Wallace at all but a traveling Scot simply passing through.

"Here's to victory!" Simon declared, meeting many eyes as he looked around the room, his next words especially bold. "Here's to Scotland!"

A fiddle and a pipe started playing as everyone raised their mugs higher in salute, their rumbles of pleasure audible but by no means loud before they drank. These were fighting men and patrons alike who were used to living in quiet corners shrouded in secrecy. Who became submissive and ambiguous until they had their chance to strike.

Lindsay smiled and drank alongside everyone. While many of her Hollywood friends would see these people as even worse off than how they were portrayed in movies, she saw something else. Something she could relate to. Had always related to in with one way or another.

Loss and heartache.

Then strength and perseverance.

She glanced at Conall, thankful that she had met him when she was young. That he, whether he realized it or not, ultimately gave her the strength to move on. To realize all the potential in her.

To finally leave that tree.

"Dance with me, lass," William declared as he held out his hand to her and grinned.

Though Grant had told her she needed to pursue Wallace now, she would not. Yes, it might ruin fate and destiny, but she was done acting for the sake of a greater good. It just didn't feel right anymore. She glanced at Conall whose eyes remained firmly on anything but her now. As always, he was willing to let her go. Maybe even ready to push her away.

Or maybe not.

"Thank you, but I've another in mind." She smiled graciously at William before she stood in front of Conall, met his eyes and held out her hand. "Care to dance, Conall?"

The music was lively, at odds with the turbulence in his eyes, before Graham nudged him from one side then Bryce from the other. While it wasn't the most flattering way for a woman to finally get a man to dance with her, it worked.

At first, his expression was guarded, but as the pipes played and the crowd grew merrier, he seemed to as well. Before she knew it, they were twirling and smiling and laughing. More than that, she was reconnecting with him in a way she never thought she would.

The Conall she had known *still* existed.

By the time they were finished dancing both were laughing and far too close, his body against hers as he tried to protect her from the crowd. Like she imagined, Conall was exceptionally handsome when he smiled. When he found joy in life. Or—so it seemed—joy in her as he pulled her even closer and wrapped an arm around her lower back.

Though she had brought herself to this very place by not listening to Grant, she wondered if she should stop it. If she was risking too much. Yet as their eyes held and the music faded away, she realized she would risk everything for Conall. Everything to have him look at her like he was now. With a fondness born of friendship and the admiration and desire of a man that adored her above all else.

It was that, his raw vulnerability, the *real* him, that made her come undone and pull his head down until their lips touched. While they had certainly kissed before and done far more, somehow this felt like the first time. Brand new.

The kiss was soft at first, teasing, before he walked her back against the wall and deepened the exchange. Their tongues twirled and searched, eager. The way he clenched her ass and lifted her to better suit their height differences drove her wild.

Impatient, she squirmed against him and ran her hands over his broad shoulders. No doubt following her every thought, he swung her into his arms and headed upstairs. She chuckled as not just Bryce, Graham, William, and Simon toasted them farewell but the entire room.

Several candles cast dim lighting as Conall brought her into a room, shut the door and didn't lay her on the bed gently but tossed her down before coming over her. The look in his eyes was predatory and intense.

She sensed his every thought as he lowered himself until their lips were inches apart. He relished her flowery, aroused scent. Her beauty. He was done holding back. Done keeping his distance.

"Do ye want to enchant me, lass?" he whispered as he slowly loosened the ties of her dress, his eyes trailing after his fingers as she struggled to catch her breath. "Do ye want to control my actions now?"

The seductive way he said it as he lowered his body until she felt his heat made her quiver and set her skin on fire.

"'Tis amazing how quickly a chilly night can turn warm, aye?" he murmured, his brogue so thick she could barely understand him as he pulled her dress off her right shoulder then her left.

He lowered his head and ran the tip of his tongue over her cleavage as he very slowly worked her dress down. As she did downstairs, she began squirming, eager, but he would not go any faster. Rather, he took his sweet time, kissing and swirling his tongue over her receptive skin before he finally slid his hand up beneath her dress.

She loved the feel of his weapon-roughened touch against her soft flesh. The way he ran his fingers painstakingly slow up her calf. Then how he dusted the hypersensitive area beneath her knee at the same time he ever-so-slightly did the same to the back of her forearm.

She shivered and arched, enthralled by how masterfully he seemed to figure out all the spots that drove her crazy. Not just the locations but how light or hard he should touch them. His lips met hers again as his hand began its journey up her inner thigh. Just the inch-by-inch pace he kept caused such a spike of anticipation that she climaxed right then and there.

He pulled back so he could watch her, his breathing as labored as hers as blazing heat filled her veins and she shuddered.

"Och, lass," he whispered moments before he brushed the pad of his thumb over her clit, and elongated the orgasm. "I love watching ye find yer pleasure."

She liked him watching her as well. The lust in his eyes as his lips fell open just enough that she knew he wanted to taste her as much as see and hear her.

Though she meant to respond, nothing came out but a throaty moan as he slid two fingers deep inside her. She gripped his forearm and whimpered in pleasure as he curled his fingers and began stroking in and out.

A budding point began between her legs and spread liquid heat up her stomach and down her thighs as he nibbled her neck then along her collarbone. Just as the sensation washing over her hit her chest, he yanked her dress down further and pulled a nipple into his mouth.

"Ohhh," she cried at the sharp, delicious feeling in combination with a climax that zipped the rest of the way through her and made everything explode.

It seemed that was the final straw as he pulled her dress off and began yanking at his own clothes. She was in such a state of euphoria she only half heard his boots thump to the floor or see their clothing go flying before he was over her.

Then he was kissing her again. This time so passionately she knew they had already gone way too far. There would be no turning back from everything blossoming between them. Not just the sex but how strongly they felt. While that thought certainly frightened her, she didn't run. Instead, she spread her legs, cupped his cheeks and kissed him back with just as much emotion.

She had tried to play similar parts to this on the big screen hoping to feel any emotion, but she had never come close. The way she became lost in the feel of him was beyond the scope of anything she had ever imagined let alone experienced.

When he, at long last, thrust and began filling her, it was remarkably intense. All of it. The look in his eyes as they held hers. The way he felt deep inside her. The pure chemistry flaring between them.

He didn't move right away but kissed her again, wrapped his fingers with hers beside her head then pulled his lips away just enough to whisper, "Lindsay," before he pressed even deeper.

She clenched his hand tighter as he began thrusting, his moves well-measured as he drew out their pleasure. She imagined the expression on her face mirrored his. Bliss and desire mixed with desperation.

He never found release the last time they were together. It was clear in the struggle she saw in his eyes now. The need to let go but unwilling to do so until she found her pleasure yet again.

"It's time," she whispered hoarsely as she wrapped her legs around him. "Let go, Conall."

Either because of her words or the way she dug her heels into his ass, he began thrusting harder. That's when all his pent up anger began to truly melt away. As he braced his arms and lost himself in the feel of her.

She bit her lower lip as he thrust so hard she could barely hold on. It felt as good rough as it did when he took his time. So good that another climax gripped her and she locked up. Thankfully, at the same moment, he thrust deep, released a choppy growl as his body shuddered and finally let go.

He held himself inside her for several minutes as their harsh breathing lessened. Then he kissed her again, just as passionately, before he pulled away. Utterly relaxed, she watched through drowsy lids as he lit a small fire on the meager hearth. By the sounds of it, the weather was worsening, and it was sleeting out.

"Are you hungry, lass?" His eyes met hers. "We've been left a small tray of bannock and some cheese."

"No," she whispered and lay on her side. "Come back, Conall. Lie with me."

"Aye," he murmured. His eyes never left hers as lay beside her, pulled her close then covered them with a blanket. Neither said a word for several minutes as they stared into each other's eyes. She knew that like her, he was coming to terms with what was happening between them.

"I'm sorry about what I said before, lass," he said softly. "About lying together until we ignited our powers." He ran a finger along her jawline. "'Twas just my foolish way of telling you I wanted to be together."

Her heart fluttered a little. What did he mean by *together*? Sex? More than that? She swallowed hard, unsure why she was having such a strong reaction.

"I'm not afraid anymore," she whispered, answering her own question with that one statement. She was ready to let him in. She was willing to take that chance...even if it meant she might lose another person she loved.

She waited with baited breath for his response. When it came, she was surprised how much lighter she felt.

"I'm not afraid either." He cupped the back of her neck beneath her hair. "Whilst I know we're supposed to come together to ignite the magic of the ring, that isnae why I want you."

"I know," she whispered, and she did. "It's because of what we shared as children."

"Aye," he murmured. "And what I suspect we can share now." His eyes never left hers as his brogue thickened. "I dinnae want ye to go back to the twenty-first century, lass." Pain flickered in his gaze. "I want a chance to pick up where we left off so long ago and see through what I always swore would happen." He cupped her cheek. "I want to marry ye, Lindsay."

Well, he certainly went from nothing to everything in a heartbeat, didn't he?

While she was ready to let him in, she had given very little thought to the life she might be leaving behind. He was a chieftain so it could only go one way. She lived here and not the other way around.

"I…" she began, not sure in the least what to say next.

How had she not given this more consideration when she knew very well that Milly would be staying? That the main purpose of these rings, above all else, was to bring true love together? Sure, things had been non-stop since she arrived and everything was overwhelming, but had she fooled herself so completely into thinking this might not happen with Conall? Now he was all but proposing, and though it made her heart somersault, she wasn't entirely sure if that was a good thing or not.

All she could manage was a weak, "This is all happening rather fast," before she frowned and mumbled, "I'm an actress…I've worked hard to get where I am."

"Aye," Conall agreed, his steadfast eyes on hers. "And I know 'tis a lot to ask of you to give up your career, but you can do as much here." A smile lit his eyes. "'Twould give my clan great enjoyment during these difficult times."

"You would want me to act here?" She frowned, knowing full well what he thought of her profession. "Isn't what I do one step up from prostitution in your eyes?" She twisted her lips. "In fact, I heard that actors are sort of at the bottom of the barrel in this era."

Which made his offer that much sweeter.

"If 'tis what you truly want to do, Lindsay," he continued, making no comment about how actors were viewed in this day and age. "Then do so with my blessing."

"That's nice of you to say," she murmured, her thoughts all over the place. Acting had always been part of her strength. It had helped pull her out of the dark place she had been.

Just like he had.

So though she meant to say, "No, I'm sorry, I just can't give it up," she instead said, "Let me think about it, okay?"

She could barely believe she said the words, but when she saw his smile only blossom wider before he kissed her again, she realized she *did* need time to think. She wasn't ready to say no quite yet.

Caught up in his excitement, desire that had barely waned flared once again, and she straddled him. This time *she* kissed him and began putting him through the same sensual rollercoaster ride he had just put her through.

She started with his chest and worked her way down his glorious body, kissing and tasting every last bit of him. Every last chiseled muscle was sampled until she got to the muscle she had been most eager for.

His eyes rolled back in his head as she brought him into her mouth. She had never had a problem with her gag-reflex, so he got far more than he likely bargained for. So did she for that matter. Using her tongue, lips, and throat, she had him groaning and twisting his hand into her hair in no time.

"Och, lass," he moaned, thrusting into her mouth as readily as she was taking him. It wasn't long before he thrust one last time and let go. She stayed until he was finished, enjoying every last bit of him. Then she gradually worked her way back up the v above his cock, to his abs then his chest, loving the way his muscles rippled and clenched as he came down from his release.

She continued to worship him as thoroughly as he had her until she was straddling him again. Though it had not been that long, he was ready for her when she sank onto him. Her eyelids fluttered as she worked her way down, rolling her hips all the while.

"Bloody hell," he whispered, lust and admiration in his eyes as he watched her.

There was no stopping her groans as she fully seated herself then, too eager to sit still, started riding him. Hands braced against his chest, she lifted then sank, rolling and rocking her hips the whole time.

It wasn't long before he gripped her hips and began meeting her thrusts. Then it was wild and sweaty and non-stop as they moved against each other. Neither held out long before letting go at the same time. She came so hard she was nothing but trembling dead weight on him. Weight he didn't seem to mind in the least as he squeezed her butt tightly as he let go then simply wrapped his arms around her.

She must have dozed off because the next thing she remembered was being cuddled back against him beneath the blankets. The fire had dwindled to ashes and based on his breathing, Conall was sound asleep.

Drowsy, she blinked several times and was about to nod off again when something caught her eye. A tall, shadowy man in the corner of the room.

The warlock.

Though frightened, she couldn't move or call out. All she could do was watch as he shifted closer, a nasty grin on his face as his eyes held hers.

Suddenly, she felt the oddest sense of compulsion. Like she needed to go to him…be with him. She watched in horror as it occurred to her what he was doing. He had learned her magic at the Skirmish at Earnside, and now he was turning it around on her.

He was enchanting *her*.

Chapter Eighteen

CONALL KNEW SOMETHING was wrong before Lindsay even opened her eyes. He felt it in the deepest part of his soul. Something was coming for his lass.

What happened next, though, was truly bizarre.

She sat up, her every movement sensual as she watched something he could not see. Something he strongly suspected was the warlock.

"*Bryce, Graham, Rona,*" he said into their minds. "*Get in here now.*"

He didn't care if they saw her nude. Something was wrong, and he might need their help. Unfortunately, nobody answered. When he stemmed out his mind, it was only to find them gone. Vanished.

That's when he saw her gem.

It was the color of his eyes.

Though that *should* make him happy he suspected it was happening because she was protecting him now. Though she seemed to have been lured away, some part of her stayed with him. It might also explain why he could not connect with his kin.

When Lindsay stood, her eyes intent on something in the corner, he went to grab her hand, but a sharp voice stopped him.

"Nay, Son, dinnae touch her or ye will be greatly harmed."

His eyes widened as his father appeared near the hearth. Though transparent, he was easy enough to see. Their eyes held for a long, tortuous moment before Darach murmured, "Look at her gem, Son, and remember well what ye two had together so long ago. Remember why she should always come back to ye. *That* is how ye might get her back now."

Though it was difficult to tear his eyes away from his da, he did, trusting him without question. He stared at the ring and worked to remember every little moment they had ever shared.

One memory, in particular, took precedence.

"I'm not afraid of the dark," she had murmured as dusk fell. "Are you?"

As he often did, he sat against the tree and stared up, hoping for a glimpse of her. "Nay, of course not."

"Good," she murmured. "Because it's always made me feel safe."

He frowned. "Safe how?"

"Safe from what I see sometimes," she said softly. "It's better to see nothing than too much."

She sounded so sad.

"Are ye sure?" he asked. "Because I was always taught 'tis best for a warrior to confront whatever might stand in his or her way."

"I'm not a warrior," she reminded, but curiosity remained in her voice. "Besides, what makes you think something stands in my way?"

"Well, ye are afraid to look at what frightens ye," he explained. "And by nature, does something not stand in our way if it frightens us? Does fear not hold us back and mayhap cause us to prefer the dark where 'tis safer?"

"You're quite wise for a kid," she remarked softly.

"Aye, I know," he said proudly, still worried about her as he stared up. "So mayhap 'tis okay to prefer the dark but why not look at what stands in yer way? Why not recognize it so ye can fight it?"

That was it.

That was how he got through to her.

He needed to remind her of that conversation. So he stood, remained close to her and thought about that memory over and over again. If his theory held true, and she was protecting him from within his own mind, she should hear it.

She should begin *thinking* it.

He stayed close, ready to pull her into his arms if need be, as she took a few more steps then stopped. A slight tremble rippled through her as he continued thinking the same thing again and again. That she should recognize and fight what she feared. That she had the power to do that.

Suddenly, a sizzling sound echoed through the room, and she fell back. Conall caught her and swept her into his arms then sat on the edge of the bed as she blinked several times and looked at him.

"I just saw it," she whispered, her eyes wide. "The warlock was here."

"Aye." He kissed her forehead, trying to offer comfort as he explained what had happened. "You did it though, lass. Just like Da seemed to know you could..." His words trailed off when he realized his father had vanished.

"I remember...sort of," she murmured, looking at her ring. "This helped." Her eyes went to his. "*You* helped Conall. You were there for me like you always were."

"'Twas mostly you, lass. *Your* strength." He frowned. "Tell me what you saw. Tell me about the warlock."

"He looked just like he did at the Skirmish at Earnside." She shook her head. "Just our roles were reversed this time."

"So he is enchanting you now?" He kept frowning as he wrapped her in a blanket, poured her some whiskey then rebuilt the fire. "How do we combat that?"

"I think we just did. At least for now." She took a few sips. "If it happens again, you know what to do."

"Assuming 'tis me you're trying to protect," he pointed out, not happy with this at all. "What if it's someone else?" He shook his head as he poured himself a drink. "They'll have no ability to save you because they dinnae share our memories."

"What if..." Her eyes lingered on the gem. "What if this is it, Conall?" Her eyes met his with a flicker of hope that made his chest tighten. "What if I wasn't just protecting you but we've actually ignited the power of the ring?" A small smile curled her lips. "Isn't the ultimate goal in every MacLomain, Broun connection to have the gem turn the color of a specific wizard's eyes?"

"Aye," he said softly, just as hopeful as her. "That being her one true love."

Their eyes held for a moment before she focused on the fire. "I think I've always loved you, Conall." Her voice grew softer. "In one way or another."

He had never been so thankful to hear those words, as vague as they sounded.

"Then use that." He sat beside her. "Use whatever love you felt back then, the friendship we shared, against this evil." He tilted her chin until their eyes met again. "Use it not to embrace the darkness you found comfort in but to confront whatever stands in your way. Whatever tries to turn your power around on you."

She nodded, her eyes soft as they stayed with his. "I can use that and so much more."

Not entirely sure what to make of that and unwilling to pressure a firm declaration of love out of her, he simply offered a comforting smile. There was nothing more difficult than having that conversation earlier. To ask her to stay and marry him, yet see such confusion in her eyes. To know that she might very well leave him. Worse yet, because he loved her, he would have to let her go. Because his only concern was for her safety and happiness, even if it was at the expense of his own.

Clearly intent to navigate around the conversation, she sipped her whisky, eyed it absently and chuckled. "Because of you, I can appreciate the taste of this, you know."

When he perked his brows, curious, she grinned. "So you haven't figured it out yet?"

"Nay." He met her grin. "What?"

"That day you threw the skin of whisky up into the tree because I was crying." Lindsay nudged his shoulder with hers. "I caught it you know." She chuckled again. "I'd never tasted such God-awful stuff. Or at least that's what I thought at first. The more I drank it, the more I liked it though." She shrugged. "Unfortunately, I never did find whisky as good as yours again."

"Well, I'm glad I helped develop your pallet." It was hard to do anything but grin as their eyes held, and desire quickly sparked between them again. Yet he worried. "I finally saw Da, lass. He was here." He shook his head. "And though I was happy to see him, I worry that he's with the warlock. That the warlock might have seen where we are."

"Assuming he knows every tavern in Scotland," she countered. "How likely do you think that is? Likely enough to wake everyone in the middle of a freezing night, start traveling and leave your grandfather behind? Will it even be safer out there?"

She made several valid points, but that didn't stop him from mentally connecting with his cousins, sharing everything that had happened and telling them to remain vigilant. They agreed with Lindsay that it was best to stay put for now until they had more information. As far as he could tell all of them had remained sober and Graham, surprisingly enough, had not taken advantage of a whore but slept alone.

"We should rest," Lindsay said softly as she set aside her drink, stood and dropped the blanket. When her eyes trailed down his body then she crawled onto the bed, he didn't hesitate to follow, stopping her while she was still on her hands and knees.

She made a throaty, pleased sound as he spread her legs just enough, didn't enter her but enjoyed the feel of her firm arse against his cock as he kissed his way up her spine. She had a sound, movement, and expression for every little thing she felt. While at first, he thought maybe she was acting, he soon realized she was doing anything but. She was embracing the *real* her. A lass, as it turned out, that was free and wild in her lovemaking. That received pleasure as heartily as she gave it.

He loved the way she began squirming in need as he nuzzled the side of her neck. Though tempted to draw it out and make her wait, it became increasingly difficult. She was way too tempting, and he was far too aroused.

So he kept nibbling at the side of her neck as he gripped one hip firmly and eased his way inside of her. His balls tightened as he clenched his jaw against sweet bliss and trembled with restrained need. It took everything he had not to thrust hard and find the release that was already so close.

"It's okay," she whispered, her breathing ragged and broken. "I want it too."

He tried, he really did, but when she ground her arse back against him, there was no hope for a slow sensual experience.

All he could do was grip her hips and thrust hard.

Her moans of pleasure only increased along with his grunts as he peered down through half-mast lids, so aroused it was near painful. Sweat glistened on them both as he increased his speed, reveling in the beauty of her arse propped up and her more than evident enjoyment.

He only vaguely saw the glow of her gem as she clenched the blanket and fire raced up his spine. Seconds later, he released a low roar, locked up inside her and let go.

"*Hell*," she groaned as her body started shaking and she climaxed.

"*Bloody* hell," he added as he breathed heavily and gradually loosened his grip on her hips. He lowered, fell to his side and wrapped his arms around her. Nothing felt this good. Her by his side and in his arms. He wanted this always. He wanted her in his castle as its mistress and her in his arms every night.

Those were the last thoughts he had as he pulled a blanket over them, might have murmured, "I love ye, lass," then drifted off to sleep.

All he dreamt about was her. When they were bairns, and he caught glimpses of her silver eyes. Then more recently including the first time he held her in his arms in Stirling. How trusting and vulnerable she had been. How she had, somehow, been very much the *real* her with him though he didn't know it at the time.

He had watched over her all night that first eve in the run down castle, staring at her without blinking it seemed. Wondering what she would be like when she was no longer under the influence of herbs. What she might be like if she awoke and they had time alone together. Because even back then, he had sensed something just out of reach.

An indefinable connection.

"'Twas never really indefinable, was it, lad?" his father said softly, somewhere off to his right in his dream. "Nay, ye saw a lifeline in her and now yer taking it as is she." His voice drew closer, more insistent. "She's followed the gem and moved beyond all the faces she wears, Son." Then he roared, "So wake up!"

Conall bolted upright, having felt the terror his father had wanted him to feel as he looked around, confused. As far as he could tell, little had changed outside of the dim daylight muted by falling snow where before it had been dark.

"Oh, God, no," Lindsay gasped as she bolted upright moments later. Her terrified eyes met his. "What happened?" She shook her head as she scrambled out of bed. "Tell me it was all a dream."

"Aye, 'twas…I think." He was right behind her, yanking on his clothes, discombobulated, still caught up in his father's vague warning. "What did you dream about?"

"I was a child again," she said absently as she struggled into her dress, trembling. "And there was so much blood."

"'Twas just a dream then," he said, trying to calm her with soft words even as he realized she must be referring to her parents.

"It..it.." She kept shaking her head before her eyes met his. "It wasn't a dream, Conall. It was *real*."

"Aye, mayhap, if you say so." He gripped her shoulders lightly and tilted his head until her eyes finally stayed with his. "Lindsay, I know..." Ashamed he had held this back when he should have told her far sooner, he murmured, "I know what happened to your parents and I know it's what triggered your gift."

Her eyes widened then narrowed as she struggled with his admission.

"I'm verra sorry I didnae tell you sooner, but I didnae know where to begin," he whispered, pained by the look in her eyes. "It happened because of our telepathic connection."

"That's why I've been able to stay in a bed with you around isn't it?" she murmured, her eyes wider still as they searched his.

What was she talking about?

He never had a chance to ask because she resumed dressing, yanking on her boots as she narrowed her eyes on the window. "Something's very wrong." Anxiety churned in her eyes as they met his. "The blood wasn't my parent's but others." She swallowed. "People I cared about."

"Aye, then, lass." He strapped on weapons and tried to reach out to his kin. *"Bryce, Graham, Rona?"*

None responded.

It was eerily quiet.

"Something's really wrong, Conall," she whispered.

"Stay behind me." He made her meet his eyes as he pressed a blade into her hand. "Do you ken, Lindsay?"

She nodded.

"Aye?" he asked just to be sure. "When we leave this room you need to stay behind me no matter what." He lowered his brows. "Can you do that?"

"I can," she assured, gathering herself, her eyes steadier by the moment. "I'll be okay."

He eyed her another moment before he nodded. "All right. Follow me."

Oddly enough, the moment he stepped out the door, he knew his world was about to be turned upside down. He experienced such an ominous feeling that his stomach lurched. When he got to his grandfather's room, there was no sign of him.

He could not have healed that quickly and left. There was no way. Conall already had his sword at the ready but pulled out his dagger as well as he started down the stairs slowly. The dread he felt only grew stronger. The moment he rounded the corner and caught a glimpse of the tavern below, ice ran through his veins, and he stopped Lindsay.

"What?" she whispered, her voice shaky. "What is it, Conall?"

Numb, unable to tell her, unable to voice it, he gestured that she go back up the stairs.

After all, how could he tell her that she was right?

That there was nothing but blood below.

He tried to steer her up the stairs but stumbled he was in so much shock.

How else could it be considering he had just seen the dead bodies of his grandfather and cousins.

Chapter Nineteen

L INDSAY FELT CONALL'S need to protect her from what he had seen. Even so, the deep pain and sudden fury in his eyes told her all she needed to know. Her dream had manifested. Before he could stop her, she slipped by and raced down the stairs only to slow then stop.

Just like in her dream, she put a hand over her mouth and choked back a sob. Everyone was dead. Slaughtered. So many. All the people they had recently laughed and danced alongside. Those they had mourned and celebrated with.

Bryce.

Graham.

Rona.

And, oh *God*, Grant.

All dead, their bodies ruined.

"This can't be happening." She tried to hold back another sob for Conall's sake, but it was no use. This was too gruesome. Too familiar.

"Come back, lass," Conall whispered as his hand clamped around her wrist. "We dinnae know if the enemy is still here."

Lindsay's eyes fell to her ring. It was still the color of his eyes.

"If he is we need to find and fight him." She locked her jaw, narrowed her eyes and ignored the tears that slipped free. "I never had the chance to avenge my parent's death." Her eyes met his. "But at least what happened ignited my gift. That has to mean something."

"Aye," he said softly, both turmoil and strength in his eyes as they held hers. "I'll be by your side every step of the way, lass." He clenched his blade, his body trembling with tightly restrained rage, his brogue so thick she could barely understand him. "Just give me a direction. Tell me what ye need of me."

She was about to respond when the front door opened.

"Adlin!" they both said at once.

"Wake up!" he roared as his blazing light blue eyes found them. "'Tis coming!"

Seconds later, everything snapped shut and went black before she shot up in bed at the same time as Conall. The moment their eyes met, they knew what had happened.

They had been given a glimpse of the future.

Based on the dim pre-dawn light, one she suspected would happen very soon.

"*The ring's gem is glowing the color of your eyes,*" she said into Conall's mind in case anyone was listening. "*I think it's trying to help us.*"

"*Aye.*" His eyes went to the door before returning to hers. "*Let's get dressed. I'll warn my cousins.*"

"*No.*" Lindsay shook her head, surprised by how strongly she felt. "*I think we need to handle this on our own.*" She yanked on her dress. "*I think this is directly related to the warlock and the fewer people we involve, the better.*"

He nodded as they dressed. "*Aye, then, lass. What do we do next?*"

"*That's a good question.*" She frowned. "*My guess is what we just saw will happen later this morning based on the lighting and the fresh...well, you know...bodies.*"

"*Aye.*" His eyes flickered from the door to her again. "*So we lay in wait?*"

"*Maybe.*" She considered the other times she had made contact with the warlock. First, to defend Graham then tonight, after having sex with Conall. What was the connection? Was there any? In the first scenario, she was coming to someone's rescue. In the second? It made no sense.

Or did it?

Darach's words kept coming back to her. *Move beyond all the faces you're willing to wear and follow the gem.*

Her eyes went to Conall. She had finally and truly done that with him, hadn't she? He knew everything now including the violence of her childhood and how she had lost her parents. When they first met at the tree, he didn't know that part. She never told him. But now he did, and it wasn't driving him away. Not in the least.

"I had wanted to go with my parents that night, but they wouldn't let me," she whispered aloud, finally saying the words for the first time. "So I crawled into their bed and waited."

Though tempted to sit she remained standing, strong as she ever was. She notched her chin and kept her eyes on his. "That night I witnessed the most horrific thing in my life through one of their eyes, and I still don't know whose. Maybe both. Maybe I was even there somehow via my gift. It certainly felt like it."

Lindsay shook her head and continued. "But it doesn't matter anymore and hasn't for a very long time." She stood up a little straighter, gathering strength as she knew all-too-well how to do. "Soon after, I was put into foster care and never slept another night through in a bed…not until now…until you."

Conall stepped closer but never said a word. His eyes were compassionate as he waited for her to say what she needed to say.

"I learned what it felt like to be vulnerable and helpless that night in my parent's bed," she said through clenched teeth. "So I began sleeping on the floor so I would *never* sleep so soundly that something like that could ever happen again. So I wouldn't be pulled from my body and see something I couldn't stop. To be held back from protecting someone I love." She shook her head. "For all the strength I thought I found I guess in some aspects I still lived in fear."

"Why are you telling me all this, lass?" he said softly as he tilted her chin and met her eyes. "Why now?"

"Because I don't sleep on the floor when I'm with you," she said softly. "Because all the fear is finally gone."

This was it.

The moment of truth in more ways than one.

She could feel it and say it, but only the ring would know for sure if she really meant it.

"Because I love you, Conall," she whispered. "I'm *in* love with you and don't want any secrets between us. I want you to see the *real* me. All of me. And nobody else."

No sooner did she say the words than the ring flared brighter and a dark shadow fled the room. Though it was clear Conall was caught by her words it was also evident that he had seen the same thing.

"Come, lass." He pulled her after him and spoke within her mind. *"Dinnae hesitate to enchant, aye? Because I'll be right there beside you using my magic as well."*

Despite the circumstances, she felt a rush of thanks to be here with him.

To have come so far.

Whatever had just happened between them, the warlock felt threatened and was moving fast. But not fast enough as she stopped, released Conall's hand and leaned back against the wall in the hallway. Seductive, determined, she focused on feeling saddened by the loss of the warlock.

She *longed* for him to come back upstairs...*longed* for him to be with her.

Conall fell back into the shadows as she kept focusing on the warlock.

It didn't take long before his reluctant, but steady feet sounded on the stairwell. When he reached the top and looked her way, she batted her lashes and made a come-hither motion with her finger.

Like a moth to a flame, he drifted her way, his expression warring between furious and bewitched as he fought her hold over him. What he likely already figured out though, was that it was far too late for that.

Especially when Conall chanted and began manipulating the air seconds before the warlock reached out to her. She smiled softly and focused everything she had on enchanting him as Conall closed the distance.

Regrettably, the warlock was strong and managed to keep him back.

At least at first.

The warlock's strength began to lose traction as she sauntered up to him and ran her fingers lovingly over his chest. As she did, she tried to get information as she murmured, "Who are you? Where did you come from?"

"Dinnae ye already know?" he sneered, his eyes all-knowing. "Yer wee witch."

Though tempted to frown, she kept her expression soft and tempting. "What wee witch?"

His grin was dark and foreboding but gleeful at the same time. "The same that saw to the archwizard so well, aye?" He chuckled, evidently knowing full well he was caught in an enchantment and they were harnessing the power of the ring. "Ye may see an end to me but know well, my kind *will* see an end to Scotland. If not for ye enchanting me and drawing me ever closer, Robert the Bruce would already be discovered, and history changed."

"Och, but 'tis not," Conall growled as the gem flared and the warlock's powers began to dwindle. As Conall's chants warred with the warlock's, and harsh wind whipped down the hallway, Lindsay did her best to keep the dark creature enchanted.

Pressure built.

The building shook.

The warlock glared at her in defiance, his body tossed about by the air being manipulated, before she and Conall truly got the upper hand and the monster fell to its knees. Air pressed in around it, locking it in place. Yet it continued chuckling, its words garbled as Conall came up behind it, yanked its head back and ran his dagger across its neck.

Yet they both heard what it said first.

Beware the Bruce's new Queen. She is promised, and she will ruin ye.

Conall didn't just settle for opening the warlock's throat but drove a sword through its heart as well. He pulled her into his arms and away from the creature as it never wailed in pain once but died what appeared to be an awful death as it liquefied then turned to ashes. She never looked away. Not once. She had not turned from horror in the past, and never would.

Just as the last ashes floated to the floor, something or better yet, *someone*, began to materialize.

Lindsay blinked back tears as Darach's grateful eyes met hers.

"Da?" Conall whispered.

"Aye." Darach was sitting on the floor where the last of the warlock had vanished. He wasn't transparent but whole as his eyes went to Conall. "Aye, Son, 'tis me."

"Da," Conall repeated, stunned, before he fell to his knees and embraced his father. "I didnae think...ye vanished for so long..."

"Aye." Darach hugged his son tightly. "I've missed ye and yer ma something fierce. I've missed all of ye."

"And we've missed ye, Son," came Grant's soft voice.

Lindsay had never been so grateful to see Conall's cousins when they appeared as well. All wore amazed but grateful expressions as Conall helped his father up then Grant embraced Darach. After that, everyone was hugging him and laughing with happiness.

"I cannae tell you how grateful I am, lass," Darach murmured as he turned her way and took her hands. "Thank you, Lindsay."

"I'm not entirely sure what I did," she confessed. "Though I *am* confused why you wanted your family to stay away yet you came to me several times. Wasn't that a little risky?"

"Aye, there is much to talk about." He embraced her before his eyes turned fondly to his family. "Mayhap over a wee dram? 'Twould taste better than ye know."

"None are up yet and 'tis verra quiet downstairs," Graham said. So that's where they went, including Grant who refused to return to bed when he had just been reunited with his son. Still, they settled him in front of a warm fire with a blanket wrapped around his shoulders.

"'Twas great power that awoke me from my slumber," Grant began as they all joined him and Darach was given his whisky. "Dark magic, indeed."

"Aye." Conall's eyes met Lindsay's with pride before they went to Grant. "We've defeated our warlock, Grandfather. That is why Da has returned."

His cousins, who apparently had not sensed a thing, listened as Conall explained what had happened from their glimpse of the future to battling the warlock upstairs.

"'Twas verra difficult seeing you all like that..." Conall left off, his words soft and his eyes grateful as he looked at each and every one of them.

"I didnae sense a thing," Rona murmured, truly troubled. "I didnae sense that so much death was coming."

"Because it didnae in the end, lassie," Grant murmured. "History, or should I say our immediate future, was changed, and it sounds like we have both the ring *and* Adlin to thank for that."

"But where is he?" Lindsay asked, looking around for Adlin and hopefully Milly as well.

"My guess is that he will show up closer to the time you had your vision," Grant informed.

Ah, well that made sense she supposed.

"So tell us what happened to ye, Son," Grant said to Darach, his eyes troubled. "Then we will try to make sense of the warlock's last words."

Darach took a deep swig from his mug then nodded, his eyes a little haunted. "I was still there that day in the village when I went missing, Da." He shook his head. "I could see ye, talk to ye, yet ye couldnae see me anymore. 'Twas verra troubling."

"Troubling," Bryce muttered. "It sounds terrifying."

"Aye," Darach said softly. "'Twas as if I had crossed over into another dimension. I was unable to use my magic or communicate in any way."

Grant frowned. "Why does it almost sound like ye've been by our side all along?"

"Because I have." Darach's eyes went to Conall. "I watched ye become laird, and I couldnae be prouder."

"'Tis yours again," Conall started, but Darach shook his head and said, "Nay, lad. Clan Hamilton is yours to lead now. I've done my part."

When Conall frowned, Darach clasped his shoulder and met his eyes. "I know 'twas not a mantle ye wanted to wear, but ye've done well by our clan. And ye did well despite your grief over losing not just Fraser but me. That is telling." He nodded, pride again in his eyes. "You're a born leader, Son." His eyes flickered to Lindsay then back. "And mayhap soon enough you'll have a wife to share it with, aye?"

"Here's hoping," Grant murmured, a twinkle in his eyes as they went to Lindsay.

Meanwhile, she tried not to blush.

"So all this time ye've been right here with us, Uncle Darach," Rona said, coming to Lindsay's rescue as she winked at her then turned her attention to Darach. "What was it like in this other dimension ye found yerself?"

"Verra lonely," Darach whispered, his eyes a little lost before he refocused. "'Twas devoid of color and scent. Even the temperature was never right. 'Twas cold when it was clearly hot out and hot when 'twas cold." He frowned. "The only good thing was, for the most part, I never saw a warlock. Not until more recently when Milly first traveled back in time, and her ring started to act up. I think 'twas that, the magic attached to these rings, that started to change my environment."

Grant frowned. "What do you mean?"

"I began to see glimpses of color here and there then..." His eyes went to Lindsay. "I saw you precisely as you are except your hair shined as did your eyes. You truly are verra beautiful, lass, not just in this world but all worlds I imagine."

"Thank you," she murmured as Conall squeezed her hand in what she suspected was agreement.

"'Twas verra difficult, Lindsay," Darach confessed. "While I was drawn to you because I knew you could connect me with home, I also knew I didnae want my kin anywhere near where I was. I worried that at any moment, the warlock might get to one of you because I had somehow led it to you." He frowned, clearly ashamed. "'Tis no easy thing being separated from your loved ones such as I was. To be right there yet not there at all."

"You might be a great wizard, Son, but you are also a man." Grant rested his hand on Darach's shoulder. "You did as any of us would have so dinnae be so harsh on yourself." He sighed. "What worries me most is that you were right there the whole time and none of us sensed it. Most especially me or Adlin." His troubled eyes went to the fire. "I knew we were dealing with powerful magic, but this is truly concerning."

"Yet Conall and Lindsay defeated it," Darach reminded. "As did Adlin and Milly." Optimism lit his eyes. "Is there not hope in that?"

"There is," Grant conceded. "But what I sensed before I woke only proves mine and Adlin's theory is correct. Each warlock that comes is more powerful than the last." His eyes went to Darach. "Because I suspect you only ever came across your warlock, aye?"

"Aye," Darach said.

Grant nodded. "Which tells me 'twas your warlock alone that kept you imprisoned."

Lindsay shook her head. "So there are stronger warlocks still coming?"

"While we can hope not," Grant murmured as his eyes flickered over Graham and Bryce. "I think 'twould be prudent to expect as much."

Graham's eyes narrowed. "So ye and Adlin, the most powerful wizards born to Scotland, couldnae sense the magic this last warlock used on Darach for *years* and there might be *more* powerful beasties on their way?"

Bryce crossed his arms over his chest, a determined, heavy scowl on his face. "Let them come. Let them face my dragon."

"A dragon ye havenae embraced since ye were a bairn," Graham reminded. "Do ye even know how to become one anymore?"

"Och." Bryce narrowed his eyes at Graham, his brogue so thick she barely caught a word. "Ye dinnae forget such a thing, ye bloody fool." He shrugged. "But then ye havenae been around as much as usual these past few years to know I *did* shift at least once."

Graham crossed his arms over his chest as well, met Bryce's frown and was about to speak when Grant cut him off.

"You two can bicker later." He shook his head at them. "Right now, we must remain focused on the warlock that was just defeated." His eyes went to Conall and Lindsay. "More so, his last words to you."

"Beware the Bruce's new Queen," Lindsay said softly. "She is promised, and she will ruin ye."

"'Tis alarming that, aye?" Graham frowned. "Because did Robert the Bruce not claim yer friend Christina was promised to him and did she not say she dreamt the same, Lindsay?"

Not for the first time since she had heard the ominous words, a chill raced through her.

"So if we're to go off the warlock's words," Bryce said, clearly confused. "Then we're to assume we are to be wary of Christina then? Would she not be the one who is going to ruin us?"

"Warlock's can turn words into riddles as swiftly as wizards can," Grant muttered. "Best to simply keep a close eye on Christina and the sooner, the better." A frown settled on his face. "Mayhap your other friend too, aye, Lindsay?" His wise eyes met hers. "Is she not the smallest of you and your friends?"

Lindsay didn't follow where he was going with that. Not at first anyway.

"You can't be serious." Her eyes widened. "You can't possibly think that the wee witch the warlock referred to is Jessie?" She shook her head. "I was in your room last night and saw the healer who took care of you and it certainly wasn't her!"

Yet even as she said it, she recalled feeling a strong sense of familiarity.

"That's impossible," she whispered without meaning to. "Downright ridiculous." Before anyone could get a word in edgewise, she continued. "The warlock said he came from her." Lindsay narrowed her eyes at Grant. "Are you telling me my sweet little country bumpkin friend from upstate Maine is sending warlocks after all of us to ultimately not only kill us but to ruin Scotland's history?"

"I dinnae know, lass," he said softly. "All I *do* know is after we get Wallace out of here safely, 'twould behoove us to keep a verra close eye on both Christina *and* Jessie."

"What's this about Christina and Jessie?" Milly said from the doorway as she and Adlin entered. Lindsay's eyes whipped to the window. It was, in fact, as light out now as it had been when they saw everyone slaughtered. She swallowed hard and met Conall's eyes.

It had been *that* close to happening.

Lindsay hugged Milly then caught them up on everything that had happened as Adlin and Darach reunited.

"I'm just so glad everyone's okay," Milly murmured as she gave Lindsay another big hug. "And that Adlin helped out even though we weren't here."

"Aye, 'twas really just a premonition on my end," Adlin said, clearly grateful as he eyed them all. "But one, it seems, that worked in everyone's favor."

"And where were you guys again?" Lindsay asked.

"With Aðísla caught in some kind of limbo I guess." Milly shook her head. "It seems the MacLomain's Viking Ancestors are starting to connect with her and its messing everything up. Most specifically Adlin's ability to time travel."

"That isnae welcome news." Grant frowned and shook his head. "Not with what lies ahead."

"It is what it is," Adlin said. "Nothing to overly worry about right now, old friend." He smiled at Darach, Conall, and Lindsay, pleased. "Not when so much has been accomplished thus far, aye?"

"Aye," Grant managed, a renewed gleam of pleasure in his eyes as they went to Darach though he spoke to Adlin. "Ye always were good at keeping me focused on the positive, Adlin."

Adlin was about to respond when a child ducked in the front door, her eyes wide on all of them before she peeked out the window and whispered, "The Sassenach are coming." Her eyes went wider still, and she started trembling. "Lots and lots of Sassenach!"

Chapter Twenty

"I CAN DO this." Lindsay looked from man to man. "Let me *do* this."

Though tempted to forbid it, Conall knew better at this point. Lindsay *could* do this, and he had faith in her. "I have seen my lass enchant the Sassenach before. Let her do it again so we can buy William time to escape."

"Speaking of Wallace." Bryce frowned. "Has anyone seen him since last night?"

"Aye," the little girl said before none other than William entered, still wearing his wig.

"They are entering town now," he said softly. "There is no way out."

"Mayhap," Grant murmured. "Or mayhap not." His eyes went to Lindsay. "Are you up to the task then, lass?"

She nodded with determination. "Absolutely."

Proud of her, Conall squeezed her hand and nodded. "I willnae go far."

And he meant that.

When Grant ordered everyone upstairs to wait with weapons ready, Conall shook his head, already anticipating his grandfather's next move.

"I know you intend to stay in front of the fire looking feeble with Lindsay by your side," he informed as he pointed to a table in the corner. "I will be passed out drunk over there."

Grant shook his head. "They will take one look at your size and see a problem."

"Not if I sit by his foot," the little girl volunteered. "And say he's my passed out da, aye? Would that not make him appear less threatening?"

Everyone looked at her with surprise. A ragged thing with a stubborn chin and defiant eyes, Conall already knew Lindsay liked her. She probably reminded her of herself at that age.

"'Twill be verra dangerous," William said as he crouched in front of her. "Are ye sure, lassie?"

The little girl offered a shy smile. "'Tis no more dangerous than all the battling ye do for us, aye, Sir William Wallace?"

"It's okay." Lindsay looked at the girl fondly. "I'll keep everyone safe. She can stay."

"Yer verra brave, lassie," William said to the girl. "What's yer name, wee one?"

She leaned over and whispered in his ear.

When he murmured, "Is that right?" she nodded.

"They're nearly here," Adlin said softly, looking out the window. "Let us go hide then."

As everyone vanished upstairs, Conall cupped Lindsay's shoulders and searched her eyes. "Stay safe, lass. If you think for a moment your enchantment isnae working give me a signal. Tap my shoulder to try and wake me, aye?"

"I will," she assured, confident in her gift.

It was hard to allow her to put her life on the line like this, but he knew he had to do it. That she could handle it. He brushed his lips across hers and nodded before he patted Grant on his shoulder in passing then plunked down at a table in the corner. He tucked his weapons behind him out of sight and sprawled his upper half across the table, hiding the majority of his face behind his hair. The little girl sat at his feet as promised.

Less than a minute later the door opened, and men entered.

"Who goes there?" called out the first soldier as he scanned the tavern.

Lindsay, who had been sitting beside Grant, stood, her eyes warm and flirtatious as they met the man's eyes. "Just my granda and I trying to keep warm on a cold winter's morn, good sir." She sauntered over, hiding behind her lashes, her accent very convincing. "Would ye and yer men like something to drink?"

"Aye," he murmured, eying her up and down with appreciation. "And something more, woman."

"Of course," she said softly. "In due time."

Their eyes held for a moment before he nodded and whispered obediently, "Yes, in due time."

"We're here in search of the rebel William Wallace," said the man behind him as he looked around. "Have you seen him?"

"Och, nay." She scrunched her nose and caught the eye of the other man as well. "If I had, you would know it right away."

The man's eyes lingered on hers, and his voice grew soft. "I would, wouldn't I?"

"Oh, aye," she assured as more and more men entered.

It didn't take Conall long to figure out the only problem she was running into was that someone in charge hadn't come in yet. That was the key. To control he who controlled the others.

One soldier stood in front of the fire warming his hands as he eyed Grant curiously. His grandfather, naturally, had a hood on and appeared very frail indeed. Another soldier was heading Conall's way, curious. When he nudged him, the little girl piped up.

"My da's sleepin' off the drink, aye?" She rested her head against Conall's shin, her big eyes weepy. "He willnae cause ye any trouble. I swear it."

"Och, nay, he's useless that one," Lindsay called out, winking at the Sassenach warrior when he glanced her way. Thankfully, that was all it took for him to fall under her spell.

"And he's just warmin' his old bones," she called out to the Sassenach watching Grant.

Unfortunately, he didn't look her way but narrowed his eyes and shifted closer to Grant. Why was the man so intrigued by his grandfather? Seconds later, he learned why as the Sassenach pulled Grant's hood off slowly.

"Did Robert de Clifford not mention an old man with a blue and green plaid being injured before his last battle?" He fingered a small scrap of Hamilton plaid at the end of one of very few tiny braids in Grant's hair.

Conall had kept one dagger tucked against his side and was moments away from grabbing it.

"He did," came an all-too-familiar voice from the door as none other than Robert the Bruce entered. "Let me take a look." His eyes went to Lindsay. "While I do, serve my men some whisky, aye, wench?"

She nodded, obedient and flirtatious as the Bruce's order effectively put everyone in front of her where she could easily work her wiles on the whole crowd. Meanwhile, Robert made a project out of tilting Grant's head back and looking him over.

"Och, he's nothing but an old man picking up scraps where he can," Robert finally muttered and winked at Grant before joining his men who were now thoroughly under Lindsay's spell. "What do ye say, lass?" he hinted. "Would ye say he's just an old harmless man surrounded by more harmless men?"

"Aye." She offered everyone a dazzling smile. The sort that made her eyes sparkle. "He is harmless as are all my friends." She flipped her hair and smiled even wider. "Friends that ye will let walk right past ye out the front door, aye? Friends that willnae trouble ye in the least as ye enjoy this fine whisky I'm servin'."

"That's right," everyone heartily agreed as they enjoyed their whisky and admired Lindsay.

"You should be able to get William out of here now," she said into Conall's mind.

He relayed the message to his kin, ruffled the little girl's hair, murmured his thanks, then stood and strapped on his weapons. As Lindsay had assured, everyone kept drinking and paid them no mind as his cousins and William came downstairs.

He was somewhat amazed at how many Sassenach Lindsay had under her spell and said as much. *"I'm verra proud of you, lass. Thank you."*

"Anytime." She smiled at him as he ushered his grandfather and kin along. He turned back to make sure the little girl was safe, but she had vanished.

They were nearly all out the door when he realized Lindsay was not following.

"Are ye not joining us, lass?" he asked.

"I can't," she murmured into his mind. *"Or it will break the spell these men are under. You guys go. I'll be all right. I'll find a way out."*

"Och, nay." Robert shook his head and winked at Conall. "Worry naught, friend. I'll see our lass to where she needs to go. Ye have my word."

He frowned, unsure how he felt about that.

"*You have enough to deal with when you get out that door*," Lindsay said. "*Focus on that. Robert will take care of me.*"

Conall's eyes lingered on her. He knew she was right, but that didn't make this any easier. Too many things could go wrong.

"*Go*," she whispered into his mind. There was a twinkle in her eyes that had not been there before. "*And the next time we meet we'll chat more about that marriage proposal of yours.*"

He managed a small smile before he narrowed his eyes in warning at Robert then exited. Leaving her behind with so many Sassenach was no less difficult than it had been on the hill yesterday, but he knew this was the best course of action. It gave them a chance to get William out of there and hopefully Simon Fraser as well.

As the little girl had warned, there were quite a few Sassenach about, but most weren't all that close to the tavern yet. So nobody saw them sneak away which worked in Robert's favor lest he have to answer to them later.

"This way." William waved them on as they stayed low and headed for the stables.

They had just rounded the corner of a building when their luck ran out.

A random soldier spotted them and alerted the rest.

"Bloody hell," Grant muttered as Rona shoved him out of the way seconds before an arrow nearly hit him. Bryce scanned their surroundings for the archer as he pulled out his bow, located the man, released an arrow, and took him down. But not before the Sassenach cried out, alerting even more men.

Seconds later, Sassenach warriors were everywhere.

"Go!" roared Bryce as he started shooting off well-aimed arrows. Men started falling but not nearly enough as everyone swung onto horses and took off. Conall kept Grant with him, worried that his grandfather was still too wounded to manage alone.

Then it was just pure havoc as Conall swung his blade and did his best to keep men at bay. They came fast and furious and seemingly from every direction. He ran his sword across one man's neck while he whipped a dagger straight into another man's forehead. After that, he kept men away by any means necessary including kicking and punching from astride his horse.

Adlin stayed as close as he could with Milly, but they were being driven apart. Fighting like a madman, Graham issued his berserker laughter, but even that sounded strained.

No matter what happened, all tried to cover Wallace as they headed out of the village but it was quickly becoming impossible. There were far too many, and William's men were no match, staggering out of bed as they were. Several were driven through with swords before they had a chance to retaliate.

"*This doesnae look good,*" he said into Grant and Darach's minds. "*I dinnae see how we can survive this without using magic.*"

"We cannae," Grant began before the last thing they expected happened.

Rona took an arrow to the shoulder that knocked her off her horse.

Moments later the Sassenach were on her.

"Go!" Bryce roared as he turned back then spoke into their minds. "*I can save her faster than the lot of us combined.*"

Clearly realizing what Bryce meant, Adlin and Grant shook their heads, but it was too late.

Color whipped and whirled behind them before Bryce embraced his dragon.

"Holy *shit*," Milly exclaimed, her words drowned out by Sassenach cries as Bryce became something out of their worst nightmare. Massive and black, the last thing Conall saw as they raced away were wings spread so wide against the sky that the entire village was blocked out.

Moments later, a deafening roar filled the air.

"Bloody hell," Grant muttered. "How are we going to erase *this* from history?"

That, unfortunately, was to be worried about later. Right now, all that mattered was helping William Wallace and Simon Fraser escape. As it turned out, Simon was not all that far behind them and soon joined them in flight.

In the end, thanks not only to Lindsay and Bryce but all of them, they officially got away from the Sassenach with William, Simon and a sizeable amount of their men alive and well. They had, in effect, made sure they escaped what would someday be known as the Action at Happrew.

History was once again on track.

Though Conall was determined to go back after Lindsay, Bryce, and Rona, none would allow it. Most specifically Adlin and Grant. Conall kept trying to reach out to Lindsay telepathically to no avail. What had happened? Did Robert get her safely out of there as promised? Did Bryce destroy the Sassenach with one mighty fiery breath? Was Rona still alive?

As they sat around a campfire later that day and snow fell softly, Milly sat down next to him. "She's going to be okay, Conall. I don't doubt it for a second. Not with Bryce protecting her...such as he was."

He didn't respond but kept steady eyes on the fire, praying all the while.

Milly slipped her hand into his after that and remained quiet. That's when he realized she was as worried as him. All they could do was wait and watch the darkening forest. All he could do was hope he hadn't lost Lindsay when he had just found her. How ironic, in its own way, that she and Bryce were once more in the hands of the Sassenach. That they were right back where they began.

Or so he thought until something brushed his mind.

He narrowed his eyes through the curling fog. Weather so much like it had been at Stirling Bridge. Weather so similar to what it had been when he kissed her for the first time. When he felt something brush his mind again, stronger this time, he didn't hesitate but raced into the forest. She was coming. He just *knew* it.

Moments later, she appeared.

He closed the distance, pulled her into his arms before she had a chance to speak and kissed her hard. A kiss that outdid all others or so it seemed as he cupped her cheeks and relished the feel of her lips against his. Relished the fact she was with him again.

"Glad to see you two aren't vanishing into thin air this time." Milly chuckled from somewhere nearby. "Because I'd like to give my friend a hug too."

Conall reluctantly pulled away so Lindsay could greet everyone else as well.

He embraced Bryce next then felt a fresh rush of relief as he spied Rona. She might be wounded, but she seemed steadfast and grateful to see him as he scooped her into his arms and headed for their small camp. "She might not have been around back there, but Aðísla is with us and will see to that wound."

"I sensed it ye know," she said softly.

"What?"

"My own death." Her eyes met his. "I would have died had Bryce not embraced his dragon. Had his beast not protected me. 'Twas humbling."

He frowned, confused. "He will always protect ye, lass."

"Aye, I know," she murmured. "But it felt more like his beastie protecting me…" Her voice softened even more. "And I havenae been so kind to beasties since Fraser fell, have I? Or anyone for that matter."

He was surprised by her words. More so, by the regret in her eyes. The acknowledgement that she had been somewhere dark for a very long time.

"It has been a hard road for us both," he acknowledged. "But one we are near the end of aye?"

She nodded and offered a small smile. "Aye."

"Sister." Graham frowned, concerned as he fell in alongside them. "How are ye, lass? Are ye well?"

"I am," she confirmed. "Better than I've been for some time I think."

Graham smiled and nodded.

As it turned out, Bryce and Lindsay had ended up working together, somehow amplifying her power of enchantment through his dragon. Even as they described it later around the fire, it seemed almost unbelievable.

"'Twas because she saved him at the Sassenach encampment in Stirling," Grant said softly. "Bryce's dragon trusts Lindsay so 'tis not such a far-fetched idea that the two of them convinced an entire village and all of its visiting Sassenach that they had only ever seen William and his men." The corner of his mouth curled up in amusement. "Never a bonnie lass with enchanting ways, her valiant protectors or, Lord above, a mythical *dragon*."

Everyone chuckled as Bryce and Lindsay looked at each other fondly.

"We do work well as a team, aye, lass?" Bryce said.

"We do," she agreed before her warm eyes turned Conall's way. "We all do, I think."

"Did you ever see the little girl again?" Conall asked. "Was she well in the end?"

"No, we never saw her again." She shook her head. "But before we left we made sure the English had no memory of her, so she should be okay."

"Oh, aye, she'll be just fine," William murmured and winked. "How else could it be with a name like Iosbail?"

Adlin laughed first followed by everyone else before Grant came to his feet and announced it was time to say goodbye. William needed to continue on, and they needed to return home. While everyone bid Simon Fraser a fond farewell, there was a particular heaviness when they turned William's way.

"Och, nay, dinnae be like this," William said softly as he eyed them. "Adlin told me that I willnae remember ye next time we meet nor all that has happened here, but I dinnae entirely believe him." He winked at Lindsay. "I cannae imagine a time in which I'm not trying to push ye into Laird Hamilton's arms because would it not benefit history? Would it not benefit my country?"

Her eyes narrowed in recognition, but she made no comment.

"Aye, much like me trying to push you into William's arms." Grant winked at her. "A means to an end."

She shook her head and muttered, "Devious Scotsmen." Then she glanced at Conall, grateful. "Not that I'm complaining."

"I'm going to miss you, William," Milly murmured, unable to hide her tears as she embraced him. "Thank you so much for—"

That's all she managed to get out before he cupped her cheeks and gave her a kiss that made Adlin clear his throat.

"Goodbye, Mildred," William whispered before his eyes turned to Lindsay and Adlin. "Take good care of her." Then he looked at everyone else. "I dinnae need to possess an ounce of magic to know yer all saying a final farewell to me." He nodded, impressed as he looked at each and every one of them. "Thank ye for all yer help and for loving this country and its people as much as I do."

He clasped hands with everyone but embraced Grant and Adlin. Men who had impacted his life for a very long time. Though it was an emotional goodbye, it was one Conall would not have traded for anything. The chance to know the great William Wallace and help him in his unforgettable endeavor to lead his country to freedom.

Less than an hour later they were home, back in his time, thirteen-twelve, and enjoying a homecoming unlike any other as his father reunited with his clan. As he figured it would be, Da disappeared early on with Ma, gone to their chamber to make up for lost time. He smiled as he sat in front of the fire in the great hall next to his grandparents and Lindsay. Everyone else had gone off to bed.

"You know what I keep wondering." Conall eyed his grandfather. "If Lindsay somehow controlled our journey, why would we travel back here first? Why our dungeons?" He shook his head. "And how, when her magic doesnae seem to run along those lines, would she subconsciously lock us in there? How could she possibly override my magic like that?"

"Mayhap she inadvertently brought you home to protect you from the Sassenach before they rushed Stirling Bridge." Grant shrugged, his eyes mischievous. "As to why the dungeons? 'Tis hard to know. Mayhap she wanted some time alone with you."

Conall narrowed his eyes. "Or mayhap *you* wanted us to have some time alone."

"Either way…" Wisdom lit Sheila's eyes as they went between her husband and grandson. "Many walls started coming down after that dungeon wall, wouldn't you say?"

"Aye," Grant agreed. "But then I never wanted that wall to begin with. 'Twas always something that bothered Conall, not me."

Conall didn't miss the innuendo and while tempted to comment, decided not to.

The truth was, he could see it all so much more clearly now. His fear of losing someone he cared about didn't begin with Fraser or his father but perhaps Lindsay and even Grant himself. Maybe, on some level, though he always remained convinced she would return, losing his tree faery was more difficult than he realized. Especially as the years ticked by and she faded more and more into the past.

As time went by, his castle dungeon became a symbol of such loss. After all, had it not once taken Grant? So he walled it off, no doubt subconsciously thinking he could stop more loss.

Yet loss still came, and that wall didn't do a thing to stop it.

As his grandfather likely knew since the moment he moved into this castle and confronted his former prison, things must be faced not avoided. Loss would always come, but God had a funny way of giving back. He glanced at Lindsay, grateful he had let her in and finally opened his eyes to the dark place he had been. The walled up place that never allowed him to heal but only made him grow more bitter.

"*Ye've come far, Grandson,*" Grant murmured into his mind, evidently following his every thought. "*And 'tis bloody good to have ye back.*"

"*'Tis good to be back.*" He met his grandfather's eyes. "*'Twas poor of me to have held so much against ye,*" he began, but Grant cut him off.

"*Nay, 'twas as Lindsay said when ye sat at my bedside in Happrew,*" he assured, warmth in his eyes. "*I knew where yer anger came from so never held it against ye. I love ye, lad.*" He shook his head. "*And dinnae ever forget it.*"

He should have known Grant was somehow listening in Happrew.

"*Aye, Granda,*" he said. "*I love ye too.*"

"So the battle here never took place because we fixed history just enough so far." Lindsay shook her head, clearly amazed as she looked around. "And what about that little girl and her parents? I've been looking for them all night but didn't see them."

"'Tis a strange thing," Grant murmured. "I've been looking for them too based on your description, but such a family doesnae seem to exist."

"I don't understand." She frowned, confused. "I saw them. They were here."

When Grant shook his head, clearly feeling it wasn't his place to continue, he telepathically relayed his conclusions to Conall who in turn spoke within her mind. "*Not only were you inadvertently protecting my clan and me, but 'tis verra likely you began something that would finally release you from the dark corners of your past. Those you didnae truly move on from.*"

She shook her head. "*I don't understand.*"

"*Either because of your magic or the ring's, you relived your past though the child and her parents though their faces were different,*" he explained. "*You manifested something similar to what first sparked your gift and that in turn enabled us to travel through time and begin our journey.*" He looked at her with pride and even a little wonder. "*You began your own healing process, lass.*"

"That's unreal…but it makes sense." Lindsay's eyes held his. "*I did more than heal though.*" She slipped her hand into his. "*I found the 'happily ever after' I gave up on a long time ago.*"

"*Aye.*" His eyes held hers. "*Though it could be a wee bit happier…*"

"How so," she whispered aloud before he stood, pulled her into his arms, winked at his grandparents then murmured a chant.

Seconds later they stood beneath the oak tree in front of MacLomain Castle.

A tear slid down her cheek as she stared up into its moonlit branches and whispered, "It's as beautiful from down here as it was from up there."

"As are you, lass," he murmured, unable to look anywhere but at her. "Never a faery but so much more."

Her eyes met his and held. "A faery you swore you would marry."

"Aye." He cupped her cheek, his brogue thickening. "And I still will if ye'll have me."

He felt her thoughts brush his. Her love for acting but also her willingness to explore her options. More than that, her love for him. The strength they had discovered so long ago together.

"I'll have you, Laird Hamilton," she whispered, never getting a chance to say more as his lips closed over hers and he lowered her to the ground.

Nothing more was said after that.

Nothing more was needed than the feel of her in his arms and what they had found together.

Battles lay on the horizon, and evil likely waited in the very near future, but for now, he and Lindsay had found something they never imagined possible.

Something old and new all at once.

More than that, something that had always been theirs.

The End

Coming Soon

Promised to a Highland Laird

Christina has made her own way for as long as she can remember and juggled men for even longer. The love 'em and leave 'em type, she finally said goodbye to Virginia, moved to Maine, and made a new start. Or so she thought until her best friends were pulled back in time. Better yet, when a stubborn Claddagh ring on her finger declares she can run but can't hide. Not when it comes to men from medieval Scotland.

First-in-command of MacLomain Castle, Graham MacLomain has more secrets than most and wants nothing to do with a lass from the future. Especially not one who is promised to King Robert the Bruce. Yet the moment he makes contact with Christina before she travels back in time, he is drawn to her. Soon enough, despite his own commitments and a life that can never include her, he's eager to be by her side.

Friends from the start, Graham and Christina devise a plan to pretend true love found them. Now they can discreetly dodge destiny and follow their own paths. The only problem? Destiny is unavoidable. Passion sparks and love ignites. Days before the Battle of Bannockburn, they'll have to face the truth and make a heartbreaking choice. Give in to how they truly feel and destroy all those they care about or turn away, and save Scotland from ultimate ruin.

Dear Reader Letter

As always, thanks so much for reading.

The MacLomain Series: A New Beginning has been a labor of love as I sift through and try to keep true to history while introducing my fantasy-driven characters into the mix. Scotland's history, as we all know, is remarkably turbulent so choosing specific battles to define this series was tricky.

The Battle of Stirling Bridge was an easy choice as it marked a great victory for Sir William Wallace near the beginning of what became a long road for him and Scotland. I specifically chose the Actions at Earnside and Happrew to use in *Taken by a Highland Laird* because there is so little known about these battles outside of the fact that they struck me as pivotal.

In Happrew, Robert the Bruce was still aiding the English, and William Wallace escaped. At Earnside? The last battle recorded of Wallace 'potentially' fighting and even then, it's debatable if he was ever truly there. More so, the battle's exact location.

That was in September of 1304.

In August 1305, Wallace was captured in Robroyston, near Glasgow, and handed over to King Edward I of England. From start to finish, England made an example out of him. Accused of high treason and crimes against English civilians, he was stripped naked and dragged through the city at the heels of a horse. He was then strangled by hanging but released while he was still alive, emasculated, eviscerated and his bowels burned before him. After all that, he was beheaded, and cut into four parts. His preserved head (dipped in tar) was placed on a pike atop London Bridge. John de Segrave delivered his four quarters to various locations in Scotland to send a very clear message.

Rebellion would be swiftly and harshly punished.

I was teary often as I educated myself about William Wallace in order to offer my readers a better story. I knew he was exceptional but had no idea how much so until I started really researching him. I wish I could cover everything I learned but this series is only so long, and I would need a *lot* more space. I can only hope I did him justice in the short fictional time I spent with him.

Meanwhile, as we bid farewell to William and move forward, I hope you'll journey with me as we learn more about King Robert the Bruce. Based on what I've already read I think he's misunderstood in many circles, and I hope to shed light on that. After all, the Bruce is as important to Scotland's history as William Wallace ever was.

If you're game, let's adventure forth and defeat evil in more ways than one as we revisit the remainder of the series in two well-known battles. The first, the Battle of Bannockburn that took place in June 1314 then the Battle of Byland Moor that took place in Yorkshire 1322.

It should be an interesting ride where we can only hope history is saved, the Sassenach defeated, and true love found.

Good health and happiness to you always!

xoxo
Sky Purington

Previous Releases

~The MacLomain Series- Early Years~

Highland Defiance- Book One
Highland Persuasion- Book Two
Highland Mystic- Book Three

~The MacLomain Series~

The King's Druidess- Prelude
Fate's Monolith- Book One
Destiny's Denial- Book Two
Sylvan Mist- Book Three

~The MacLomain Series- Next Generation~

Mark of the Highlander- Book One
Vow of the Highlander- Book Two
Wrath of the Highlander- Book Three
Faith of the Highlander- Book Four
Plight of the Highlander- Book Five

~The MacLomain Series- Viking Ancestors~

Viking King- Book One
Viking Claim- Book Two
Viking Heart- Book Three

~The MacLomain Series- Later Years~

Quest of a Scottish Warrior- Book One
Yule's Fallen Angel- Spin-off Novella
Honor of a Scottish Warrior- Book Two
Oath of a Scottish Warrior- Book Three

Passion of a Scottish Warrior- Book Four

~The MacLomain Series- Viking Ancestors' Kin~

Rise of a Viking- Book One
Vengeance of a Viking- Book Two
A Viking Holiday- Spin-off Novella
Soul of a Viking- Book Three
Fury of a Viking- Book Four
Her Wounded Dragon- Spin-off Novella
Pride of a Viking- Book Five

~The MacLomain Series: A New Beginning~

Sworn to a Highland Laird- Book One
Taken by a Highland Laird- Book Two
Promised to a Highland Laird- Book Three
Avenged by a Highland Laird- Book Four

~Calum's Curse Series~

The Victorian Lure- Book One
The Georgian Embrace- Book Two
The Tudor Revival- Book Three

~Forsaken Brethren Series~

Darkest Memory- Book One
Heart of Vesuvius- Book Two

~Holiday Tales~

Yule's Fallen Angel
+ Bonus Novelette, Christmas Miracle

About the Author

Sky Purington is the bestselling author of over thirty novels and several novellas. A New Englander born and bred who recently moved to Virginia, Sky was raised hearing stories of folklore, myth, and legend. When combined with a love for nature, romance, and time-travel, elements from the stories of her youth found release in her books.

Purington loves to hear from readers and can be contacted at Sky@SkyPurington.com. Interested in keeping up with Sky's latest news and releases? Visit Sky's website, www.skypurington.com to download her free App on iTunes and Android or sign up for her quarterly newsletter. Love social networking? Find Sky on Facebook and Twitter.